THE DUKE'S DEFENDER

The Duke's Guard Series,
Book Six

C.H. Admirand

ARE YOU SIGNED UP FOR DRAGONBLADE'S BLOG?

You'll get the latest news and information on exclusive giveaways, exclusive excerpts, coming releases, sales, free books, cover reveals and more.

Check out our complete list of authors, too!

No spam, no junk. That's a promise!

Sign Up Here

www.dragonbladepublishing.com

Dearest Reader;

Thank you for your support of a small press. At Dragonblade Publishing, we strive to bring you the highest quality Historical Romance from some of the best authors in the business. Without your support, there is no 'us', so we sincerely hope you adore these stories and find some new favorite authors along the way.

Happy Reading!

CEO, Dragonblade Publishing

Additional Dragonblade books by Author C.H. Admirand

The Duke's Guard Series
The Duke's Sword
The Duke's Protector
The Duke's Shield
The Duke's Dragoon
The Duke's Hammer
The Duke's Defender

The Lords of Vice Series
Mending the Duke's Pride
Avoiding the Earl's Lust
Tempering the Viscount's Envy
Redirecting the Baron's Greed
His Vow to Keep (Novella)

The Lyon's Den Series
Rescued by the Lyon
Captivated by the Lyon

Dedication

For DJ, the keeper of my heart, and love of my life. I miss you.

For Arran McNicol, my editor, who gets me back on track when my brain is moving at a different speed than my fingers on the keyboard.

For my loyal readers, thank you for reading my books and letting me know how much you love my stories.

Author's Note

Dear Reader:

Hardheaded Heroes and Feisty Heroines…what's not to love?

This book is for all of you who continue to read the books that live in my mind and my heart, with characters that continue to whisper to me long after I've written their story and shared it with the world. Thank you, from the bottom on my heart.

Settle into your comfy reading spot with a cup of tea (or tasty adult beverage) while I tell you a story…

CHAPTER ONE

AIDEN GARAHAN ENTERED Gavin King's office on Bow Street, surprised Captain Coventry, the duke's London man-of-affairs, had yet to arrive. "Am I early?"

"Garahan!" King rose and walked around the desk, hand extended to greet him. "Coventry sent word he has been detained. No need to wait for him to begin."

"I've only just arrived in London," Aiden said. "Has something urgent arisen in me absence?"

King nodded. "The duke's latest missive to Coventry and myself had a special request in it."

"How can I help?"

"Lord Montrose, a very good friend of the duke's father, recently passed away, leaving his only child—a daughter—without the protection of his family or the title he earned in battle."

Aiden noted what King had not said. "An inheritance is involved, then."

"Aye."

"But no worry of a distant cousin trying to stake his claim to Montrose's property—or the fortune from his daughter."

"Apparently Montrose had the devil's own luck filling his coffers," King explained. "He left his daughter with a large dowry, and his sizeable fortune. Miss Emily Montrose is an heiress."

Aiden blew out a breath. "'Tis a relief, for his daughter's sake, that her inheritance is not entailed." He frowned. "Once word hits the streets, fortune hunters will be crawling out of the woodwork."

King agreed. "I have two of my men on assignment at the moment protecting a wealthy lord's daughter from that very situation."

"The bloody bottom feeders won't be granting Miss Montrose time to mourn her da before they start clamoring at her door."

"Precisely. Three months ago, Montrose amended his will, arranging for his daughter's protection—should anything happen to him before his daughter wed."

"A wise man provides for his family," Aiden remarked. When King remained silent, a knot formed between Garahan's shoulder blades. "Ye're thinking there was a reason for his lordship to make such a provision for his daughter." It wasn't a question. "Had his lordship received threats, or was he being blackmailed?"

When King remained silent, Garahan asked, "Were the circumstances surrounding his death suspicious?"

King rubbed his neck, and Garahan wondered if it was where the older man felt the prickling of a warning sign—Aiden felt it between his shoulder blades. King ignored the question to say, "Upon Lord Montrose's death, the Duke of Wyndmere became Miss Emily Montrose's guardian."

"Well now, 'tis not unexpected, as His Grace is known for going to great lengths to protect his family, extended family, and friends," Aiden said, "with the help of me brothers and cousins."

King held Aiden's gaze. "The duke has assigned her protection to you and two of Coventry's men while Lord Montrose's affairs are being settled."

Aiden accepted the assignment, pleased to have been singled out to perform the duty. The niggling sense that there was a specific reason he was chosen was something he'd ask Coventry later. "And after Lord Montrose's affairs have been settled?"

"The three of you are to escort Miss Montrose to Wyndmere Hall, where she'll reside with the duke and duchess for the foreseeable future," King replied. "Or until an offer, acceptable to the duke, has been made for her hand."

"I do not envy the duke the task of selecting a husband for Miss Montrose."

"Apparently she received a number of offers for her hand during her first Season," King informed him, "but not one during her second. My preliminary information gleaned that Miss Montrose has only attended a handful of functions this Season."

"Had she been ill?"

"It was not mentioned."

Garahan's gut clenched at another possibility. Best to ask now. "Was Miss Montrose compromised?"

"Not to my knowledge, but after receiving the request from the duke, I put a man on it. I should hear something soon and will keep you informed. What I do know is that Lord Montrose, a former soldier, was diligent escorting and—if the *on dits* are to be believed—guarding his daughter during any societal functions she was allowed to attend."

"Well now," Aiden said, "there must have been some reason her popularity fell off."

King shrugged. "In my years working for the Bow Street Runners, I have seen every level of society. What I do know about the *ton* is that every Season has one or two young women of uncommon beauty or personality that are claimed to be the Incomparables. If your daughter does not share similar hair or eye color—or have a figure that rivals that of the one, or ones, claimed to be the reigning beauty—she will be overlooked in favor of those collecting offers from every empty-headed lord in the market for a biddable, rich wife."

Aiden thought the idea laughable. If a woman was comely and pleasant to speak to, why wouldn't she capture some gentleman's eye? Then again, what did he know? He was raised on a farm back home in Ireland. He'd learned, at a young age, to work hard from sunup to sundown, using the strength of his back and his talent with his fists…for a bit more than tending the land.

A knock interrupted his thoughts. "Enter. Ah, Coventry!" King greeted the tall, broad-shouldered, light-haired man sporting his signature frockcoat—a nod to the deep blue coat he had worn before he was forced to retire from the life he loved, as a captain in the King's Royal Navy.

Garahan noted Coventry still wore the black sling his brother James had confided the man no longer needed, and the matching eye patch that he did. Misjudging the captain was something Coventry counted on—it gave him the edge in a fight. More than one miscreant in the past had thought the captain would be an easy mark, but they had been wrong.

"Glad you could make it," King said. "I have explained the assignment to Garahan. Have you anything to add?"

"I met with Tremayne and Bayfield and advised that they will be part of Miss Montrose's protection detail."

Aiden had worked alongside both men recently and admired the skills they'd honed during their time in the military—until they'd been injured and been forced to retire. "When do we start?"

"Immediately," Coventry answered.

"Well then, I'd best be going. Is there anything else I need to know?" Garahan watched Coventry closely, and noted a hint of unease in the captain's single-eyed gaze.

Coventry drew in a breath and said, "Miss Montrose has been dealing with her father's wishes regarding his funeral and internment. Until the reading of his will, she will have no idea she is to become ward to the Duke of Wyndmere."

Aiden had experience with the women in his family—strong-minded, big-hearted Irishwomen—and every last one of them would balk at being told what to do. He sighed. Balk was too weak a word—*fight* against being told what to do was more like it. He wondered if Miss Montrose was a shy flower of a lass—given her lack of marriage offers the last two years—or a woman who preferred to butt heads against orders. "Why hasn't the lass been told?"

"The duke did not say," King replied. "It shouldn't have any bearing on your assignment."

Coventry agreed and told Garahan, "As per her father's instructions, she will have been informed of her new status as ward to the Duke of Wyndmere by Lord Montrose's solicitor this morning. Tremayne and Bayfield are waiting for you outside."

Aiden would have to see what he could find out about Miss Montrose from his contacts—and his cousins—in and around London. He bade the men goodbye, but paused in the doorway. "Has she any relations to support her in her grief?"

Coventry shook his head. "Miss Montrose is truly without family."

Aiden immediately disagreed. "As ward of the duke, she has the duke and duchess, and a host of their relatives as her own now… And me and mine to protect her."

No one argued with him as he took his leave and walked outside, where Coventry's men waited.

Tremayne and Bayfield hailed him as he stepped through the door.

"We can discuss our plans to protect Miss Montrose after we reach the Montrose town house," Garahan said.

The men agreed, mounted, and turned their horses in the direction of Mayfair. Aiden had no idea what would be waiting for them. A distraught young woman. A termagant, or a biddable lass. The unknown. Preparing himself for whatever came his way defending the duke and his family was what made his assignments interesting.

One thing was certain—he and his companions best be prepared for anything.

CHAPTER TWO

EMILY MONTROSE IGNORED the urge to escape to her bedchamber, lock the door behind her, and weep. She'd handled the details from her first meeting with Father's solicitors, and knew there was the possibility of additional instructions in his will. Hand to her racing heart, she still could not believe what she had just learned.

"A ward—at my age?" She paced in front of the fireplace in her father's library. "I have never even met the Duke of Wyndmere, but I know of him. Anyone and everyone heard about that disastrous first ball he and his duchess held—and the madman who held the duke's sister at knifepoint before slashing the duke's brother in the arm."

Emily paused as a shiver raced up her spine, remembering other rumors—both true and proven false—about the duke in the last two years. One thing stood out above the rest—the Duke of Wyndmere protected his family at all costs. Mayhap that was why Father chose him as her guardian.

She turned, put her hands on her hips, and glared at her father's empty desk chair. Sorrow twined with frustration inside of her. "I am one and twenty and do not need a guardian!"

But her father didn't answer her…and would never grumble at her again. Dear God, she wished their last conversation had never happened after she refused yet another suitor. What she wouldn't give to have been the biddable daughter he'd often claimed to wish for. Why had she refused to listen to his advice, and ceased speaking her mind at the *ton's* functions? Why had she refused so many offers to dance from those select—and very few—gentlemen Father approved of?

She waged an internal battle, beat back the tears too close to the surface, straightened, and continued pacing. Why had Father arranged for this happenstance, when she would turn two and twenty a few months from now? He had promised if she had not received an offer for her hand from an eligible member of the *ton* they both agreed upon by her twenty-second birthday, she would be free to pursue her scholarly interests with her father's full support.

She walked over to his favorite dark brown leather chair. Touching the seat, she smiled. It was worn and had fit him like a glove. Placing a hand to the back of it, she thought it odd that it felt cool to the touch, but would warm once one sat upon it for a bit. Thoughts of her father's passing had so many questions swirling inside her until she ached with the need for immediate answers.

But whom could she ask? Whom could she trust?

Gazing out the window, she wished she could see more of the sky so she could look for the brightest, whitest cloud she always envisioned as Heaven. But that was impossible in London with the town houses and buildings so close together. Mayhap if she were in the park, early in the morning, she would be able to see the sky.

Her throat tightened as grief washed over her. Hand to her heart, she whispered, "Have you found Mother's cloud yet?" A tear escaped past her rigid guard. "Are her wings iridescent like one of the Fae, or are they feathered, like that of a pure white dove?"

The thought of her parents finding one another, now that her father had left this world, eased the sharpest edge of her sorrow. Picturing them with angel's wings added to the new image of them in her mind's eye. She'd much rather see them both that way, than in those few moments she saw her mother before she used the last of her strength to give birth to Emily's stillborn younger brother. Dear Lord, please let her imagine what her father would look like as an angel, and erase the last image of him—bloody, battered, and lifeless—as he was carried into the house the night he joined her mother.

Reality settled in, along with the fact that she was without family…truly alone. "Who shall I converse with over a morning pot of tea?" she asked her father's empty chair. "Who will eat the cream tarts Mrs. Christian bakes by the dozen because they are your favorite?" Tears welled, and this time, she was too tired to stop them.

In the quiet of her father's library, no one would bear witness to her sorrow. Her father's ancient chair and well-loved books comforted her. The volumes and tomes they'd explored together were where they'd last been shelved, standing as silent witnesses to her sorrow. Only the shadow of the strong, confident man, who had been larger than life for as far back as she could remember, remained. He was her rock, the firm foundation of her existence. She felt as if she were now standing on shifting sands, about to sink.

She caught the anguished sob with the back of her hand. Swallowing the sound—and her bone-deep grief—she whispered the question foremost in her mind since that night: "Father, how did you not hear—or see—the carriage that struck you down?"

She spun around. Had she heard a wisp of sound—the familiar, deep rumbling of her father's voice? Was Father here in spirit?

The knock on the door caught her off guard. But she'd hidden from the staff long enough for today. Besides, they always knew where to find her. "Come in."

Their butler opened the door.

"Yes, what is it, Wilcox?"

He was frowning when he answered, "Messrs. Garahan, Tremayne, and Bayfield to see you, Miss Montrose."

"Who are they? Their names are not familiar." She wondered if news of her good fortune—if one could call losing one's father to gain an inheritance good—had already spread. "Please ask them to leave their cards. I am in mourning and not receiving callers."

"Yes, miss."

With the closing of the door, she whispered each name softly. "Do you recognize their names, Father?"

The knock on the door interrupted her father's reply—silence. "Come in."

Wilcox stood in the doorway, his frown more pronounced. "Messrs. Tremayne and Bayfield have agreed to call again, though neither produced a proper calling card."

That was curious—mayhap they were not fortune hunters. "What of the third gentleman?"

Instead of answering right away, the butler motioned her closer. Worry filled her. Wilcox had never gestured to her in that manner that she could recall. Something must be amiss—aside from the fact that Father was dead, and she was now ward to a duke.

"What has happened?"

The butler pitched his voice low, so as not to be overheard. Emily did wonder who else, but one of the footmen, would be near enough to hear their conversation. "Mr. Garahan refuses to leave, and in fact insists upon an immediate audience with you, Miss Montrose."

"You will kindly tell that rude gentleman that I am not receiving callers, no matter how insistent they may be."

"Ye'll want to amend yer last statement, lass, as I've been sent by His Grace, the Duke of Wyndmere."

Her lips parted at the sight of the tall, broad-shouldered, dark-haired, dark-eyed, handsome man garbed in black standing just behind Wilcox. For a heartbeat she wondered if he were a dark angel who'd come to take her to her parents. *Ridiculous thought.*

She gathered her gumption and replied, "I do not care who

sent you! A gentleman would never venture past the entryway until and unless he were bidden to do so." When the handsome man's lips twitched, and the hint of a dimple winked at her, she stiffened. "Your manners are deplorable."

"I beg yer pardon, Miss Montrose. I should be warning ye, I never claimed to be a gentleman." His pleasant expression disappeared, and a neutral one took its place. "I'm here on business for His Grace. I'm thinking ye'll be wanting to hear what the duke requires of ye."

"I have never met the duke, and refuse to bow to his dictates before I meet the man!"

Mr. Garahan's jaw clenched, and she expected harsh words in answer to her statement, but he surprised her. "Well now, part of me shared duty—"

"Shared?" she interrupted, knowing it was rude of her. "With whom?"

"Lieutenant Tremayne and Captain Bayfield," he answered.

She was digesting that information, and their rank, when it hit her. "Did you say duty?"

"I was hoping ye'd have heard the news from yer da's solicitor by now."

Emily knew then what he had hoped. "That the duke has proclaimed me as his ward?"

Mr. Garahan shook his head, and she noticed strands of fiery red nestled among the dark brown hair that brushed against his collar. Her mind drifted as she wondered, would his hair feel silky and warm?

The clearing of his throat to get her attention had her pushing that inappropriate thought aside. For a brief moment she hoped what the solicitors had told her was a mistake. But the man standing before her was proof that there was no such error.

He corrected her assumption. "'Tis yer da who asked it of His Grace. I've a note for ye from Wyndmere Hall."

She gripped her gown with both hands to keep from snatching the missive from him and ripping it to shreds. Doing so would not change the contents, or instructions in her father's will, but it would certainly make her feel better.

"Ye may want to loosen yer grip, lass, lest ye wrinkle yer gown."

Appalled that the man would mention something so personal as her clothing, or bring attention to the anxiety that had her by the throat—evidenced in her grip, as he put it—she glared at him. "You will kindly remember to address me as *Miss* Montrose."

He remained stubbornly silent. Would he be this difficult to deal while waiting for the duke to arrive? A second, more appalling, thought filled her with dread: if the duke were not in London, would he expect her to put herself in the hands of Mr. Garahan and travel to meet him? Did the duke have a country residence?

Ridiculous. Of course he had a country residence, and probably a handful of other estates. How would she handle a journey that would no doubt take a couple of days, at the very least, in the company of strangers? *I'd have Helen, my maid,* she remembered, so she would not be totally alone. Mayhap they could take one of the footmen with them, too.

"And I'll thank you to keep your opinions regarding my person to yourself, Mr. Garahan."

He raised an eyebrow but did not reply, simply held out the missive with the ornate wax seal, waiting for her to grasp it.

She dug deep to snuff out the anger flaring to life inside of her, knowing her temper would have her speaking when she should be silent, and in a tone of voice her father warned her, more than once, was far from circumspect. Drawing in a deep breath, she slowly exhaled and accepted the missive from the duke. The tips of her fingers brushed against Garahan's. Tingles spread to her palm and all the way to her heart.

That had never happened before! Unsure of what it meant or what to think, she buried the feeling. She needed to appear in control, so that Garahan and the others would not assume she didn't have the wherewithal to handle the situation she'd been thrust into. In a more conciliatory tone, she thanked him.

"Sure and ye'd be welcome, lass."

"*Miss,*" she corrected him.

Much to her irritation, his warm brown eyes softened, reminding her of the rich cup of chocolate she enjoyed on occasion, distracting her when she needed to have her wits about her. She would need to make him understand. She was not one of the typical women Society expected—biddable, quiet, and retiring, without a thought in her head. "I take it you are new to your position of delivering missives from your employer, the duke."

He snorted with laughter before collecting himself enough to answer, "Faith, is that what ye think?" When she narrowed her eyes at him, he said, "His Grace has sixteen men in his personal guard—meself, me brothers, and me cousins. We protect his family—and his extended family. As the duke's ward, ye're now among those under our protection."

Appalled, she took a step back and drew in a breath to refute the man's claim—but before she could, Wilcox interrupted again. "Messrs. Tremayne and Bayfield wish a word with Mr. Garahan."

She flung her hand at Garahan and said, "Thank you for delivering the missive. Please do see that Messrs. Tremayne and Bayfield accompany you on your way out."

"Begging yer pardon, miss, but we aren't leaving." He paused for a moment, then said, "I'm not familiar with the word *messers.* 'Tisn't an insult to the lieutenant and the captain, is it?"

Was he laughing at her? That would not be borne! "You, sir, are no gentleman!"

He sighed. "Faith, did ye not hear me a few moments ago, when I agreed with ye? I never claimed to be a gentleman."

"Trouble, Garahan?" a deep voice asked from the doorway. Wilcox stood flanked by two men equal in stature to Mr. Garahan. One had a slashing scar across one side of his face, and the other sported lace cuffs that did not hide the wicked scars on his hands.

She had a feeling she knew who the men were, but knew it

would be prudent to ask, "Wilcox, who are these gentlemen?"

Mr. Garahan frowned. "Wilcox already announced who they were and that they needed to speak with me. Lieutenant Tremayne stands on the left of Wilcox. Captain Bayfield on his right."

Her throat taut from the need to shout and demand everyone leave now, Emily sent up a silent prayer for patience and the return of her normal calm. Tremayne was the gentleman with the slashing scar, coal-black hair, and bright green eyes. Bayfield, who wore the lace cuffs, had dark brown hair and blue eyes.

Though equal in stature and form to Mr. Garahan, neither one captured her attention like the irritating Irishman who'd forced his way into her home. She couldn't say what bothered her the most about Mr. Garahan: his intimidating size, the musical lilt of his voice—or was it the way he was able to remain calm while she was on the verge of shouting?

"I distinctly recall telling Wilcox that I am not receiving callers and am in mourning."

The lieutenant inclined his head to her, saying, "I beg your pardon, Miss Montrose, but we are not here on a social call, but to assume our positions as your guards."

"Guards?" A sinking feeling had her hands trembling. She clasped them to her waist to still the motion. Was she to be kept under lock and key?

"Aye, Miss Montrose," the captain agreed. "His Grace has asked Captain Coventry, his London man-of-affairs, to lend his support regarding His Grace's guardianship. In this case, Lieutenant Tremayne and myself. We are to assist Garahan, guarding you from this moment until we safely deliver you to Wyndmere Hall."

The ball of fear forming in her belly had the bile in her stomach simmering. She fought to tamp down her fear, and with it the bile. She would not disgrace herself by losing the contents of her stomach in front of them. Hanging on to her composure with as much dignity as possible, she asked, "And where, may I ask, is

Wyndmere Hall?"

"In the Lake District, Miss Montrose," Mr. Garahan answered.

"That far?" she asked, as the anger that bubbled dangerously close to the surface at Mr. Garahan's intrusion drained quickly—too quickly. Her head felt light, and she desperately wished she'd remembered to have her vial of hartshorn at the ready. She had had it with her when meeting with Father's solicitors. It was nearly impossible to fight against the weakness, but she absolutely refused to swoon in front of these behemoths—her new protectors. She needed to appear stronger than she felt!

Silently wishing the trio of men to perdition, she did something completely foreign to her nature—she *capitulated*. "Wilcox, would you please ask Mrs. Christian to send a tea tray for four?"

"At once, Miss Montrose."

"Thank you, Wilcox." Turning to the men, she asked, "Won't you please be seated? If I am to acquiesce to your claims that you are to guard me, I must first read the missive from His Grace."

The men nodded, but did not take a seat.

Exasperated, she motioned for them toward the empty chairs, then sat behind her father's desk. The men stubbornly remained standing, forming an arc of protection between herself and the open door. Ignoring them, she broke the wax seal to read the duke's message.

Dear Miss Montrose,

I am deeply sorry for your loss and know the contents of your father's will may come as a shock to you. Trust that there is no mistake. Your father asked me to act as your guardian upon his death.

Until your father's affairs have been settled, I am asking you to cooperate with Garahan, Tremayne, and Bayfield, who will heretofore serve as your private guard. When you have settled your father's affairs, the men are to accompany you on your journey to Wyndmere Hall.

Sincerely,
Wyndmere

Hands visibly shaking, she placed the missive on the desk, stared at it, and rasped, "Why?"

"I'm certain I wouldn't be knowing," Mr. Garahan answered.

She looked up and met his dark gaze. "I beg your pardon, Mr. Garahan?"

"No mister, just Garahan," he corrected her. "No need to beg me pardon. What we're after is yer understanding."

Lieutenant Tremayne nodded. "It would simplify matters if you will allow us to do our job as we see fit."

"Without questioning us every step of the way," Captain Bayfield added. "It would make for a smoother transition until we deliver you to His Grace's country estate in the Lake District."

She glared at Mr. Garahan. "Understanding?"

"Aye, lass."

"It's miss," she reminded him, this time without heat.

He appeared to be holding back a smile—drat the man.

Wilcox returned, followed by her lady's maid, and one of their footmen carrying a large tea tray.

"Shall I pour for you, Miss Montrose?" her maid asked.

She was about to refuse when she noticed her hands hadn't stopped trembling. Rising from where she sat behind the desk, she held them to her waist and answered, "Yes, if you would, please, Helen."

She took a seat on her father's favorite chair. "Gentlemen, if we are to get on amicably, please do take a seat. Our cook has prepared a lovely tea tray for us. It would cause her worry if the tray was returned with half of pot of tea and a plateful of scones."

Thankfully, the men sat. Her maid poured, and Emily was finally able to steady her hands enough to serve the scones.

Thank God Mrs. Christian had not sent a tray of Father's favorite cream tarts, or she would have been reduced to tears in front of these strangers. Strangers who were sent for her protection.

Did the duke suspect her father's untimely death was no accident, or was he being overly cautious where she was concerned? Her breath hitched in her chest as she wondered—did the duke think she needed protection from whoever had struck her father down and left him to die? Her vision grayed around the edges, until she remembered to exhale.

A glance at the footman, and his slight nod, confirmed her suspicion that Wilcox had instructed him to remain. Oddly, she was relieved that the footman did not budge from where he stood off to the left, behind where she was seated. Bless Wilcox for sending the young man to act as her protector. She was so frazzled, she hadn't she thought to summon her maid to act as chaperone. Thank Heaven for their stalwart butler.

"Addlepated," she whispered. Someone cleared their throat, and she glanced up and noticed the merriment in the depths of the lieutenant's brilliant green eyes. He was definitely a charmer. She imagined he had broken more than one heart before his injury. She shifted her gaze to the man next to the lieutenant— Captain Bayfield, who was as handsome as the lieutenant, though neither one held the appeal of the annoying Irishman who had trouble remembering to address her properly.

Emily set her teacup and saucer on the occasional table near her chair. "Now then, gentlemen—"

Mr. Garahan interrupted, "Ye never answered me question before—what does *messers* mean?"

She quelled the frustration building inside of her. Mayhap Mr. Garahan was unfamiliar with the term. "When addressing a group of gentlemen—" she began, only to be interrupted—again!

"There the lass goes again." Mr. Garahan had a pained look on his face, while the other two chuckled.

Ignoring the outburst, she continued, "As I was saying, when addressing a group of gentlemen, one can use the shortened version of *monsieurs*—which is *messrs.*"

"French, is it?"

Was Mr. Garahan trying to incite her temper? He had no idea she had one—did he? "Yes, Mr. Garahan—"

"*Just* Garahan," he interrupted. "If ye please, Miss Montrose."

Surprised, and pleased, that he'd addressed her correctly, she smiled. "I shall endeavor to remember you prefer to be addressed by your surname."

"We prefer it as well," Lieutenant Tremayne announced.

Captain Bayfield nodded, and she acquiesced. "Very well, I shall use your surnames when speaking to you."

"And we shall call ye *lass*," Garahan said with a broad grin.

Her gasp was loud. The amusement on the faces of the men irritated the breath out of her. It took every ounce of her control to remain calm. She did not bother to correct Garahan again—she ignored him.

Exhausted from her morning meeting with Father's solicitors, and trying to keep ahead of the conversation with the three men apparently assigned to her protection detail, she stood and announced, "I am expecting one of Father's solicitors to return at four o'clock. Until then, I shall remain here sorting through the documents I received this morning."

The men rose, and Garahan asked, "Does Wilcox know the man?"

"Yes, why?"

"Is he a trusted friend of your father?" Bayfield asked.

"I assume so. I never asked," she replied.

"How long has he been your father's solicitor?" Tremayne asked.

She stared at Tremayne and finally shrugged. "I'm afraid I cannot give you the exact number of years—fewer than ten, more than five, if I could hazard a guess."

The group of men seemed to accept her response. "We'll be speaking with Wilcox and the footmen." Garahan looked over his shoulder and nodded to the footman behind her. "Yerself included."

After Emily's maid set the last of the dessert plates and tea-cups and saucers on the tray, the footman carried it from the room. When he passed Garahan, Emily thought she heard him whisper, "Thank you."

There was definitely more going on beneath the surface than she knew. Would any one of the servants speak to her about it? The sickening thought that others questioned the way her father had been struck down by a carriage racing along the streets of London filled her. Unsure of whom she could ask, she kept the worry to herself...for now.

Nodding to the men as they filed out, she hoped that once she was more acquainted with them, she would feel she could trust one of them enough to ask the questions that had caused so many sleepless nights. Had Father been murdered? If so, why? More importantly, by whom?

"Do you need me to stay, miss?"

"I'll be fine, Helen. I need some quiet to digest all that I've just learned, before I return to the task of reading the documents my father's solicitor left with me."

"Very good, miss. Ring if you need me."

"Thank you. I will." At the close of the door, she sighed audibly, relieved to finally be alone. Retracing her steps, she sat behind her father's desk once more. There were so many questions, tangled with the fear that her father's death had been engineered by someone. Again, the twofold worry, of whom and why, had a nagging ache forming at the base of her skull.

Studying one document after another, she tried in vain to ignore the intensifying pain. Finally she finished, gathered them into a neat stack, and returned them to the leather case they'd been delivered in. Father's solicitors had explained the contents earlier, but she wanted to read them for her own edification. She smiled, remembering her father teaching her the importance of reading documents before signing anything.

Picking up the duke's missive, she read it again. Her thoughts may be muddled about the circumstances surrounding Father's death, but one thing was crystal clear—she had a temporary personal guard who would be with her until they delivered her to the duke's doorstep whether she liked it or not!

Well, the Duke of Wyndmere was in for a shock. Emily had no intention of being a biddable ward, nor would she acquiesce to marrying a man of the duke's choice. She had no plans to marry—ever!

CHAPTER THREE

"THERE'S WORRY IN the lass's eyes," Garahan told the men, waiting to meet Lord Montrose's staff.

"Has there been an investigation?" Bayfield asked.

"Did Montrose owe a debt he could not pay?" Tremayne wondered aloud.

Garahan clenched his jaw and shook his head. "I'll be asking King and Coventry why they made no mention of this."

The grumbled agreement from the men flanking him eased the tight knot in his gut. There was more to the situation than they'd been told. The question was, why?

Wilcox arrived with the staff. The suspicion that it was no accident Montrose had been run down lay heavy in the air. Did the staff sense it too, or did they suspect the lord had purposely stepped in front of the fast-moving coach? Neither option sat well with Garahan. The question remained—why hadn't King mentioned there were unsettled circumstances surrounding the death of Montrose? Was it his way of getting the gut reaction from Garahan, Tremayne, and Bayfield?

He'd be asking King before the day was out. First he had to convince the lass—*Miss* Montrose—to trust Tremayne, Bayfield, and himself. Had she had the time to grieve? If she were like his ma, she'd hold on to her grief to be strong for those around her, until she was alone, and allowed it to rage out of her.

His gut settled with the realization that he wanted be the man to offer his shoulder to weep on when the lass finally let go of her grief.

He turned his attention to those gathered. They needed to be prepared for their household to be inundated with unwanted callers once word got out that Miss Montrose was an heiress with a sizeable dowry. Scanning the group, he was pleased to note that, though young, the footmen appeared strong enough to fend off any fortune hunters, if the need arose.

"Me name's Garahan. I am part of the Duke of Wyndmere's personal guard and have been chosen because of me skills to protect his lordship's daughter. To me left is Lieutenant Tremayne, to me right, Captain Bayfield. Both men have been chosen because of their skills protecting our country. The retired Lieutenant Tremayne served in the King's Royal Dragoons, and retired Captain Bayfield served in the King's Royal Navy. Both are revered for their bravery under fire... Both were injured in battle."

The staff gathered were oddly quiet.

"We ask that ye help us protect Miss Montrose, and appreciate your assistance. We're dividing the staff between the three of us. Would the gardener, stable master, coachman, and stable lads follow Tremayne? He'll speak to ye and answer yer questions. Would the housekeeper, cook, and maids follow Bayfield? Wilcox and the footmen remain here."

The staff followed Garahan's request, dividing into three groups. One of the footmen glanced over his shoulder at Tremayne, and then back. "My father was in the dragoons."

The look on the younger man's face was telling. Garahan knew the lad's father had given the ultimate sacrifice. "Me belated thanks to yer da, and yer family for his service. What's yer name?"

"Honeywell."

"Are ye the sole support of yer ma? Do ye have any siblings?"

"I have an older brother. The two of us support Mum and

our four younger sisters."

Garahan placed a hand to the footman's shoulder. "You and your brother do yer family proud. If ye need anything, let me know. Me brothers, me cousins, and meself understand the importance of family, and support ours by sending our wages home."

He was pleased to note the admiration in the eyes of the other footmen at his pronouncement.

"Is there anything ye've observed while performing yer daily duties that ye think we should know?" Garahan hoped someone would say something that indicated the state of Lord Montrose's mind prior to the tragic accident—*if* it was an accident.

He noted two men shifting from foot to foot, avoiding his gaze.

"Well then, if ye think of anything, let one of us know. Bayfield will be on duty inside, while Tremayne and I will guard the perimeter of the building."

"Aye, Mr. Garahan," Honeywell was quick to assure him.

"Just Garahan. Now then, I've received the information from Wilcox as to where ye're stationed throughout the day, and who has been entrusted with sending missives at his lordship's request. I have a missive that I need sent to Gavin King of the Bow Street Runners."

The group murmured, and one footman raised his hand. "My name's Brewster. I usually handle—" He cleared his throat and continued, "I *handled* delivering his lordship's missives." The flash of sorrow in the young man's eyes spoke louder than words. Lord Montrose was well loved among his staff. "I have been to Bow Street on occasion, and will ensure your missives get into Mr. King's hands and no other."

"Well then, Brewster, I'll be thanking ye now, as ye'll be kept busy delivering messages between here and Bow Street, as well as to Captain Coventry, the Duke of Wyndmere's London man-of-affairs, on the corner of Hart and Lumley." Garahan thanked the group, reminding them where he and the others would be stationed. "I'll let ye return to yer duties. Ye know where to find me if ye need me."

The chorus of *ayes* pleased him. They may be on the young side for footmen—which had him wondering if Montrose hired young men who were supporting their families instead of seasoned footmen. Watching the group disperse, he noted they were all different heights, with varying builds and coloring—not what the cream of Society usually expected to see in a lord's household. Most had footmen of similar coloring, height, and physiques, who wore well-tailored livery. As the *ton* no doubt intended, it left a distinct impression.

Tremayne and Bayfield were still addressing their groups. Garahan nodded to them and walked over to where Wilcox stood off to the side. "A question, Wilcox. I've noticed the footmen are all young."

"But strong and determined to work," Wilcox added.

"How many are the sole support of their families?" Garahan asked.

The look of surprise on the butler's face did not deter him from answering, "More than half."

Garahan filed that knowledge away. "Have their fathers all served in His Majesty's forces?"

Wilcox locked gazes with Garahan before answering, "Aye. There's not one among them who has not lost a father or uncle in service to the Crown."

"Only Honeywell spoke up."

"It's not something they willingly speak of," Wilcox told him.

"Wasn't it the reason they were hired?" Garahan asked.

"In part," Wilcox admitted. "A very large part. But they're a proud group and will do whatever task I assign them—and do it well."

"Good to know. If any of them are in need of coin for any reason, I'd like to help."

Wilcox nodded. "His lordship would have highly approved of you, Garahan."

"As I know he valued yerself taking the young footmen under yer wing and advising his lordship as to who needed an extra hand now and again. Ye've done well, Wilcox."

Wilcox turned to study the other members of the staff still speaking with Tremayne and Bayfield, and Garahan realized something.

"I should have asked, but was impressed with Brewster when he said he'd delivered messages for Lord Montrose."

"He has been trusted to handle *delicate* matters for his lordship in the past. Will he be expected to deliver missives to all parts of London?"

When they were alone, Garahan intended to ask Wilcox what those delicate matters were. "Just two locations," he answered. "Gavin King of the Bow Street Runners, and Captain Coventry, the Duke of Wyndmere's London man-of-affairs."

Wilcox's eyes widened, but he did not remark on the men Garahan would be in constant contact with.

Tremayne's group filed out, with Bayfield's right behind them. "I think we should be able to do our job with minimal interference," Tremayne said.

Bayfield agreed. "The housekeeper returned while you were speaking to the footmen. Mrs. Minnover was handling a personal errand for Miss Montrose."

Garahan frowned. "I didn't realize she wasn't here. Did she say what the errand was?"

"Nay."

"I will make a point to speak to Mrs. Minnover. There will be no secrets while we're on duty."

The two men agreed and left to man their posts. Garahan went in search of the housekeeper.

Wilcox sent him to the sitting room, where Mrs. Minnover would be meeting with Miss Montrose. As he drew closer to the room, he heard soft voices. He slowed his steps, not wanting to intrude. He could give the housekeeper and Miss Montrose a little more time.

Standing with his hands behind his back to the side of the doorway, he wondered if they planned to spend the next hour chatting. He smiled remembering how the lass with the cool gray eyes and fiery auburn hair had stood up to him, arguing with him, when she should have been thanking him!

The sounds of skirts swishing signaled their conversation was at an end, but it wasn't the housekeeper who emerged.

"Begging yer pardon, Miss Montrose."

Her eyes flashed with irritation before she quickly buried the emotion. "What are you doing standing outside the sitting room? I thought you had a job to do."

He ignored her sharp tone and stared into her eyes. As he'd hoped, his silence confused her. When she lifted her hands to her waist—a gesture she'd used earlier when her hands were trembling—he took pity on her. "I can do me job in any part of yer household. I was waiting to speak with Mrs. Minnover. As ye were already conversing with the woman, I have been patiently waiting for ye to finish."

Her troubled gaze lifted to his. "Is there any reason you need to speak with our housekeeper?"

"A number of them. Most have to do with the changes that were agreed upon while she was away from the town house doing yer bidding."

Her flash of irritation added roses to her cheeks and deepened the hue of her eyes to the color of summer storm clouds. "Are you questioning my decisions already?"

The tremble in her voice hinted that something besides her father's passing may be weighing heavily on the lass. Never one to skirt around a situation—preferring to meet them head-on—he asked, "Is there something that has ye worrying, something ye need to unburden?"

Tears welled in her eyes. She blinked, transferring the moisture to her long eyelashes. She ignored the tear that got past her guard and stared at her feet. "Nothing is wrong."

He knew that wasn't true. Avoiding eye contact was a sign a

person was either uncomfortable, or hiding something. Mayhap both. "As ye have yet to meet His Grace, 'tis best ye know, he never shirks his duties."

She lifted her head to meet his gaze.

"His Grace always keeps his promises, and would die before breaking a vow. Agreeing to become yer guardian, should anything happen to yer da, is a vow the duke will not break. Do ye understand?"

He waited for her to decide. Finally, she nodded.

"How long do ye think it'll take ye to trust me?"

She blinked. "I have no idea."

The housekeeper joined them in the doorway. "Mr. Garahan, I understand you and Messrs. Tremayne and Bayfield will be staying with us for a time."

Garahan coughed to cover the fact that he'd laughed at the way the woman phrased her statement. "We will be staying—but not as guests, mind. We're here to see to Miss Montrose's protection until Lord Montrose's will has been executed to the satisfaction of his solicitors."

"I see," the older woman murmured, with a sharp glance at Miss Montrose. "That was not what I was led to believe."

"Then 'tis a good thing we're having this conversation, Mrs. Minnover. And by the way, just Garahan—no mister."

The housekeeper smiled. "There have been a few troublesome moments in the last sennight."

Miss Montrose frowned. "That have been settled and are no longer of any consequence."

"I'll be the judge of that. Why don't ye fill me in before I return to me post?"

Mrs. Minnover's eyes widened. "Your post?"

"Aye, at the moment Tremayne and I are guarding the perimeter of Lord Montrose's town house. Bayfield is stationed inside."

"Do you expect intruders to storm the front door?"

He fought the urge to smile at the housekeeper's question.

"Anything is possible when a man of wealth and means passes, leaving his only daughter, who is now an heiress, to navigate the world alone."

"I'm not alone," Miss Montrose grumbled. "You're here trying to control our comings and goings."

"Have ye ever had a gentleman ye did not know barge into yer sitting room insisting he speak with ye alone?"

She slowly smiled, and he was momentarily distracted by the entrancing sparkle in eyes. Her plump lips tempted him to lean close and taste them. Would they be sweet—or tart?

"Yes, though he did say he never claimed to be a gentleman… You!"

Frustration would give way to anger if he did not control his roiling emotions. "Wilcox announced me."

"After I refused to see you."

"Ye cannot refuse to see a messenger from the Duke of Wyndmere."

Her eyes narrowed. "But you are not a messenger, are you, Garahan?"

He clenched his jaw to keep from saying something he may regret. Squaring his shoulders, he decided to show his displeasure. She needed to understand who was in charge here, and by all that was holy—it was not her!

Mrs. Minnover tugged on Miss Montrose's arm. "I do believe you owe Mr. Garahan an apology, Miss Montrose. The duke's message was quite clear, as was Lord Montrose's reason for having Wilcox and myself present as witnesses when his will was being read."

Miss Montrose refused to meet his gaze. He found it humorous instead of angering. "Ah, Miss Montrose, ye'd get along well with me ma. She's a strong woman, determined to have her way in all things."

That surprised a smile out of her. "Oh? And does your mother get her way in all things?"

He laughed. "Nay, though Da appreciates her willingness to

hold out until the last moment before giving in."

Her shoulders slumped. "Does your mother always give in?"

He sensed she needed coddling, and wondered how long her mother had been gone. His tone softer, but respectful, he replied, "Not even half the time. If she isn't right, she'll have convinced Da to change his mind."

"Is your mother such a persuasive speaker?"

He smiled. "Aye—'tis funny, but she usually uses the same argument every time, and faith if me da isn't a smart man who'd rather not be sharing the horse's stall in the barn to sleep in instead of his bedchamber."

The feminine snort of laughter charmed him. The fact that she didn't beg his pardon for the unladylike sound warmed his heart. He was coming to appreciate the stubborn lass and hoped she would soon see he was not the enemy, but the man who would protect her to the last beat of his heart.

When she swept past him, he decided to grant her a little while longer before pressing for an explanation as to what had occurred in the last sennight. An hour ought to be enough time.

CHAPTER FOUR

TREMAYNE'S SIGNAL, THE short, sharp whistle, had Garahan striding to the end of the alley. He frowned at the handsome cab slowing as it approached the Montrose town house. He nodded to Tremayne and started walking toward the front door. Tremayne did the same.

They met in the middle as the carriage rocked to a halt and the door swung open. A well-dressed man stepped down onto the sidewalk, ignoring the two of them. *Fortune hunter.*

Irritated, Garahan, ordered the man, "State yer business."

The man kept walking—and suddenly found himself flanked by two tall, very broad men. This time it was Tremayne who gave the order. "State your business."

The lordling lifted a quizzing glass to his eye and frowned. "My business is none of your affair." When he took a step, he found himself tightly wedged between the larger men.

"Well then, boy-o," Garahan said. "If ye do not want to have to explain to Gavin King of the Bow Street Runners what business brings ye to the Montroses' front door, ye'll answer our question."

"Now," Tremayne added.

The man's attempt to square his shoulders resulted in the men pressing against him.

Their meaning was clear—neither Garahan nor Tremayne

said another word. They waited. When the caller remained stubbornly quiet, Garahan said, "Faith, I cannot seem to remember what King suggested we do with any man who came calling uninvited."

"I believe he wanted us to summon the Watch or the constable," Tremayne answered. "If we have the time, we were to personally escort him to King's office on Bow Street for questioning."

The man's sharp intake of breath was music to Garahan's ears, but he wasn't about to let the stranger think he had the upper hand. "Ye take hold of his left arm; I'll grab the right."

"You are not serious about taking me to Bow Street. Are you?"

Garahan clamped a hand around the man's right arm. From the startled squeak, he knew Tremayne did the same, preventing the man from moving toward the front door.

"Wilcox will need to know I'm off to Bow Street," Garahan said.

"I cannot let you have all of the fun—in a closed carriage all the way to Bow Street," Tremayne said.

"What if I let ye have the next caller all to yerself?" Garahan asked, keeping an eye on the startled expression of their prisoner. Good—the man needed to know he was not in charge of the situation and would not be admitted without an invitation.

Tremayne grinned. "Done. Need help loading the prisoner?"

"Nay. Tell Wilcox I'll be back as soon as I can."

The man struggled against Garahan's grip as he dragged him over to the carriage and gave their direction to the hack driver.

"The fee is double if I'm transporting a criminal."

"Well now." Garahan paused as if considering his options. "I'll be letting ye accompany me into Gavin King's office and let ye explain why ye planned to charge me double."

The driver's face blanched. "The usual fare, then."

Satisfied, Garahan helped the prisoner into the carriage, climbed in behind him, and tapped the inside of the roof, signaling the coachman to be on their way.

He didn't mind the silence—it gave him time to wonder what the other man's tale was. It had to involve coin, or it wouldn't be worth a trip to Bow Street to be questioned by one of the more daunting men in charge of the Runners.

Halfway to Bow Street, the man spoke. "If you order the hack to turn around, I'll make it worth your while."

Garahan didn't bother to respond.

"The wager has reached a staggering amount for whoever wins."

A wager? That piqued Garahan's interest, but he remained silent.

"Any member of White's will verify that it is in their betting book," the man insisted.

Garahan turned to stare at him until he shifted on the seat. Knowing the power of silence, he waited.

Finally, the man told Garahan what he wanted to know. "Greenwood, Michael Q."

"What business do ye have other than wasting me time and that of King's?"

"Did you not hear what I said?" Greenwood repeated his offer.

The man had *bollocks* for brains if he thought Garahan could be bought. He never accepted coin, whether it be a gift, which usually came with strings attached, or a bribe. Bribes always came with consequences that the one offering the bribe never antici-pated.

The hackney pulled to a stop, and Garahan quickly stepped down from the cab. When Greenwood attempted to follow him, he shut the door in his face. "Wait here—ye'll be needing a proper escort to King's office."

One of the men outside the building recognized him. "What brings you here in the middle of the day, Garahan? You usually arrive in the middle of the night."

"Ye have the right of it, Proctor. I have a prisoner who insisted on an audience with King."

The Runner glanced at the carriage, noting the pale-faced occupant. "He's in a meeting, but I'd be happy to escort your prisoner and wait with him. The meeting should be over in an hour or two."

"You cannot keep me here!" Greenwood shouted.

Garahan grinned. "I'm thinking me prisoner hasn't realized we can keep him here as long as we like. Be sure to have King ask Greenwood about the wager involving me current assignment, what it entails, who placed it, and where. Oh, and he tried to bribe me—apparently the wager has reached a staggering amount."

"That would depend on whom you are speaking to, would it?" Proctor asked as they walked over to the carriage.

"Aye, though it wouldn't matter how much coin were offered. I cannot be bribed."

"I enjoy wagering at darts," Proctor said, "though it's the winner who buys the next round of ale." They were chuckling when Proctor opened the door and reached inside the carriage. "I believe King is going to enjoy interrogating you, Greenwood." With a nod to Garahan, he hauled the prisoner toward the building.

"It is not against the law to refuse to tell a stranger what business I have with Lord Montrose's daughter!"

"Ah, there's where you'd be sadly misinformed, Greenwood," Proctor told the man as he opened the door. "Garahan is a member of the Duke of Wyndmere's private guard and is on special assignment guarding Miss Montrose—the duke's ward. It's Garahan's duty to ask, and yours to answer."

Greenwood tried to plant his feet but, to Garahan's amusement, ended up stumbling as Proctor dragged him over the threshold.

Satisfied, Garahan grinned. "Well now, word will soon spread that no visitors will be allowed entrance to the Montrose town house." The last thing he heard was Greenwood whining that he didn't realize who Garahan was.

THE HACK DRIVER stopped behind the third carriage lined up in front of the town house. "Bloody hell!" Garahan pushed the door open and tossed his coin to the coachman.

Tremayne was nowhere to be seen, which had his hackles rising. The door opened before he could reach for the handle. "Wilcox! What are all these carriages doing here?"

From the grim expression on the butler's face, it had to do with the lovely heiress. "Miss Montrose is serving tea to three gentlemen in the sitting room."

"Where are Tremayne and Bayfield?"

"In the sitting room."

"Having a bloody cup of tea?" Garahan demanded.

"Standing guard," Wilcox corrected him, following.

Garahan waved him away. "Ye don't have to announce me."

"His lordship would never approve if I did not," Wilcox protested.

Garahan slowed his step. "Under other circumstances, I'll not interfere with yer duty, but right now, ye're interfering with mine. Why is the bloody door closed?" Instead of giving in to the need to kick it, he shoved it open, hard enough to slam it into the wall.

Neither Tremayne nor Bayfield moved a muscle, which took the edge off Garahan's anger. They'd been expecting him.

Given Miss Montrose's wide eyes and pale-as-flour face, she had not.

One of the three men stood and stalked toward him, demanding, "Who do you think you are bursting in on Miss Montrose and her guests?"

"'Tis yerself who will be answering me questions—later." Garahan turned his back on the man and said, "Tremayne, no one leaves until I get me answers."

Tremayne closed the door and stood in front of it. Bayfield remained on the opposite side of the room, behind Miss Montrose, where he had been poised to defend her.

It was a struggle, but Garahan kept his tone civil. "Suppose ye tell me why ye're serving tea, when ye told us earlier ye weren't receiving guests, as ye were in mourning?"

She met his censorious look with one of defiance, and he nearly laughed. The woman had grit to spare. "I was not receiving guests earlier," she told him. "I am now."

"Ah, there's where ye'd be wrong, then, lass."

She narrowed her eyes and spat out, "It's Miss Montrose to you."

Ignoring her outburst, he faced the three men, not bothering with pleasantries. "Miss Montrose is in mourning, and not taking callers for the foreseeable future. Before ye leave, ye'll tell me who are ye and why are ye here."

"How dare you come in here and start making demands?"

Garahan sighed. It was the cockerel who'd spoken up a few moments ago. He didn't bother to answer the question. Instead, he turned his attention to the two men still seated. "I just returned from escorting someone by the name of Greenwood to Bow Street. I left him in good hands." He smiled at the men and added, "He'll be meeting with Gavin King."

The two set their teacups on the table in front of them. The thinner of the two spoke first. "Gerald Ainsley, and my associate Francis Johnstone."

"Associate, is it? Not yer friend?"

The men glared at one another. *Not friends.*

"And ye just happened to call on Miss Montrose at the same time as—" He paused, shook his head, and said, "Faith if the *bollocks* for brains has yet to give his name."

"Do you have any idea who you are insulting?" the now-red-faced man demanded.

"Aye," Garahan answered. "Ye're the next man I'll be escorting to Bow Street to be interrogated by Gavin King."

The braggart's face turned ashen. Satisfied he finally had the man's attention, Garahan asked Ainsley and Johnstone, "Are either of you associated with Greenwood?"

The two shifted on their seats. They were. *Damn that bloody wager!* He'd have to send word to King that they needed to get to the bottom of whatever the wager was—and quickly. He'd not have Miss Montrose's reputation compromised because he did not perform his duty protecting her.

"Well now, as ye both are acquainted with the man, I'm thinking Tremayne will be the one escorting ye to Bow Street while I speak with Miss Montrose."

"See here—!"

Garahan strode over and got in the man's face. "Ye'll want to watch yer tone when speaking to me, boy-o."

"You are obviously hired muscle and far beneath my social standing," the man declared.

Garahan's control cracked. He grabbed the man by his cravat and lifted him off the floor. "It'll be me pleasure to relay yer thoughts to me employer, the Duke of Wyndmere."

The man's eyes rolled wildly from side to side. "Duke?"

"Meself, me brothers, and cousins form the duke's personal guard," Garahan said as he let go, smugly pleased when the man wavered on his feet.

"Best not utter another word, Wayne," Ainsley warned, "or you'll end up staying the night on Bow Street."

"He wouldn't dare."

Garahan grabbed the man by the arm and hauled him toward the door.

Tremayne raised an eyebrow in silent question, and Garahan answered, "If ye wouldn't mind. I'm thinking Wayne—"

"Baron Anthony Wayne," the man said through clenched teeth.

"As I was saying, Wayne is eager to spend a few hours being questioned by King. I wouldn't want to disappoint the man."

"Use my title, damn you. It's baron!" Wayne shouted. "I'm a member of the *ton* and demand your respect!"

Garahan glared at the shorter man. "Ye have to earn me respect."

Tremayne's eyes showed his silent agreement.

"If you'd accompany your cohort," Bayfield told the others, "I'm certain King would be happy to entertain you for the rest of the day."

"It isn't a crime to call on a young woman," Ainsley said.

"She was more than happy to receive us," Johnstone added.

Bayfield glared at the men. "I had just stepped into the hallway when you three arrived, reminding one another to go with the *ruse* that Miss Montrose sent for the three of you."

The gasp from behind him was all answer Garahan required. He would beat the bloody *shite* out of the men on the way to Bow Street. "I've changed me mind, Tremayne. Ye stay here with Miss Montrose, and I'll—"

"I need to have a private word with King," Tremayne interrupted. "Bayfield needs to fill you in on what happened in your absence."

Bayfield nodded. "And you wanted me to remind you that you wished to speak to Miss Montrose."

Tremayne stepped aside as the men filed past him into the hallway. "I'll send word if I expect to be longer than anticipated."

Garahan shoved the baron toward Tremayne, who grabbed hold of him before he could brush past and head for the door. Though he hated to miss the opportunity to be alone with the blackguards, he knew he'd have his chance to pummel them later.

TWO AND A half hours later, Gavin King looked up from the missive he was reading, nodded to Proctor, and glanced at the man entering behind his runner. "Greenbrook—"

"Greenwood," the gentleman corrected him.

King chose not to respond. "Be with you in a moment."

"I have been waiting for over two hours! I demand—"

King rose from behind his desk. "I'm a busy man, and right now you are interfering with an escalating situation that I am personally handling for the Duke of Wyndmere."

The man's face turned ashen.

King was satisfied with the man's reaction. He would use that emotion to his benefit. He ignored the newcomer and turned to his man. "Show Greenwood to one of the holding cells. I need to respond to an urgent missive."

"You cannot—" Greenwood began, only to pause when King looked at him. "As a busy man, I am certain you understand the importance of being prompt."

King held up his hand for his man to wait, deciding to let Greenwood spout while he digested Garahan's report and the one he'd received a few moments before. In Garahan's absence, three men—Ainsley, Johnstone, and Wayne—had coerced their way into Montrose House, using the ruse that Miss Montrose had sent for them in order to gain entrance. The wager in White's betting book—and the rumors surrounding Miss Montrose and her inheritance—had been confirmed from three different sources. It was time to take action.

"Are you aware of a wager involving the Duke of Wyndmere's ward, her inheritance, and her dowry?" King asked.

Greenwood shifted uncomfortably before denying any knowledge of the wager. "I have never even met the chit! Why would I have knowledge of her sizeable inheritance or dowry?"

King hid his smile. The titled buffoon had just implicated himself with the word *sizeable*. "Are you acquainted with Gerald Ainsley, Francis Johnstone, or Baron Anthony Wayne?"

For the second time, Greenwood shifted his weight before answering. "I have heard of Wayne. Why?"

"Thank you for waiting, Proctor. Escort Greenwood to one

of the cells while I question the other men. I believe I shall speak with the baron first."

"Baron Wayne is here?" Greenwood looked distinctly worried.

King didn't bother to respond. He had the information he needed. It was time to find out how many others, besides the four currently cooling their heels waiting to speak to him, were involved.

CHAPTER FIVE

EMILY WATCHED TREMAYNE leave with the three men who'd lied to gain entrance into her father's town house—no, not her father's any longer. It had been willed to her along with his sizeable fortune.

She was his only child and, fortunately for her, his title was not hereditary, or else some distant relation of her father would have already appeared at their door to claim his right to Montrose House. Father had earned his title in battle, and now that he had passed, it would return to the Crown. No part of her father's wealth and possessions were entailed… She was a very wealthy woman. Dear God, she'd rather have her father back.

Was this at the very heart of why Baron Wayne, Ainsley, and Johnstone had prevaricated in order to gain entrance to her home? She was heartsick that she'd been duped by three elegant calling cards. What possessed them to insist she'd sent for them? What would they have to gain by doing so? Did they not think she would eventually discover the truth? And why, in Heaven's name, would their butler think she had?

She could not countenance the idea that Wilcox thought she'd sent word to three gentlemen she did not know to call on her when she was in mourning. He and Mrs. Minnover had been with her family for as long as she could remember. He would never willingly put her in danger. There must be another reason why he allowed the men entrance. Mayhap it had something to do with the two men guarding her.

Fear slashed through her belly. Did this have to do with what she'd overheard about her father's accident?

Garahan interrupted her troubled thoughts. "I take it ye had no idea those three lied to gain entrance to yer home."

"If I had, do you think I would have admitted them?" She wanted to take back the words and amend her sharp tone, but she did not have the strength.

Garahan glanced at Bayfield before answering, "To tell ye the truth, Miss Montrose, I have no idea. From this moment forward, I'll ask ye to refrain from accepting callers."

Bayfield moved to stand beside Garahan. "This is a difficult time for you, Miss Montrose," Bayfield said. "In order to protect you, as was Lord Montrose's last wish, we're asking—not demanding," he added.

"Either way," Garahan said, "we expect yer cooperation in this. We have reason to believe that these three are only the first of those who will try to gain an audience with you."

Emily frowned at the serious expressions on the men's faces. "I cannot imagine why. Even though Father inherited his title for his bravery on the field of battle, he was accepted by those whose older brothers or uncles—who bore hereditary titles—had purchased their colors."

She smiled, recalling the fuss she'd made trying to refuse when her father insisted he gift her with a new wardrobe for her eighteenth birthday. He had hoped she'd take the *ton* by storm. After all, he'd reminded her at the time, she was the image of her beautiful mother. It had become clear even to Father that no matter how greatly she resembled her curvaceous mother, auburn hair and gray eyes were simply not *de rigueur*. The reigning Incomparables from her first two Seasons had ink-black hair and flashing green eyes. The previous Season's Incomparables were statuesque blondes with sky-blue eyes.

"Miss Montrose."

Mother would never have allowed the baron and his cohorts to call on her.

"Miss Montrose!"

She blinked. "Forgive me. I was woolgathering. What did you ask me?"

Garahan frowned at her, while Bayfield's expression remained neutral. She had no idea what either man was thinking.

"Circumstances have changed, and we need yer word that ye'll cooperate."

Irritated, she reminded him, "I have already agreed to cooperate."

"Yet the moment I leave," Garahan said, "ye invite three ne'er-do-wells into yer home."

The censure in the man's voice had her blinking back tears. "I apologize. I had no idea."

Bayfield was quick to add, "We are awaiting word from Bow Street, at which time we will be at liberty to explain the situation more fully. You'll understand we are not being unreasonable in our request."

Unhappy with having one more aspect of her life snatched from her hands, she wondered how her assigned protectors, closer in age to her than was comfortable, could be so immovable. There had to be a way for her to continue with her normal routine: early-morning walks, carriage rides in the park, shopping on Bond Street, and stopping for tea or an ice at Gunter's. She would go mad if she couldn't, but she was in no place to make any demands until she knew the reason why they were being overly protective of her.

Knowing she had to agree, she inclined her head. Clenching her hands into tight fists, she drew in a calming breath—and then another. "I appreciate what you are trying—"

"We are not *trying* to do anything, Miss Montrose," Garahan said. "By yer da's last request and the missive from the Duke of Wyndmere, we are yer guards until we deposit ye at Wyndmere Hall. Like it or not, lass, ye will obey us."

She felt a flush heat her belly and rush to the top of her head. Incensed, she shot to her feet. "Botheration! I'm not a blasted package to be ferried from one town to another! And for your information, I obey no man!"

The frustration in Garahan's eyes had shame washing over her. Her anger fizzled out as she struggled to regain her equilibrium. "Please, forgive me. I normally am quite easy to get along with."

"Are ye now?" Garahan asked, as Bayfield coughed to cover the fact that he was laughing.

She frowned at both men, irritation breaking through her hard-won surface calm. "As a matter of fact, I am."

"And ye've been bending over backward to do as yer da asked until matters have been settled and we journey to the Lake District?"

Emily lifted her chin and narrowed her eyes at the irritating Irishman. His dimple deepened as his lips curved into a devastating smile. Oh, that was unfair, using his good looks and charming smile to get his way. "I have."

Bayfield cleared his throat and asked Garahan, "Have you spoken to Wilcox and asked what occurred before I arrived in the entryway?"

Garahan shook his head. "I'm about to. I wanted to speak to Miss Montrose first."

Tired of being spoken about as if she were not in the same room, she drew on the persona she used when attending Society functions—that of an imperious young heiress. "You may leave, Garahan."

The man stiffened and turned to glare at her. "Ye'll want to remember Bayfield and I have His Grace's permission to lock ye in yer room until matters are settled."

Her mouth gaped open—but she was unable to utter a sound.

"As I told ye, His Grace will honor his word to Lord Montrose, seeing to yer safety at all costs. If it be at the cost of yer freedom for a fortnight, or however long it takes to finish the bloody paperwork required to settle yer da's affairs, then so be it."

While she struggled to calm her racing heart and tamp down her temper, she heard Bayfield ask if he wanted one of the footmen to join him standing guard on the perimeter.

She could feel the weight of his gaze upon her, though she'd be damned if she'd give the man the satisfaction of acknowledging his look—or his leave taking.

"Best send two."

Garahan left the sitting room, and seemed to suck all of the life out of her when he departed. Why in Heaven's name would she feel that way?

"I hope that once we receive the missive from King, you will be more amenable to cooperating, Miss Montrose," Bayfield said. "It is difficult enough to give your vow to protect someone with your life—but to have the one you are guarding act is if your life is of no consequence will have the others, and myself, questioning whether you are used to demanding your way or if you are simply unkind." He bowed and left the sitting room.

She did not feel her tears until they dampened the bodice of her gown. "I'm not unkind," she told the empty room. "I'm devastated and frightened… Whatever happened to Father was no accident."

GARAHAN'S GAZE MET Bayfield's. "'Twas as we feared. She is holding something back from us."

Bayfield agreed. "Aye, but I cannot imagine Miss Montrose confiding in us yet. King should have received your missive by now. Should we wait until Tremayne returns to discuss the matter further?"

"Aye, we wait," Garahan said. "King has men in even the darkest corners of London. He'll already have heard a rumor about the wager—and confirmed it—along with the matter of her inheritance and dowry."

Bayfield added, "Or already suspects Montrose was murdered."

The two approached Wilcox, who was waiting for them. "I had no idea the men were lying," he said. "Given all Miss Montrose has had to deal with, I thought a visit with those she invited would cheer her."

"From all that we know of Lord Montrose and his household," Garahan told the butler, "you, Mrs. Minnover, and the rest of the staff are loyal and would never dream of putting Miss Montrose in harm's way."

Relief flashed on the older man's face. "If I could get my hands on those men…"

"Get in line," Bayfield said. "Behind Tremayne and me."

The butler ask Garahan, "What about you?"

"They're behind me."

Wilcox nodded. "I take it Miss Montrose was difficult?"

"She can't be helping the way she feels right now," Garahan said. "The grief has her in its grasp. No stranger to it, I know that we have to give her the time—and grace, as me ma would put it—to grieve in her own way and her own time."

"But not at the cost of her protection," Bayfield added.

Satisfied, the butler drew in a breath and asked Garahan, "How many footmen do you need to stand guard with you while you wait for Tremayne to return?"

"I'm thinking two outside with me, and two outside whatever room Miss Montrose is in."

"I shall see to it," the butler said.

"Where is her maid?" Garahan asked.

Wilcox frowned. "Poor Miss Helen, she was another youngster his lordship took on as staff to keep her from starving—or trying to earn enough money for food by picking pockets."

"Is she with Mrs. Minnover?" Garahan asked.

The butler nodded. "The housekeeper and Mrs. Christian are plying her with whiskey-laced tea."

"Why didn't she remain with Miss Montrose?" Garahan asked. "Surely they could have comforted on one another."

Bayfield answered, "The poor young woman broke down, sobbing right when the men arrived to call on Miss Montrose. What else could Miss Montrose do but send her to her bedchamber, or the kitchen, until she could compose herself?"

"Well then," Garahan said. "In the future, if her maid is indisposed, we'll have to ensure that either Mrs. Minnover or Mrs. Christian are with Miss Montrose at all times for propriety's sake."

The darkness in the butler's gaze confirmed what Garahan suspected—Wilcox suspected Lord Montrose's death was no accident. "What do ye know that ye haven't told us?" Garahan asked.

Wilcox was quick to answer, "I do not have any hard facts, but I'll be happy to discuss it after I send Mrs. Minnover in to sit with Miss Montrose."

Garahan and Bayfield watched the man leave his station, and took up his post.

"Carriage wheels rumbling over cobblestones make a racket," Bayfield said.

Garahan agreed. "A fast-moving carriage is even louder."

"How many enemies do you think Montrose had?"

Garahan clenched his hands into fists at his sides and slowly opened them. "I'm thinking we're about to find out. We'd best be sending word to our eyes and ears about London. There's far more at stake here than the duke, King, or any of us suspected."

"Miss Montrose's life could be in imminent danger," Bayfield said. "The fact that there is a wager, which has the bottom feeders of the *ton* seeking her out, is our warning to double our defenses. Masterson and Hennessey should be returning to London soon. I'll send word to Coventry to let him know we need to add them to our guard."

Garahan wished he could counter the notion, telling Bayfield he was overreacting, but his gut knotted—a sure sign trouble was headed their way. "We could ask King to loan out Franklin, Jackson, Greeves, or Thompson. They've worked closely with us before."

Bayfield met Garahan's gaze. "We will not let anyone get past our guard."

"What about those bandy-legged cockerels?" Garahan asked.

Bayfield snorted with derision. "Tremayne and I kept a close eye on them. We needed to see what Miss Montrose's reaction would be. She seemed flattered...but surprised they had called."

"What if one of them—"

Bayfield interrupted, "Tremayne or I could take on all three at once with one hand tied behind our backs."

"'Tis the truth ye speak, but 'twas beyond aggravating arriving to see the lineup of carriages and not one of ye standing guard outside!"

"It was imperative that we were in the room guarding Miss Montrose."

Garahan finally gave in, admitting, "Ye're right, but 'tis galling just the same."

"Even you cannot be in two places at one time, Garahan."

"Faith, it doesn't mean I won't try."

Later that night, Garahan's words would be put to the test.

CHAPTER SIX

EMILY SMOOTHED HER hands over her skirts as she stood, though truthfully, not a wrinkle marred the soft batiste gown in a color she had never worn before...the daily reminder Father was gone.

She cried herself dry after the three lords, who'd professed to be devastated by her loss and hoped to be of comfort to her, were summarily removed from the sitting room. It was time she accepted her responsibility and role as mistress of Montrose House...though she may not be for long. Her housekeeper and cook should not have to try to guess what meals would be served—or the sleeping arrangements for His Grace and Captain Coventry's men.

One last glance in the looking glass above the washstand in her bedchamber, and she was ready to return to her duties.

Mrs. Christian looked up from the pot she was stirring when Emily entered the kitchen. "Are you feeling more rested, Miss Montrose?"

"Yes, thank you. I'm here to go over the menu for our staff—which, surprisingly, has grown since I breakfasted."

Mrs. Minnover walked into the kitchen a few moments later. "Were you able to rest?"

The housekeeper's direct look left no doubt in Emily's mind—she'd been weeping. "I was, thank you. I planned to go over the menus with Mrs. Christian, and now that you are here, we can go over the sleeping arrangements for His Grace's guards."

Mrs. Minnover shook her head. "No need to worry about the sleeping arrangements. Apparently the men have already discussed the matter with Wilcox and the stable master. They only need one cot—in the stables."

Emily frowned. "There are three of them—surely they intend to sleep at some point."

The knock on the doorframe had her spinning around. She should not have been surprised to find Garahan standing there, his broad shoulders filling the span of the doorway.

"Ah, here ye are, Miss Montrose. I have a few questions for ye, now that Tremayne has returned."

Had the men who'd gained entry to her home by spouting falsehoods been dealt with already? "Is Tremayne ready to speak with me and advise what occurred?"

"Tremayne has already given his report to me. *I* need to speak with you about another matter."

"I beg your pardon?" She strove to keep the edge from her voice when she asked, "Did you say he's already given his report?"

"Aye."

His neutral expression was irritating, his words galling. "As mistress of this household, he should have reported to me immediately upon his return."

"Mrs. Minnover, would you and Mrs. Christian excuse us? I need to have a word with yer mistress."

Emily balked at the suggestion. "I have nothing to say to you."

His dark eyes sent a silent message, one of impatience. "Ah, but I've something important to discuss with ye. If ye don't mind, Miss Montrose."

"While you were resting," Mrs. Christian said, "Mrs. Minnover and I put together a menu we felt you would approve of. You can make any changes you feel necessary after your discussion with Garahan."

Emily nodded to the cook and frowned at Garahan. "I do hope you will be quick about it."

His lips twitched, but he did not smile. She wondered if it would add to his handsome visage—or detract from it. As he motioned for her to precede him, she suspected it would only add to the man's appeal.

Once they reached the door to the main side of the town house, he reached around her to open it for her. "After ye, Miss Montrose."

He was close enough that she could see flecks of gold in the depths of his eyes and inhale his masculine scent—a heady combination of soap and man.

"I hate to rush ye, lass, but I need to be at me post."

His words snapped her out of her reverie. She had absolutely no business whatsoever daydreaming about his distracting lips or getting a closer look—and sniff—of the man! Though she was afraid before too long she would have to satisfy her overwhelming curiosity and find out for herself if his mouth would be firm, demanding a response from her…or soft, coaxing a response.

"I know ye're suffering, Miss Montrose," Garahan said. "But I need ye to try to set that aside for a few moments." He strode down the hallway, and she found herself practically skipping to keep up with him.

They reached her father's library—the room the trio had commandeered while they were here. He opened the door and waited for her to enter.

She brushed past him, careful not to touch him, though it was a challenge, as the man was immense. His size distracted her, but not because she feared him—oddly enough, it comforted her.

Angry with herself and her wandering mind, she marched over to her father's favorite chair and sat. It was time to take back control of her life and her home.

Garahan closed the door behind him and walked toward her.

The frown on his face warned her she was not going to like what he would have to say.

"I'll get right to the point, Miss Montrose. It has come to me attention that there are questions concerning yer da's accident and that ye sent Mrs. Minnover on a errand for you. An errand that would garner information confirming yer suspicions about his death."

His death. Her stomach flipped over and bile rushed up her throat. Drawing on every ounce of strength in her body, she forced it back down. She would not cast up her accounts in front of the man! Biting on the inside of her cheek, she was able to control the urge to retch.

When she remained silent, he said, "I see."

She rose to her feet. "How could you? I did not say anything!"

"I could not miss the terror in yer eyes, or the way yer throat worked to control the need—"

"Am I not allowed to retain any of my dignity?"

"Forgive me for speaking plainly, lass, but do ye need me to fetch ye an urn or chamber pot?"

Mortified, cheeks burning with embarrassment, she asked, "Dear God in Heaven, whatever for?"

He looked down at the softly faded carpet at their feet. "I've been on the receiving end of me ma's considerable temper the time or two when I lost me lunch on the carpet she treasured."

Shock had her mouth gaping open, but the laughter in his eyes had her closing it with a snap. "You, sir, are no—"

"Gentleman," he finished for her. "We've been over this before, lass. How many times before ye accept it as fact?"

She closed her eyes and willed herself to her favorite reading spot—the wide, padded bench Father had specially crafted for her beneath the window in her bedchamber overlooking the garden. Warmth spread from her heart all the way to her toes. She sighed deeply and opened her eyes, surprised to find the reason for the warmth was not her memories—it was the Irishman who'd vowed to protect her holding her in his arms.

"Are ye steady now?"

"Now?"

"Ye started swaying. I could not let ye fall, lass."

The sound of his voice and the emotions swirling in the depths of his dark and dangerous eyes called to her. She shook her head, and his grip eased a moment before he let go of her.

"I did not mean to startle ye, lass."

"It's miss," she reminded him.

"Aye, that it is. Now then, why don't ye take a seat and ye can tell me where ye sent Mrs. Minnover?" She wavered, and he immediately reached out to steady her. "When was the last time ye ate?"

"I don't recall."

He guided her back to the chair then turned around and walked to the door. He leaned out, and she heard the soft rumble of his voice, though not his words.

He stepped back into the room. "Do ye want to wait until yer meal arrives, or do ye think we can finish our discussion?"

"I'm not hungry," she protested. Her stomach chose that moment to grumble.

"You may not be, but yer gut is. Ye need to be strong for yer da's sake. If there is more to what happened, ye'll need to face it with the strength yer da knew ye have."

She clasped her hands in her lap and stared at them. "How would you know?"

"Ye've been holding yer emotions in check since the moment we arrived on yer doorstep. I'm thinking ye've a spine of steel. Now is the time to prove me right."

She lifted her head and met his gaze. There was no censure there…only the calm expression he'd worn before, as he waited for her to acquiesce to him. "He used to tease me that I had inherited his stubborn streak."

"And it will aid ye in what may lie ahead of us. Now then, tell me what ye've been holding back."

Emily sensed she could trust the man, though it went against her nature to trust too quickly. If only Father were still alive... If only she hadn't overheard that conversation between Wilcox and one of the footmen.

"Lass, ye need to trust someone in yer hour of darkness... Let it be me."

The depth of his voice and sincerity in his tone had her blinking back tears. "It's not in my nature to trust easily." He held her gaze and waited. She sighed and said, "I overheard a conversation that has had me wondering if my father was involved in something dangerous."

When he handed her the linen square from his pocket, she stared at it for a few moments before she realized her face was damp with tears. "Er...thank you, Garahan." She blotted her face and gripped the handkerchief as if it were a lifeline.

"Did ye hear any particulars? Names or a place?"

She finally accepted the fact that he would not be leaving anytime soon. He was here to protect her at her father's behest through the Duke of Wyndmere. She could and would put her trust in Garahan. "I heard Wilcox say Father was pushed."

Garahan's face lost all expression. "Did ye now."

"Yes."

"Are ye certain ye did not mishear what was said?"

Irritated that he would question her, she snapped, "If I am to trust you, Garahan, the very least you can do is not question my word."

He shook his head. "I question everyone's word—even the duke's. Ye can ask him when ye meet him."

"Why is that?"

He shrugged. "Ma likes to remind me I'm the son who always questioned everything—even from a young age."

It didn't erase the irritation she felt, but it did help her to understand it was his way. "I know what I heard."

"Do ye remember when ye heard it?"

"Why?"

He shook his head. "Ye may want to trust me, but I'm thinking ye still don't."

She needed him to understand. "I am trying. Can that be enough for now?"

"When did ye hear Wilcox say yer da was pushed?"

"Right after Father's physician came to attend him."

"Was yer da still alive when the physician came?"

The stark memory of her father being carried into their home—too covered in blood to determine where the injury was—filled her.

The large, callused hand that grabbed hold of hers was just what she needed to calm her, center her. Drawing on her inner strength, she cleared her throat and felt the tightness ease. "I could not tell—and did not ask. He was covered in blood."

The compassion in Garahan's eyes was nearly her undoing. She had the overwhelming urge to throw herself into his arms. The memory of his strength…his warmth…would chase away her sorrow.

No! She needed to be strong.

"The physician was not here long," she murmured. "My heart hoped my father was badly injured—not fatally. But my head did not agree."

"What ye've said will help us determine the truth. If there is a culprit to be detained and charged in this matter, we will find him! Where did ye send Mrs. Minnover?"

She wavered in her resolve not to tell anyone. "There is an angel in London who helps women who have nowhere else to turn. I hoped our apothecary would know her name or how to get in touch with her."

When she lifted her gaze to meet his, he gave a brief nod. "Thank ye, lass. Ye have me word as a Garahan."

His declaration was a balm to the turmoil roiling inside of her. The bright spot in the darkness that had surrounded her since the night Father was carried inside…mumbling.

"I just remembered something!"

Garahan waited expectantly.

"He had to have been alive—he was mumbling something, but I could not make out what he was saying."

"I need to speak with Wilcox," Garahan said as Mrs. Minnover bustled into the room.

"I trust you two have finished your conversation?" she asked.

"Aye, Mrs. Minnover. Thank ye for allowing us the time. I'll be leaving Miss Montrose in yer care. I need to speak with Wilcox, then I'll be back to ask you a question."

The housekeeper promised, "I will see to it that she is not left alone."

Immediately wary, Emily said, "You make it sound as if I am not to be trusted."

"Just not left to yer own devices until we know the truth," Garahan corrected her. "Now then, if ye have need of me, I'll be with Wilcox before returning to me post outside."

"Thank you, Garahan," Emily rasped. "I promise to try not to vex you or the others further."

"We'd appreciate it, but understand ye're grieving, Miss Montrose." With that, he bowed and left the study. As before, the room seemed to have the life sucked out of it. Mayhap it was simply the loss of one strong, capable man's presence.

What would it felt like if a man like Garahan had courted her? Would he be genuinely interested in someone like her, or would he find her lacking because her hair and eye color were not *en vogue*? Did she even want to find out?

She shook her head to gather her wandering thoughts back to where they should be, tucked away in the back corner of her mind. "Now then, Mrs. Minnover, about that menu..."

CHAPTER SEVEN

"**I** NEED TO know everything."

Sorrow flashed in the butler's eyes for a moment before a neutral expression settled on the man's face. "I haven't been able to uncover any hard facts."

"About?" Garahan asked as he followed Wilcox to a door a few feet from the grand entryway to the town house.

"What Lord Montrose told me before he died."

Garahan entered the room and looked about him. A small desk and chair had been pushed into one corner, while a bookshelf with a few stiff brushes and cloths—probably used to keep Lord Montrose's guests' top hats and greatcoats pristine— nestled alongside a few books.

"Is this where ye spend yer time?"

The butler seemed surprised that Garahan didn't immediately ask what Lord Montrose said to him. A good sign that he had unsettled the man to the point where he would most likely get the truth out of him. "Er…yes, actually. When I have more than five minutes to myself, which has not happened since that night."

Garahan did not bother to ask which night. "Who brought Lord Montrose home?"

Wilcox hesitated, then answered, "A rather rough-looking character."

Garahan sighed at the vague description. "Could ye be more

specific? Was it the condition of the man's clothing, or was it his expression, or his manner of speaking?"

Wilcox sighed. "All three. He was a big man—similar in build to yourself, Tremayne, and Bayfield. He wore dark clothing—rather coarse, a working man's clothing, although not torn or soiled. The look on the man's face surprised me. If I hadn't been so concerned with the urgency of taking care of his lordship, I would have asked the man how he knew Lord Montrose."

"Ye believe there was a connection there?"

Wilcox nodded. "He had a hint of a brogue, very faint."

"Did he now?" Interesting, Garahan thought. Could he be one of Garahan's contacts? If he were, why hadn't the man arranged to speak with him?

"Not like yours, Garahan," Wilcox added. "A proper Scots brogue."

"Proper, is it? Tremayne has a connection with a former dragoon who hails from Scotland, although the man hasn't lived there in more than a decade. I'll be asking Tremayne to see what Cameron can tell us."

"We have exhausted every possible lead through our connections," Wilcox told him.

"Have ye been in touch with the Runners?"

Wilcox hesitated. "Not directly."

Interesting. "Ye have a connection?"

Wilcox hesitated. "I do not place my trust blindly."

"A man after me own heart. 'Tis the same for meself."

"I sense that you are a man of your word—so are Tremayne and Bayfield. The fact that you are all connected to the Duke of Wyndmere, a man his lordship trusted with his greatest treasure—"

"His daughter," Garahan interrupted.

"Aye, Miss Montrose. Factor in that you have close ties with the duke's man-of-affairs, and a higher up within the Bow Street Runners, and I would have to be bacon-brained not to trust you."

"Thank ye—I think." At the subtle lift of the other man's lips,

Garahan knew the butler fought not to smile—probably from years of keeping his thoughts and emotions to himself. "I will ask me contacts if they have heard who found Lord Montrose. Whoever it was may have witnessed the incident."

"Don't you mean the accident?" Wilcox asked.

"Well now, I've heard that ye've speculated aloud 'twasn't an accident."

"I never meant for Miss Montrose to hear that conversation. It was right after the physician left, and Mrs. Minnover, the staff, and I were all in a state of shock."

"As was Miss Montrose," Garahan reminded the man.

"She absorbed the physician's news as if it had been a blow. She never shed a tear that night."

"Shock affects people differently."

"I am not normally given to showing my emotions," Wilcox confided, "but I confess, the only way to hide the uncontrollable trembling of my hands was to fist them at my sides."

Moved by the man's declaration, Garahan sensed Wilcox would be the staunchest of allies in what he feared would be a web of deceit with a vicious enemy at the center of it—waiting to steal Lord Montrose's heart and fortune. "I normally resort to going a few rounds with one of me brothers or cousins."

"A few rounds?" Wilcox repeated.

"Bare-knuckle is one of our talents," Garahan explained. "Keeps the mind sharp and the reflexes toned."

"So it would seem," Wilcox replied. "Will you keep me apprised of anything you learn?"

Garahan held Wilcox's gaze for long moments before finally answering, "I may. Depends on what ye be wanting to know."

"Everything," Wilcox said. "Lord Montrose was a good man—the best of them—who deserved far better than to be run down in the prime of his life." As if he felt he'd shown too much emotion, the butler closed his eyes, drew in a deep breath, and apologized, "Forgive me. Of course it is up to you what you chose to disclose. I shall accept your decision, Garahan. Thank you."

"Ye mentioned delicate matters and the last sennight. Now would be the time to fill me in," Garahan said.

Wilcox sighed. "Before his lordship went out that last night, he'd received more than one missive via messenger."

"During the day, or was it in the middle of the night?" Garahan asked.

"Both."

"And were ye in the vicinity when the missives were delivered?"

"Aye. Both times, his lordship retreated to his private study on the second floor."

"Did he discuss the missives with ye?"

"Nay. But the day after each missive was delivered, a man called on his lordship."

"Do you remember his name?"

"Aye. Baron Hardwell," Wilcox answered. "There was something distinctly disturbing about the man—his demeanor and the way he raised his voice to his lordship. That had never happened in this house before."

"Do you remember any part of the loud conversation?" Garahan asked.

Wilcox's shoulders slumped as he replied, "'Bring the coin, or you'll never see her again.'"

Every muscle in Garahan's body tensed. "He threatened Miss Montrose?"

The butler nodded. "He had to have been, because his lordship has never kept a mistress, and only occasionally escorted one or two widows of officers he served with to a ball or musicale."

"Thank ye for trusting me with the name and the information. Ye're certain ye heard correctly?"

"Aye. I'll admit, I was concerned and did not like the look of Hardwell. I felt it my duty to listen outside the study, in case his lordship had need of me."

"Ye acted on what yer gut told ye, Wilcox. No one will fault ye for that. Ye may have given us the information we need to track down the bloody blackguard who orchestrated Lord Montrose's accident. Is there anything else ye can think of that may be useful to us?"

Wilcox shook his head. "I need to return to my post."

"Thank ye, Wilcox."

"I hope you find Hardwell. You know where I'll be, if you have need of me."

"I do. Thank ye."

Garahan noted the way Wilcox's left hand trembled as the man opened the door and returned to his station in the entryway. He would uncover the truth, though he suspected Hardwell was behind Montrose's death. They would need to be vigilant, because now that Montrose was out of the picture, Hardwell would think the way was clear for him to abduct the lass. And that would be his second mistake. The first would be to underestimate Garahan. One way or another, the truth, and the killer, would be brought to light. Justice would be served.

"Wilcox?"

The butler turned at the sound of his name. "Aye?"

Garahan strode over. In a low voice, he said, "Ye can count on us to ferret out the man and pry the truth from him."

Wilcox nodded.

"Ye'll know as soon as we've apprehended the bloody bastard."

Wilcox narrowed his gaze. "I could—"

"Remain here, with the others who will be arriving soon to strengthen our protective net around Miss Montrose."

The frustration in Wilcox's gaze disappeared as determination replaced it. "You can count on me, Garahan."

"Faith, I know it." Satisfied that he'd garnered every ounce of information from the man—and believed every word—Garahan went in search of Bayfield. He needed to share this latest information while they waited for Tremayne to return.

GARAHAN WAS AT his post, guarding the perimeter, when Tremayne returned. He waited for him to disembark from the hack. The other man's black look was telling. "What's happened?"

"One of King's men arrived when I was escorting our three guests into King's office," Tremayne answered.

"News of the wager, or do you have a name?" Garahan asked.

"Both," Tremayne said. "It seems a friend of the duke—the *fifth* duke—has returned from abroad and started a campaign to smear all that the present Duke of Wyndmere holds dear."

"His name, his family, extended family, and friends," Garahan rasped.

"Aye."

"What's the bloody bugger's name?"

"Not one I've heard mentioned before," Tremayne admitted. "Baron Hardwell, a lesser lord who was on the fringes of the fifth duke's crowd when he made his nightly forays into the underbelly of London."

Garahan stilled. "Hardwell?"

"Aye," Tremayne replied. "Do you know the man?"

"I don't, no. But that's the name of the man who sent missives via messenger to Lord Montrose the week before the incident."

"When did you find this out?"

"Just now, speaking to Wilcox, after Miss Montrose confessed she'd overheard Wilcox speculate that her father's accident was no accident."

"Is that all?"

"Nay," Garahan answered, "Hardwell apparently arrived to speak to Montrose in private the day after his missives were delivered." Before Tremayne could ask another question, Garahan added, "Stout man that Wilcox is, and determined to protect his lordship, he listened outside Montrose's private study and overheard Hardwell threaten to bring the coin or he'd never see her again!"

"We'll have to get this information to King immediately," Tremayne said.

Garahan asked, "Does King have any other information on the man?"

"Aye, apparently Hardwell went missing the night the fifth duke was shot in the back."

"Leaving the bedchamber of one of his married paramours," Garahan added. "'Twill be an uptick in the gossip involving His Grace and his family for sure." He met Tremayne's grim look. "King's certain Hardwell is the only one involved in this latest campaign to sully the duke's name?"

"He did not say, although from the black look when he imparted the information, I gather King suspects where one rat is feeding, more will have gathered."

"'Tis what they are," Garahan agreed. "Vermin in need of being exterminated."

Tremayne shook his head as they approached the side door to the town house. "I agree with you, but you and I have our orders to wound—not kill—those who seek to harm the duke and his extended family."

The urge to pummel something nearly overwhelmed Garahan. He drew on his reserves of patience and determination and blew out a breath. "I'm well aware that ye cannot be coaxing information from a dead man."

Tremayne's snort of laughter had Garahan able to fully contain his anger. It was odd for him to feel a connection with someone who was not family. "I'm thinking Ma would adopt ye if ye ever find yerself in need of family, Tremayne."

"I'll keep that in mind, Garahan. Thank you." Tremayne cleared his throat. "Anything else noteworthy happen while I was gone?"

"Aye." Garahan quickly filled the other man in on what had

occurred. "I've sent a missive off to Coventry alerting him to the ne'er-do-wells arriving earlier."

"Sound decision. Wouldn't you think that the man who brought Lord Montrose home after the accident would have identified himself?"

"Wilcox did not mention a name," Garahan said. "I'm thinking he didn't ask. He's been with the family for years and was no doubt in shock."

"Then we'll see what we can uncover with our connections, and Coventry's," Tremayne said.

"Ye'll be asking yer friend Cameron?"

"I'll send word around. He'll either respond…or show up on our doorstep."

Garahan nodded. "We'd best alert Wilcox. Can't have him sounding the alarm, when it'll be one of our own."

Tremayne hesitated before agreeing.

"Ye'd best spit out what ye were just thinking, Tremayne."

"What if Hardwell is not the only person we need to be on the lookout for?"

"We stand ready to defend, no matter the day or the hour," Garahan reminded him. "'Tis expecting trouble from within that has the hair on the back of me neck standing on end."

Tremayne glanced around them, shrugged, and said, "If the situation rapidly disintegrates, the three of us will stand shoulder to shoulder, form a triangle, and take on all comers!"

Garahan grinned. "We'll use it as one of our alternate plans."

"One of them?" Tremayne asked.

"Aye. Faith, it always pays to have more than one," Garahan said.

"What are you going to do about Miss Montrose?"

"Protect her with me life," Garahan answered without thinking.

Tremayne stared at him and asked, "And when her life is no longer in jeopardy?"

Garahan's gut clenched at the thought of having to move on

to his next assignment, leaving the lovely Miss Montrose in the duke's excellent care until a suitable match could be made for the lass. "I'll probably ask His Grace if I can spend me next rotation at Penwith Tower on the coast of Cornwall." He had best start distancing himself from the fair *cailín* with the entrancing gray eyes and sunset hair.

Tremayne seemed to be considering the notion. "Cornwall might just be far enough away."

CHAPTER EIGHT

CHASING AFTER THE shadow of a man who'd dared to attempt to breach their defenses, Garahan growled low in his throat, "Lord, why did I think I could be in two places at the same time?"

As if the Lord heard his prayer, the man he was following hesitated at the door to the stables, opened the door, and slipped inside. The sound of a scuffle and fists connecting with flesh had Garahan grabbing the handle and opening the door. Bayfield had the intruder by the throat up against one of the stalls. Whickers and whinnies of protest had him whistling between his teeth.

The horses immediately settled down, as he'd expected. They'd have to wait for their apple until after the intruder had been dealt with. "What have we here, Bayfield?"

"Apparently a man without a name."

Garahan noticed that Bayfield had yet to set the man back down on his feet. "Never met a nameless man before. I'm thinking he must be fatherless, too."

Bayfield's gaze met his, and Garahan knew Coventry's man had not intended to do serious injury to the intruder, but wasn't about to let the man go without a reminder of his folly this night.

"Best let him draw in a breath, Bayfield."

With a snort that sounded suspiciously like laughter, the former naval captain relaxed his grip enough to let the man draw in a breath. "You'll be sorry you—"

Before the man could finish speaking, Garahan had him by the lapels. "Ye'll be wanting to save yer breath and yer threats for yer meeting with our connection on Bow Street."

In the dim lamplight of the stables, Garahan noted the angry flush draining from the man's face. "Here now, there's no reason to call in the Runners."

"Then we are mistaken that you were trying to gain entry to Lord Montrose's town house without an invitation?" Garahan asked.

"At half past midnight," Bayfield added.

"I had a verbal invitation from Miss Mon—"

Garahan silenced the man's lie with a solid jab to his jaw. "I'll be going after this Hardwell meself," he said. "I'm thinking he needs a lesson in manners."

Bayfield handed Garahan his handkerchief, nodding to his bleeding knuckles. "My father taught me never to hit a man when he was speaking."

"Bloody waste of time where I come from. We're known for having the gift of words."

Bayfield chuckled. "Father was quick to add, if the scoundrel did not cease to speak falsehoods, or if he defamed someone of your acquaintance, an uppercut beneath the chin would be the best choice to silence the blackguard."

"Yer father sounds like a gentleman," Garahan said. "Me da isn't, and wasn't one to mind scraped knuckles. 'Twas Ma who took exception to injuries to our hands, as they were needed to help run the farm."

Bayfield nudged the man's foot and sighed. "Well-placed jab. Grab that bucket, will you?"

Garahan looked at the bucket hanging from a nail near the tack room and back to Bayfield. "'Twill be a waste of the horses' water. I've a better way to bring him 'round." Before Bayfield could stop him, Garahan lifted the man by his shoulders and shook him.

"Easy—you don't want King to think that we beat the man

senseless."

Garahan snorted with laughter. "'Twas one well-placed jab, and ye know it."

"You hit me!" the man accused the moment he opened his eyes.

"Aye."

"You aren't going to deny it?"

"Why would I?" Garahan asked.

"You'll soon find out when you are summoned before the magistrate—"

"Ye insulted the Duke of Wyndmere's ward," Garahan said. "I'm thinking ye'll be the one to answer for yer actions." The man's eyes rounded, but Garahan couldn't decide if it was in fear or awe. "Shall we start again, this time with the truth?"

A loud whistle had him spinning around and shoving the man toward Bayfield. "Tie him up! Tremayne's in trouble." Garahan shoved the door open and sprinted toward the walled garden at the rear of the town house. The sound of another scuffle made him wonder what in the bloody hell had happened since they dropped off the first load of fortune hunters into King's lap.

He rounded the corner in time to see Tremayne lift a man off his feet and toss him at two others. "Ye don't appear to be needing me help," Garahan said.

Tremayne didn't bother to look away from the pile of tangled arms and legs. "Apparently the wager has been increased again."

Garahan's anger burned. "Bayfield has another one in the stables. The bugger tried to run from me when I stopped him from going in the side entrance."

"That's where these three were headed," Tremayne replied. "As soon as one of them deigns to tell us their name, we can summon the Watch and wash our hands of them."

The man on the top of the pile moaned and sat up. "You will never find another footman's position among the *ton*!"

Tremayne bent down until he could look the man in the face when he replied, "Would you hire me as your footman?" When the man violently shook his head, Tremayne smiled. "My talents with a blade and pistol, earned serving as one of the King's Dragoons, are put to better use than that of a footman." He turned toward Garahan. "Wouldn't you agree?"

"Aye. As are me talents."

The other two intruders stirred and slowly got to their feet. Garahan studied them closely—though they were a bit worse for wear, they appeared to be well dressed. When there wasn't a sign that they were about to fight back, he asked, "Are ye surrendering yerselves, then?"

"Whatever for?" one of the men asked. "We have a verbal invit—"

Garahan delivered a right cross, silencing the man. "Anyone else care to lie about why ye are at the Montrose town house— after midnight—to call on Miss Montrose, who retired in the company of her lady's maid three hours ago?"

"We were told—"

Tremayne stepped in front of the third man. "Unless you are prepared to give us the name of whoever paid you to repeat that falsehood, you will be remanded into the custody of the Watch and be transported to Bow Street."

When the men fell silent, Garahan demanded, "Was it Hardwell?"

The identical look of surprise on the three faces was all the answer he required.

"Do ye plan to surrender, or do ye prefer that we bind yer hands?"

"You would not dare!" the first man he'd punched said.

Garahan had the man's hands bound behind his back before he could blink.

"Do you know who I am?"

"Aye, the scoundrel who thought he could break into the home of the Duke of Wyndmere's ward."

Three jaws fell open and silence ensued, making it easy for Tremayne and Garahan to tie up the other two men. "I'll fetch the Watch," Tremayne said as Bayfield approached.

"Where's yer prisoner?" Garahan demanded.

"The Watch arrived," Bayfield said with a nod toward the burly man walking toward them with a lantern and stout stick, leading a now-silent man behind him.

"Who summoned him?" Tremayne asked.

Bayfield shrugged. "I didn't have the time to ask. My guess would be Wilcox?"

The watchman nodded. "I've been summoned to Lord Montrose's home twice in the last fortnight."

Garahan stiffened, curled his hands into fists, and slowly relaxed them at his sides. "I see."

"Just to be sure whom I am speaking to," the watchman said with a nod to Garahan, "you are Garahan, one of the Duke of Wyndmere's private guard?"

"That I am."

"I've already met Bayfield, one of Captain Coventry's men," the burly man continued, "and you would be Tremayne, another of Coventry's men."

"Aye," Tremayne agreed. "Thank you for your timely appearance. One of us will accompany you to Bow Street. Gavin King will be expecting these four men."

"We are gentlemen," one of the men insisted.

Garahan walked over and got in the man's face, pleased when his Adam's apple bobbed up and down. *Good! The blackguard should be nervous.* "No gentleman calls on a lady in the middle of the night." The other man did not reply...nor did he move. Satisfied he had the man's attention, Garahan added, "But I'll be sure to report yer names to the Duke of Wyndmere, and their lordships."

"Lordships?" one of the other prisoners asked.

"Aye," Garahan answered. "The duke's brother, Earl Lippincott, and his cousins, Viscount Chattsworth and Baron Summerfield."

The mention of the duke and his family, well known among

the *ton* for rebuilding their families' fortunes and restoring their good names, was what turned the tide and had the men ceasing to struggle.

Surprised that the situation could be handled with words, Garahan wondered if he shouldn't have tried that tack first. As he followed the watchman, Tremayne leaned close and said, "Fists followed by the threat of someone higher up the social ladder than oneself always silences the worst of braggarts."

"More of yer father's advice?"

Tremayne shook his head and nodded to Bayfield. "His."

"Works every time," Bayfield said. "If Tremayne accompanies them, we'll need three of the footmen to stand guard with you, Garahan."

"And two others with you inside, guarding Miss Montrose," Garahan added. Had their scuffle been loud enough to wake her? Would she be concerned that whoever had run her father down was coming back to finish the job?

That reminded him of the watchman's words. "Tremayne, you and Bayfield guard the prisoners. I need to speak with the Watch."

The men did as Garahan bid, confident that he would fill them in later. "Was Wilcox the one who told you who we were?" he asked the watchman.

"Aye. Wilcox is a good man. Sad circumstances, that incident."

Garahan's ears perked up at the word *incident*…not *accident*. "Were the other times you were summoned here due to intruders trying to break into the Montrose home?"

"Aye, three different intruders. The last time was the night before Lord Montrose died."

"In the accident," Garahan finished.

The watchman shook his head. "I've heard whispers on the streets that there is a witness to what happened—and it was not an accident."

Garahan laid a hand on the man's arm. "Does the witness

have a name?"

The watchman looked over his left shoulder and then the right before answering. "Aye, her name is Miss Michaela. She's the angel who helps battered women find shelter. Her shadow is a former dragoon, like Tremayne. Cameron's his name."

Angel...that's who the lass sent the housekeeper to try to find. "Alasdair Cameron?"

"Aye," the watchman said. "Do you know him?"

"Tremayne does. Thank ye for the information—ye've been helpful."

Garahan returned to the men. "There's a witness. Find out all you can about a Miss Michaela—"

"Is Miss Michaela in trouble?" Tremayne asked. "Does Cameron know?"

"Aye." Garahan noted the concern in the other man's eyes. "She's in hiding."

Tremayne nodded. "Then Cameron is aware."

"Will ye seek him out before ye return?"

Tremayne was quick to answer. "I need to reassure Michaela that if she speaks to us, she will be under our protection as well as Cameron's."

"Oh, one more thing before ye leave. Wilcox mentioned that the man who brought his lordship home was built like us, wore coarse clothing, and had a Scots brogue. Ask Cameron what he knows—could be a friend of his."

"I'll ask him. Anything else?" Tremayne asked.

"Send word if ye don't expect to be home before dawn."

"I will."

Bayfield hailed a hack, and helped load the subdued quartet into the conveyance.

Watching the hack drive off, Garahan murmured, "Best speak to Wilcox. Find out if anyone in the house was disturbed."

"Why don't I take the rest of your shift on the outside perimeter?" Bayfield asked. "You can speak to Wilcox about what happened while you take my shift inside."

That Bayfield understood without words that Garahan had an unspoken need to look out for the lass should be cause for concern. At the moment, the only concern he had was whether or not she had been frightened into thinking the bastard who killed her father was coming for her.

CHAPTER NINE

"HOW MANY, GARAHAN?" Wilcox asked the moment Garahan stepped inside the town house.

"Four."

Wilcox frowned. "Claiming to be gentlemen, like the others?"

"Aye. Not one of me brothers or cousins have ever claimed to be gentlemen, and not one of us would ever attempt what those four just now tried to do. Bloody blackguards!"

The butler met Garahan's gaze. "A true gentleman does not need to proclaim it to all and sundry. It will be evident by his words. And his deeds."

"Me da and me ancestors all worked the land," Garahan said. "But not one of them would ever mistreat a lass. We were brought up to respect, and protect, women."

"We're cut from the same cloth, Garahan, as was Lord Montrose. From what I've heard, the Duke of Wyndmere is much the same."

"Ye'd be right. His Grace would die to protect his family—nearly has, on more than one occasion."

"Even though he has a private guard?"

Garahan shrugged. "'Tis work for the lot of us to keep an eye on himself every hour of the day, while doing the same for Her Grace and their twins."

Wilcox ran a hand through his hair, making it stand on end.

Surprised by the butler's show of frustration, Garahan asked, "Was it the same for ye? Trying to protect his lordship and Miss Montrose?"

Wilcox hung his head. "Aye, and I failed to protect his lordship that last night."

"What could you have done differently?" Garahan asked.

Wilcox shook his head. "Not a thing. His lordship tasked me with protecting Miss Montrose."

"'Tis a hard thing to absolve yerself of any guilt ye may be feeling, but if ye did the task put to ye, and seeing as how Miss Montrose is unharmed, I'd say ye did as his lordship asked…and still are."

"How many more do you think will try to gain entrance in order to 'see' Miss Montrose?"

"If what Tremayne, Bayfield, and I suspect has happened, and the wager has increased," Garahan said, "I'm thinking we'll be fending off a steady stream of fortune hunters, and lords down on their luck in need of an infusion of ready coin."

"Poor Miss Montrose," Wilcox murmured. "She's been through so much in the last fortnight—and now this."

"Where is she? I need to have a word with her."

"She won't want to be disturbed," Wilcox predicted.

"If I have to search the house room by room, I will, but the longer she stays hidden, the longer she'll worry. Do ye want that for yer mistress?"

The butler shook his head. "I do not. But with all that's happening, is it any wonder she locked herself away?"

Garahan stiffened at the news. "Has she? Where?"

The butler sighed. "The only place she feels safe…secure."

"Even with myself and the others guarding her?"

Wilcox's shoulders slumped. "If I tell you what I know," he said, "I'd be breaking my word to Miss Montrose. If I don't tell you, I'll be breaking my word to his lordship."

The man seemed torn. "What if I were to guess, and ye don't actually tell me anything?"

The worry in the butler's eyes lifted. "Yes. That would work. I'd hate for Miss Montrose to feel she cannot trust me. She desperately needs to trust someone."

Garahan stared at the man, trying to decide which question to ask first. Given how close father and daughter were, he went with his gut. "Has she locked herself in her father's room?"

Wilcox nodded.

"Has she hidden there recently?"

"After showing his lordship's physician out, we could not find her at first."

Remembering that she had lost her mother, Garahan asked, "Did Miss Montrose go there the night her mother died?"

"Aye," Wilcox rasped. "Ten years past. We only found her that night because one of the maids searching the second floor heard her sobs."

"Do ye have the key to his lordship's bedchamber and dressing room?"

The butler reached into his waistcoat pocket and handed the key to Garahan. "Mrs. Minnover has the keys to the rest of the upstairs rooms. I have the keys to his lordship's bedchamber, the rooms on the ground floor, and the wine cellar."

When Garahan turned toward the staircase, Wilcox stopped him. "You'll need to coax her out of the room. She only goes there when she cannot hold any more sorrow inside of her."

"Thank ye for telling me, Wilcox."

"Garahan?"

He turned to look over his shoulder. "Aye?"

"The last two times, she's cried herself to sleep. Try not to startle her if she's sleeping."

"Ye have me word, Wilcox."

Unsure of what he'd find, the young heiress sobbing, or in a deep sleep brought on by the purge of her pent-up fear and grief through tears, Garahan decided he'd be as gentle as he could with her. He would cut off his right arm before willingly hurting the lass.

CHAPTER TEN

G ARAHAN OPENED THE door at the top of the servants' staircase and stepped into the dimly lit hallway. Every other sconce had a candle burning to light his way. Treading softly, he walked to the door to his lordship's room, fit the key in the lock, and slowly turned it. The soft snick was barely audible. He closed the door quietly behind him and locked it. It would not do to have any of the well-meaning servants barging in on Miss Montrose when she had sought the solitude of her father's dressing room.

But isn't that what you're doing?

He was not barging, he reasoned, but looking out for her welfare. The lass needed rest, reassurance, and a good night's sleep.

The thick carpet muffled his footsteps as he approached the dressing room door. Inserting the second key, he paused before unlocking it. "Lord, please don't let the sound wake her, if she's sleeping."

A whisper of sound had him silently thanking his Maker as he slowly opened the door and stepped inside. A quick scan of the room revealed an alcove with a huge copper tub and washstand off to the left. To the right, two wardrobes stood side by side.

The silence was worrisome. Had she cried herself into a state of exhaustion?

He heard the sound again—like a gentle breeze rustling newborn leaves back home. Following the sound, he walked toward the window overlooking the walled garden and stables at the back of the town house and nearly missed the alcove hidden by a large wardrobe. She was sitting on the floor, her knees drawn up to her chest and her head on her knees, quietly crying. The sound wrenched his heart. What could he say that would not frighten the breath out of her?

"Go away, Wilcox...please?"

Brave lass, he thought. "I'm sorry to be disturbing ye, but I wanted to assure ye that the threat is over."

There was a brief silence, and then she asked, "How did you find me?"

"Ye're frightened and still grieving for yer da. Where else would ye go aside from his library?"

He heard her sniffling and wondered how many tears she'd shed worrying that her home—which should be a safe haven—was about to be breached. Hoping to draw her out, he said, "I've asked Mrs. Christian to prepare a pot of tea for ye, but if ye'd rather, a spot of the Irish will set ye straight."

"I don't like whiskey."

"Tea, then. Won't ye come with me now? I'll escort ye to the library. Wilcox is lighting the fire there so ye'll be warm, when ye sit in yer da's favorite chair and sip yer tea."

When she didn't move, he added, "Mrs. Christian will be worried when I don't come to collect yer tea tray."

"Very well."

Garahan did not want to give her the chance to change her mind. He moved a step closer as she lifted her head. In the candlelight he could see the tracks of her tears still damp on her face. It was his fault, and tore at his gut. Could he have handled the situation differently? He'd think about that later.

She winced when she straightened her legs.

"Have a care—if ye've been sitting in that position for too long, ye'll need to wait for the pins and needles to pass."

She rubbed a hand on her knees and bit her bottom lip. Aching for all the lass had had to handle on her own, he offered, "Why don't ye let me help ye up?"

She looked up at him and finally gave a brief nod. He bent and scooped her into his arms. She shivered. Was it was from fear or was she chilled? Deciding not to ask, he said, "Ma always swears when ye're chilled on the outside, ye need warming from the inside. Tea or a sip or two of the Irish is her cure for what ails ye."

Instead of stiffening up on him, the lass relaxed in his arms. "Do ye need me to ask Miss Helen to bring yer shawl?"

"I think the tea, and the fire you mentioned, will be enough."

"Are ye ready for me to set ye on yer feet?"

In answer, she placed her hand over his heart and rested her cheek on her hand. That simple motion and innocent trust had Garahan's gut tangling with knots that he knew would forever bind him to the lass. No matter where she was or what she was doing, he'd feel this connection to her. He carried the woman who'd captured his heart down the main staircase.

Wilcox looked up as they were descending, and gave him a brief nod. "The fire's been lit in the library."

"I've asked Mrs. Christian to prepare a pot of tea for Miss Montrose."

"I sent one of the footman to let her know Miss Montrose is ready for her tea, and to sit with her while she drinks it," the butler said.

"Thank ye, Wilcox."

"All's quiet," the butler added.

Garahan breathed a sigh of relief as he carried his precious burden. *How in the bloody hell will I ever forget the feel of her in me arms, nestled against me heart?* The feel of her, as well as the image of her in his arms with her hand to his heart, would be branded on his soul, keeping him company for eternity.

Mrs. Christian entered the room as he settled Emily in one of the chairs facing the fireplace. "There you are, Miss Montrose.

Are you chilled? You are a bit pale."

He stepped back to let the cook fuss over the lass and coddle her—the way he wished he had the right to. Shoving that dangerous thought to the back of his mind, he bowed to her. "I'll be standing guard with the others. If ye have need of me, ye've but to send word."

Tear-swollen gray eyes, and a rosy-red nose, could never detract from the beauty of the auburn-haired lass staring up at him. "Thank you, Garahan."

The longing, twined with uncertainty, in her eyes held him captive. He had to sever the connection now—before he lost his head and broke his vow to the duke. "Ye're welcome, Miss Montrose."

Turning to the cook, he said, "I'm in yer debt for staying with Miss Montrose while she finishes her tea. If either of ye are ill at ease about anything at all—a sound, the wind, what have ye—send for me."

Before his control was ground to dust beneath the soulful gaze of the woman he'd been assigned to guard, he turned and walked away. Surprised by the empty feeling in his gut, he had no choice but to ignore it as he closed the door behind him and strode toward the side entrance and his post for the remainder of the night.

Tomorrow he expected to hear from King and Coventry, or see the whites of their eyes. Either way, he and the others would stand their ground and guard the heart of Lord Montrose's home…his daughter.

EMILY WAS GRATEFUL for the company of their cook. Mrs. Christian and Mrs. Minnover had been kindness itself after her mother passed away. They'd taken her under their wing and been the ones she took her questions to when her body became a stranger to her. They'd answered her questions honestly that day, and many times over in the last ten years.

"Have I ever thanked you for your kindness after Mother passed away?"

The cook smiled. "More than once, miss."

"You and Mrs. Minnover have always treated me as if I were your own daughter. It would have been so much harder on Father if I had to go to him with my delicate questions."

Mrs. Christian's lips twitched, and Emily knew the cook was trying not to smile.

"It is all right to smile…and to speak of Father, isn't it?"

"Of course it is, miss. You are correct in thinking it would have difficult for his lordship to answer questions about the changes your body was going through at that time." The cook paused before adding, "Smiling and speaking of your father is a way of remembering him and keeping him alive in your heart. It is how I have been able to bear the loss of Mr. Christian."

Emily had never asked before, but now she had the overwhelming need to know. "Do you still miss him?"

"Every day."

"Will I always ache for the loss of my mother and now my father?"

Mrs. Christian patted Emily's hand. "The ache dulls as the years go by, and the loss will no longer feel as if it is shredding what is left of your heart."

Emily's eyes met hers. "Yes, that is exactly what it feels like at this moment, as if my heart has been torn to bits."

"When the ache is too much to bear, remember that you now have another guardian angel watching over you. And don't forget Mrs. Minnover, Wilcox, and myself will always watch over you, too."

Emily frowned into her teacup. "Until I have to leave you all. How am I to survive leaving all of you, the memories of my childhood, and my life behind while I answer the summons from His Grace?"

"It isn't a summons," Mrs. Christian reminded her. "You will be honoring his lordship's last wish that the Duke of Wyndmere accept guardianship of his lordship's precious daughter."

Unsure of how to respond to that, Emily asked, "What will you do when I leave?"

Mrs. Christian sighed. "Did you not pay attention to that part of your father's will?"

Emily shrugged. "I must not have if I cannot remember. Would you remind me?"

"We are to maintain the household for you," the cook told her. "And to keep it in readiness for when you return with your husband to either take up permanent residence, or for whenever you travel to London."

The words stole Emily's breath. With concerted effort, she regained it, rasping, "My husband?"

"It was his lordship's wish that you not be alone. He hoped you would find a man who will honor you and take care of you. Were you not paying attention to any of the reading of his will?"

She ignored the question, asking another. "What if I want to be alone?"

"You will have to speak to His Grace. Mayhap your father has made an allowance for you to do so." Reaching for Emily's hand, the cook gave it a quick squeeze before letting go. "Promise me you will not hold His Grace responsible for what was so obviously his lordship's last wish for you—happiness and security."

Emily wondered how in the world her father could expect her to be happy married to a man the duke would undoubtedly select for her—a stranger? How could she be happy when she had lost the man she'd adored the whole of her life? "I'm afraid I shall never know happiness again."

"I once thought that, too," the cook said as she rose to collect the teacups and saucers. "Until I realized that my man would not want me to spend the rest of my life wrapped in grief. He would want me to live life—not hide from it."

Emily had no idea what to say to Mrs. Christian, but she did recall Father's struggle after losing Mother. He had been inconsolable at first, but then seemed to pull himself together—for her sake.

"Why don't you wait here?" the cook suggested. "It's warm. Let me take this tray to the kitchen. I'll return with one of the footmen. He'll bank the fire while I escort you to your room."

"That won't be necessary," Emily told her.

"Even if Garahan had not asked me to ahead of time, I would accompany you. It wouldn't bear thinking that you might change your mind and head back to his lordship's dressing room."

Emily couldn't decide if she was grateful or irritated. She was not a child to be coddled, or infirm and treated as if she were made of spun glass and likely to dissolve into torrents of tears at the sign of the next crisis or disappointment.

Deciding to be grateful, as she knew that was the cook's intention, she vowed to try to accept her fate—and resign herself to it. "Thank you, Mrs. Christian."

Alone, she wondered if there was a way to avoid traveling to Wyndmere Hall. Her mind raced with impossible, and improbable, thoughts. Plots from romantic novels that she had read and squirreled away—to avoid a lecture from her father about reading books that would improve her mind, not encourage it to flights of fancy—filled her. Mayhap she could be in charge of her own destiny!

What if she were to send a missive to one of the gentlemen who had asked for her hand—the ones she had previously turned down? Mayhap she could offer her dowry, and a bit of her inheritance, in exchange for one of them to agree to wed her—*in name only.*

She shuddered at the memory of the kisses one or two of the gentlemen who'd offered for her had stolen. One had been too noisy and, for lack of any other description, sloppy. The other had claimed her lips as his hand slid to the base of her spine. She pushed out of his embrace before he could grab her bottom.

Mrs. Christian and Mrs. Minnover had warned her of such things as she prepared for her first Season. They'd also spoken of the marriage bed and what she could expect. Both women had surprised her with their enthusiasm for the marriage act and obvious love they felt for the men they had married.

Drawing in a deep breath, she remembered how it felt when Garahan lifted her into his arms. The strength of his arms combined with the breadth of his heavily muscled chest had allayed her fears in that moment, and earlier, when she'd heard intruders trying to break into her home. What she had not expected was the steady beat of Garahan's heart as she laid her hand and then her cheek upon it. She hadn't given much thought to the fact that the beat had increased for a few moments, until he'd drawn in one breath…and then another. When it returned to normal, the rhythmic beat soothed the rest of her worries. For a short time, she'd felt protected. Cherished.

If only… She sighed. There was no use wishing for what one could not have. It would only make one bitter—a lesson Father had taught her when trying to explain why Grandmother Renfrew had cut off communication with them. She could not remember who had said those words, but she remembered hearing them after her mother had died and taking them to heart. She needed to be strong and face her future.

She *would* be strong. Even though he was no longer among the living, it was what Father would want and expect. The more she thought about it, the more a feeling of utter rightness filled her. She would take back control of her life for the short time she had left here in their town house on Mayfair. She—Miss Emily Montrose, heiress—would send missives to the few gentlemen she thought she could tolerate looking at over her morning cup of tea.

Suddenly Garahan's dark eyes, dimple, and lovely, sculpted lips filled her mind and had it wandering to her bedchamber—

She slammed the door on thoughts she had no business thinking. Thoughts that would never be a part of her life if her offer of marriage was accepted.

CHAPTER ELEVEN

GARAHAN READ THE response from the duke, pleased that His Grace gave them *carte blanche* to do whatever they deemed necessary to protect Miss Montrose. He handed the missive to Tremayne, who in turn gave it to Bayfield. Garahan believed in doing so, as not every one would interpret the missive in the same way. 'Twas best to discuss what they thought and felt before acting on behalf of the duke. "I'm thinking His Grace wants us to do whatever necessary to protect Miss Montrose."

Bayfield frowned. "I agree, with a caveat."

"Aye." Tremayne sighed. "We cannot *accidentally* kill any-one."

Garahan was about to disagree when Bayfield crossed his arms over his chest. "Aye. Coventry has drilled that into our heads."

Garahan frowned at him as Bayfield continued, "We can break a few bones and knock a man unconscious—"

Tremayne interrupted, "Even a leave a reminder with a slice or two of my blade, but we must render aid if it appears the blackguard will bleed to death."

Garahan put his hands behind his back and paced in front of the horses. One by one their equine heads appeared at the top of the gate to their stalls to watch him. He scratched behind the ears of the gelding closest to him. "What if we don't notice that they're close to bleeding out?"

Tremayne snorted with laughter. "Only you or your brother James would pose that question."

Bayfield shook his head. "We do our best not to hit any vital organs. Whether it be from a lead ball from one of our pistols"— he paused to glance at Tremayne—"or from the slice of a knife or saber."

"Noted," Tremayne said. He looked at Garahan, who had stopped pacing, and warned, "Or any blunt object you happen to have on hand to subdue intruders or attackers."

Garahan grumbled. "Fine, then. I won't be putting all of me strength into a blow to anyone's head."

Tremayne and Bayfield grinned. Bayfield said, "Uncross your arms."

"Now repeat what you just said," Tremayne told Garahan, who threw his hands up in the air before complying.

"Satisfied?"

"Aye," Bayfield said.

"Now then," Tremayne began, "are we planning to arm the footmen, too, or just Wilcox?"

"Wilcox surprised me just a short while ago, informing me he has a blunderbuss stashed in the tall urn in the entryway, a knife in his boot, and a pistol tucked into his waistband beneath his waistcoat," Garahan replied.

"Does he?" Bayfield asked.

"Good man," Tremayne said.

"I'm thinking we ask Wilcox his thoughts," Garahan told the others. "We wouldn't want any of the lads we've conscripted to aid in the protection of their mistress to accidentally injure one of his lordship's solicitors." Relief filled him as the men agreed. "Now then, when are Hennessey and Masterson due to arrive?"

Bayfield answered, "Midday, mayhap later."

"Be sure to give their descriptions to Wilcox," Garahan said.

"Why don't I do that now," Bayfield replied, "and tell him you'll be speaking to him about arming the footmen standing guard?"

"That's fine, then." From the determined look in their eyes, Garahan knew these men would give their life to guard Miss Montrose. He would do the same. "In case me brother James hasn't mentioned it, he's already adopted yerselves, Hennessey, and Masterson into our clan. Yer actions were vital during the last few times ye've been called upon to add to our numbers—especially in Cornwall with me cousin Finn O'Malley—and the lot of us are grateful."

He noted the surprise on Tremayne and Bayfield's faces and continued, "Ye're part of the O'Malley/Garahan/Flaherty clan now, and as such, we've all vowed to protect ye with our lives."

Tremayne tilted his head to one side and asked, "Do we have to swear allegiance in blood?"

Garahan chuckled. "The lot of ye have already bled for the duke and his family—and, for that matter, me family as well. Like it or not, lads, ye're both one of us."

Bayfield and Tremayne shared a glance, before Bayfield asked, "Does this mean that you'll be introducing us to your cousins?"

Garahan snorted. "Ye already know me cousins."

Tremayne slowly smiled. "Ah, but we've yet to meet Siobhan Fitzpatrick, Brigid O'Ghill, and Aisling McGreevy."

Garahan clenched his hands into fists and raised them. "And ye won't, if I have anything to say about it."

"Didn't you just say we're family now?" Bayfield asked.

Garahan ran a hand through his hair until it stood on end. "Aye, but 'tisn't just meself that's protective of me female cousins—me uncles and their sons are too. Besides, there isn't a need for ye to meet them, as they'll never be traveling to London."

Tremayne grinned. "Well then, when this assignment is over, Bayfield, you and I will have to make a grip to Tipperary to meet Garahan's parents—and lovely cousins!"

A fist to Tremayne's solar plexus was Garahan's response.

Tremayne recovered quickly and shoved Garahan back two paces.

Bayfield reached for the bucket of water beside the horse's trough and tossed it in Garahan's face as the door to the stables opened and a soft gasp had them freezing in place.

EMILY HAD HEARD a commotion as she was reaching for the door to the stables, and, thinking one of the stable lads was in trouble, she pulled the door open wide—and nearly swallowed her tongue. Aiden Garahan stood feet spread, brown eyes blazing, his fist poised to strike Tremayne.

Her sharply indrawn breath had Garahan looking over his shoulder. And that was when she noticed he'd removed his frockcoat and waistcoat, and was soaked to the skin. His black cambric shirt was plastered to muscles that rivaled the statues she'd seen depicted in more than one of her father's tomes on ancient Greece and Rome. Garahan looked as if he'd stepped off the pages of the ancient myths of gods and heroes. She couldn't help but stare.

His eyes met hers, and he smiled. A warmth began to fill her from the tips of her toes to the top of her head. Unable to speak, she marveled that she felt the heat of his dark brown eyes in places she knew it was not proper for an unmarried lady to feel.

As she gathered was left of her composure, her gaze drifted to his abdomen and lower…to his heavily muscled thighs. The fabric molded to reveal every sinew, muscle, and tendon of his powerful legs. Her head light from lack of air, she noted the interior of the stables growing dimmer.

"Breathe, lass!"

She felt herself falling before she was swept against warm, wet heat and the very familiar chest of her rescuer.

"Tremayne!" Garahan barked. "Do something!

"You're doing what Bayfield or I would do."

"The rear door to the town house is closest," Bayfield said.

As her head spun and darkness engulfed her, she heard her rescuer's deep voice as it resonated through the depth of his broad chest. "Bloody fecking hell! What am I supposed to do with the lass?"

"Bring her inside," Tremayne answered.

"I'll alert Wilcox and Mrs. Minnover." Bayfield sounded farther away than the others.

Garahan's grip tightened as he strode from the dim stables into the wan light of early morning. "Breathe!"

This time, her brain obeyed. She pulled in one breath and then another, until she was breathing normally. Good Lord, she'd never imagined how beautiful all those muscles would be. In her wildest imaginings, she could not conceive of heat like this radiating off his body. It warmed her as he strode toward the rear door.

Wilcox's eyes widened, though he did not question why Garahan was dripping wet—or why he carried her. Mrs. Minnover waved him into one of the small rooms off the hallway leading to the kitchen.

"In here, Garahan," the housekeeper said, pointing to a vacant chair in the room that had the large chest containing the silver serving dishes, three silver tea sets, and flatware—Wilcox's domain.

Garahan eased her onto the chair, stepped back, and swiped a hand over his still-dripping hair. "Are ye ill, Miss Montrose?"

Mortified at her reaction to his physicality, she finally managed to mumble, "Er…no."

"I need to get back to me station." Turning to the housekeeper, he asked, "Ye'll send for me if Miss Montrose needs anything?"

Mrs. Minnover did not answer at first, and it was all Emily could do not to giggle at the way their housekeeper's eyes widened as she took in the wondrous, wet vision before them.

Garahan clenched his jaw, spun on his heel, and strode from

the room.

Emily was embarrassed, and was not about to admit the beauty of the Irishman had stolen her wits and her breath.

Mrs. Minnover cleared her throat. "I believe I know what happened, Miss Montrose."

Surprised, Emily asked, "You do?"

When the housekeeper wrapped a drying cloth around Emily's shoulders, she whispered, "Garahan's face alone is dangerous to a woman's heart, but drenched and dripping, *sans* frockcoat and waistcoat…"

When her voice trailed off, Emily sensed Mrs. Minnover had been as awed by Garahan's damp physique as she had been. Instead of agreeing, which might lead to a discussion she was not ready to have, she murmured, "I do hope Garahan has a dry shirt out in the stables."

Mrs. Minnover's muffled laughter had Emily looking up into the older woman's face. The merriment there had her letting go of the giggle she'd been suppressing. "Why couldn't any one of the men who offered for my hand look like Garahan?"

The housekeeper bit her lip before responding, "Gentlemen of the *ton* are a very different breed. Nobility always has been. Mr. Minnover earned a living working loading and offloading cargo from ships. He was broad and strong like Garahan and his men."

Emily met Mrs. Minnover's soft gaze and smiled. "The ladies of the *ton* would never understand why we are so distracted, would they?"

Mrs. Minnover agreed. "Not in this lifetime." The housekeeper tucked the cloth around Emily. "There is plenty of water for a hot bath to chase away the chill, Miss Montrose."

Emily stared in the direction Garahan had gone, blinked, and admitted, "I do not think I'll ever be cold again."

BAYFIELD WAS IN his position in the alleyway. Garahan did not bother to call out to him—he was too busy trying to compartmentalize the feelings that were rioting inside of him. What in the bloody hell happened? Just what was that feeling that shot from his loins to his heart when he'd scooped the lass off her feet before she hit the floor?

"Is Miss Montrose all right?"

He looked over his shoulder at Bayfield and gave a brief nod. He couldn't have formed the words even if he wanted to. His power of speech left him the moment he'd walked away from her.

At the door to the stable, he glanced around to ensure the stable lads were busy on the far side where the carriages were kept. Satisfied he was alone, he closed the door behind him, strode over to the horse trough, knelt, inhaled a deep breath—held it—and plunged his head into the water. The cold made his head ache, but it distracted the part of him that had come to attention the moment she was once again in his arms. He could not afford the distraction. It was his duty to protect her life...and her virtue! *God, please give me the strength to purge her lovely face and form from me thoughts, me head, and me heart.*

He placed his hands on the edge of the trough, lifted his head out of the water, and spun around at the creak of the door. Head still aching from the cold, he barked, "Well, what are ye looking at?"

Bayfield's lips twitched. "It's not your head that needs to cool off. You should have sat in the trough."

Garahan's mouth dropped open, and for a moment, all he could think of was planting his fist in Bayfield's face to wipe the smirk from it. Swiping at the hair still dripping in his eyes, he dug deep and was able to regain the threads of his control and slowly weave them back together. "I may just try that the next time."

Coventry's man shook his head. "If you know what you're about, you will see to it that there isn't a next time."

Garahan's shoulders slumped. He wished James was here—

his brother would understand what he was feeling. From what he'd heard from their cousin Emmett O'Malley, James had been attracted to his wife Melinda from the moment they met. Each time he'd had to rescue Melinda, his feelings had grown stronger. If the scuttlebutt was true, James had offered for Melinda's hand three times before the she finally said yes.

"Garahan?"

"Aye, Bayfield. Ye have the right of it." More's the pity, because he had a bone-deep feeling that Emily Montrose was the woman Ma had warned would find him one day. He already felt as if she were the other half of his heart. How in the bloody hell would he be able to deliver her to Wyndmere Hall and walk away from her? He knew the duke would be considering offers for Emily's hand in marriage.

She's not for the likes of ye, boy-o. Ye aren't worthy.

"I'm sorry I tossed the bucket of water on you. I had no idea how deep your feelings for Miss Montrose went."

"Neither did I," Garahan admitted.

"Now isn't the time for you to challenge Tremayne," Bayfield told him. "He was only trying to get a rise out of you about your cousins. He won't thank me for telling you, but Tremayne gave his heart away years ago to a young woman who tossed it back in his face when he was fighting for his life. He buries what he feels behind his taunts and bravado."

"Is that why ye hide yer scars beneath the lace at yer wrists and throat?"

Bayfield's blue eyes iced over. "Astute of you to notice."

Garahan shrugged. "Ye'll find there isn't much I do not notice."

Bayfield held Garahan's gaze, as if his stare and silent challenge would warn Garahan to hold his tongue. Garahan didn't have time for a staring contest or battle of wills with one of the men he depended on to have his back.

"Ye should know that I take a man's measure by his word, his strength, and his heart."

Bayfield looked away, then back. "You do not know what it's like to be the object of pity. Since surviving the fire on my ship, I have been shot at, stabbed, and clubbed on the head. Nothing compares to what it felt like suffering through the treatment for the burns…except the pain of having your heart handed back to you by the woman you thought would love you unconditionally for the rest of your life."

Bayfield shoved up one of his sleeves, revealing the puckered flesh from the fire that nearly stole his life. He lifted his head and looked at Garahan. "My back and arms are covered with scars just like these. What woman would accept such scars?"

"'Twas the very thing that had my sister-in-law refusing James's offer of marriage."

"Your brother has scars on his back?"

"Nay." Garahan's heart pinched at the thought of what his sister-in-law had suffered at the hands of her own kin. "Me sister-in-law does." He curled his hands into fists, unable to speak the words without imagining those hands around the neck of the bloody bastard who'd whipped his brother's wife. He slowly uncurled his fists.

"She suffered from burns?"

Garahan shook his head.

"Has your brother exacted an eye for an eye?"

The intensity in Bayfield's eyes eased a bit of Garahan's anger. "Aye. The earl gave his blessing."

Bayfield frowned. "To beat the man senseless?"

"Nay, retribution, though I'm thinking the man got off easy. According to me brother, Earl Lippincott had rules. James could not go alone—he had to take Tremayne, me cousin Emmett O'Malley, and one of King's Bow Street Runners along to witness the retribution."

The need to avenge his sister-in-law filled him, but he'd been warned to leave it be. Needing to change the subject, Garahan said, "'Tis nearly teatime. We should be ready for the next onslaught of visitors."

The men parted, and Garahan entered the stables and the room they'd claimed as their quarters for the duration of their assignment at Montrose House. He changed out of the damp clothes into dry ones, carefully draping the shirt and trousers over the backs of two of the chairs.

He had a hand on the door when he realized it would be best to remember to wear the bloody cravat and waistcoat he hated. It wouldn't do to have anyone report to Coventry, who would feel it his duty to report to His Grace that Garahan hadn't been properly attired.

He walked back to their room and put the bloody garments on. "Best not to give anyone grist for the rumor mill."

Garahan was in his appointed position when the first carriage pulled up. Silently cursing, he kept his expression neutral as he stalked over to the carriage to greet the first caller of the afternoon.

When the occupant stepped from the coach, Garahan informed him, "Miss Montrose is in mourning."

The man raised a quizzing glass and frowned at him before continuing toward the front door.

Garahan stepped in front of him, repeating, "Miss Montrose is in mourning."

Irritation spilled off the man in waves, pleasing Garahan. It more than matched his own irritation. "I am well aware, and it is the reason for my call."

When the man tried to step around him, Garahan held out a hand. "If ye wish to speak with Miss Montrose, I suggest ye write to her. She is not receiving callers."

Black eyes flashed with anger.

Good! Garahan's temper was nearing the point where he'd have to struggle to contain it.

Again the man took a step, but this time he hesitated, staring at something—make that someone—behind Garahan. He knew without turning around it was Tremayne. While not all gentlemen of the *ton* were wise enough to be wary of the members of the Duke's Guard, Tremayne's scar was enough to have even the more arrogant ones halting in their tracks.

"Problem, Garahan?"

Garahan didn't bother to turn around to answer. "Nay, Tremayne. He was just leaving."

"Do you have any idea to whom you are speaking?" the man demanded.

"Do you?" Garahan countered.

"You are obviously hired muscle, trying to protect a young woman who does not require your protection!"

Tremayne chuckled. "Have you noticed that every gentleman who has come to call on Miss Montrose has made the same mistake, Garahan?"

"Aye. That I have," Garahan answered. "I'm thinking His Grace has the right of it. Even the most talented tailor can clothe a man, but 'tis what is inside of a man that ranks him as a gentleman."

"Now wait just a moment—" The man's face paled. "Did you say 'His Grace'?"

"Aye," Tremayne answered. "His Grace, the Duke of Wyndmere. Garahan is one of the duke's personal guard. I have been drafted to assist him in protecting the duke's ward."

The man swayed on his feet. "Ward?"

Garahan took the opportunity to guide the unsteady man back to his carriage. "Did ye not know Miss Montrose is the duke's ward and, as such, is under his protection?"

"I… Er… No, I did not. Mayhap I will send her a note."

Garahan opened the door to the carriage and closed it after helping the man inside. With a wave, he sent the coachman on his way.

"Did you get the man's name?" Tremayne asked.

"Bloody hell!"

"We need it for our report."

Garahan took off after the carriage. Due to the number of horses and carriages already traveling along the street, he easily caught up with them. He gave a shrill whistle, and three carriages pulled to a stop. Ignoring two of them, he leaned into the window of the third one. "Forgive me for not asking earlier. I need to be knowing yer name."

"Viscount Trembley," the man answered, holding out a heavily embossed calling card. "Please see that Miss Montrose knows that I called for her and was refused entrance."

"'Tisn't why I chased after ye. I'll be needing yer name to add to the me report."

"Report?" Trembley asked.

Garahan stepped back and signaled to the coachman once more. "Aye, for His Grace." More than pleased with the way the man's face turned from gray to green, he turned and made his way back to the Montrose town house, where Tremayne waited.

"I gather from the smirk on your face that you have the information," Tremayne said.

"Aye. Viscount Trembley."

Tremayne waited a beat, then said, "I should apologize for trying to get a rise out of you earlier, asking after your cousins."

"Bayfield already explained. We'd best return to our posts. No doubt there will be others who will try to slip past us."

By the time Hennessey and Masterson arrived two hours later, the mood around the town house was grim. Garahan and Tremayne had turned away a handful of fortune hunters, all of whom insisted they had been invited by Miss Montrose. The sooner they confronted Hardwell, the sooner this would stop.

But first Garahan had to introduce the two new additions to her guard. He hoped she was feeling up to it.

Chapter Twelve

Emily felt as if she were surrounded by giants! She was just becoming used to Garahan, Tremayne, and Bayfield…and now she had somehow acquired two more!

The five men were standing in a semicircle in front of her, hands behind their backs. If they were trying to appear harmless—less intimidating—they should have found a stance that would not accentuate the breadth of their massive chests and shoulders. Even with the neutral expressions on their faces, she had no doubt they would give anyone pause before crossing them.

"Miss Montrose, I'd like to introduce ye to Colonel Ian Masterson, formerly of the Fifth Northumberland Regiment of Foot."

Emily managed a tremulous smile and hoped she didn't appear as unnerved as she felt. But the austere man with the iron-gray hair and dark eyes was imposing. Digging deep for composure, she managed, "It's a pleasure to meet you, Colonel Masterson."

His dark brown eyes studied her closely. "Just Masterson, if you do not mind, Miss Montrose."

Garahan nodded to the auburn-haired man standing beside him. "Lieutenant Hennessey, formerly with the Royal Marines."

"Lieu—"

She hadn't even managed to complete the word before the

lieutenant interrupted her. "Hennessey, if you do not mind, miss."

She closed her mouth and shook her head. "Of course, Hennessey. It is a pleasure to meet you, too." She turned to Garahan and frowned. "Are there any more of you expected?"

A cough, which sounded suspiciously like a snort of laughter, had her scanning the faces of the men standing not three feet in front of her. A broad wall of impenetrable warriors…her personal guard. But had they been assigned to keep her safe, or to keep her from leaving the town house? The idea had occurred to her after Garahan carried her into the house earlier, then quickly left her to change into dry clothes. She would pose the question to him later, when she could speak to him privately.

Not one of the men dared to meet her questioning gaze, though Hennessey and Masterson seemed to be fighting the urge to smile. Enough was enough! She was not a prisoner—and would not be treated as if she were one. She rose slowly, smoothed her gown, and lifted her chin—a touch higher than she normally would have, but she wanted to see their expressions when speaking to them. Lord, the men were tall! "If that is all, I would ask that you please confer with me before refusing admittance to any and all callers."

As one, the men turned to Garahan, who stood in the middle. She noted his frown and expected him to disagree with her. He did not. The irritating man ignored her!

She took a step closer to him. "As mistress of Montrose House, I expect to be obeyed."

"Begging yer pardon, Miss Montrose, but we've orders from His Grace. No one is to be admitted, unless and until the solicitors have dotted every *i* and crossed every *t*."

She took another step closer and had to tilt her head back further in order to frown up at Garahan. "Whose orders?"

Drat the man! His lips twitched. "If ye have to be asking me, I'll be thinking ye haven't listened to a word I've said to ye just now, or in the past few days."

Rumbling chuckles sounded to the left of Garahan, snorts of laughter to the right. She wanted to chastise the men for their reaction, but did not dare look away from Garahan—she wanted him to know she was challenging him for the right to do as she pleased! "I have heard each and every word you have said!"

"If ye have, then why are we having this conversation, lass?"

"It is Miss Montrose!"

"Begging yer pardon, Miss Montrose, but ye have yet to answer me question, or agree to follow orders."

"If I may, Garahan?" Masterson's deep voice broke through the tense silence. "Mayhap Miss Montrose has a specific request. It would not do any harm to listen to her. With the addition of two more guards, we may be able to allow her a bit more freedom."

"Aye," Hennessey agreed. "She may be in mourning, but a ride in the park or trip to her favorite shop may lift her spirits. A lighter atmosphere may benefit all concerned."

Garahan appeared as if he wanted to shove the men flanking him for speaking up on her behalf. "I do not think—"

"Past your own interpretation of His Grace's instructions," Emily finished for him, attempting to regain control of the conversation and, thereby, her life.

If the man towering over her were a thundercloud, she was certain that a bolt of lightning was about to strike! He clenched his jaw and curled his hands into fists at his sides. Miraculously, his voice did not sound strained when he said, "I vowed to protect the duke, his family, and extended family with me life. When ye became His Grace's ward, ye became part of his extended family. It is my duty to include ye in those I protect with me life."

She would have been touched by his declaration, if he had not been scowling and biting off each word as he said them. "I am honored to be included, but—"

This time Tremayne interrupted, "Miss Montrose. Trust that Garahan knows what he is about. There have been attempts on the duke's life, and that of his duchess, his brother the earl, and their sister."

She thought he was finished, until Tremayne continued, "Three kidnapping attempts to steal their twin babes, countless slanderous attacks on his cousins and their wives. Garahan, his brothers, and the O'Malley and Flaherty cousins have stood between danger and the duke and his family since the duke formed his sixteen-man personal guard."

"Heed his words," Bayfield said. "And for your own sake, follow his instructions."

Her need to shout at the men had her biting the inside of her cheek. She decided then and there not lower herself to arguing with them. They did not appear to be listening. Rather, she would appear to acquiesce to following their rules, all the while planning a way to sneak out of the house to meet whomever she pleased.

Happy with her decision, she asked, "Is there anything else you need to tell me?" When no one answered, she smiled. "If you will excuse me, gentlemen, I believe I shall retire to my father's upstairs study to read."

Garahan sighed audibly. "Have ye forgotten already? We're not members of the *ton*."

She narrowed her eyes, adding a frown in the hopes he would understand he trod on dangerous ground constantly reminding her of their status as her guards. When he stepped back and motioned for her to proceed him, she quipped, "No need to escort me. I know the way."

When he did not follow her, relief filled her. Miraculously, she felt her anger begin to drain away, leaving her feeling as if she'd been arguing for days. Come to think of it, she had been butting heads against an immoveable wall—Aiden Garahan— since the moment he arrived.

"SHE'S GOING TO be a handful," Masterson predicted.

"Definitely difficult," Hennessey added.

Garahan scrubbed a hand over his face. "Ye have no idea."

Bayfield chuckled, and Tremayne said, "Miss Montrose is holding up well, under what has to have been a complete shock to her."

Garahan sighed. "Aye, but she doesn't seem to grasp the severity of her situation."

Masterson cleared his throat. "As Hennessey and I have only just arrived, mayhap we will be able to see the situation from a new perspective."

Hennessey snorted. "My perspective is she's a difficult female, who dared to butt heads with Garahan."

Tremayne eyes lit with humor. "That about sums it up."

"Are ye forgetting what we've learned about his lordship's incident?"

Masterson stared at Garahan. "Don't you mean accident?"

Jaw clenched, gut uneasy, Garahan replied, "'Twasn't an accident."

"Do you have proof?" Hennessey asked.

"A witness," Tremayne answered. "I'm expecting verification from Cameron. I served with him in the dragoons."

Masterson leveled a glance at him. "Do you trust this man?"

"With my life," Tremayne replied.

Masterson nodded. "Will he send word, or show up?"

Garahan listened to the conversation, but his thoughts were on the lass. For a brief moment, the memory of her curves pressed against him as he swept her into his arms distracted him.

Abruptly, he buried that thought, and the want that threatened to swamp him whenever their eyes met. Bloody hell! He had no time for headstrong, feisty women ignoring his orders! She needed to follow his commands, the same as the men standing behind him.

"Faith, I hope Cameron shows up soon. Me brother James trusts the man—though he admitted his first reaction was to plant his fist in the man's face."

Tremayne laughed. "I was there at the time and thought they were going to come to blows before reason returned."

"Me brother isn't entirely without reason," Garahan replied.

Masterson looked from Tremayne to Garahan. "A woman has a way of interfering with a man's thoughts, whether she intends to…or not."

"Aye," Hennessey agreed. "I think we should consider the current situation from Miss Montrose's point of view."

Garahan did not want to, but if she was going to disagree with everything he said, and countermand his orders, he may have to rethink his strategy. "We may have to allow her to go on an outing—with her maid and three or four of us guarding her."

Masterson hesitated before suggesting, "Three might be best. One riding atop the carriage, two flanking it."

"That leaves two of us guarding the town house—no telling who'll try to sneak inside if they find it unprotected," Bayfield added.

"She'll balk at the guards," Tremayne predicted.

Garahan's mind was made up. "No guards, no outing."

When the others agreed, Masterson said, "Now that that's been settled, I'd like to see the list of the fortune hunters and rakehells who have attempted to call on Miss Montrose." Garahan raised one eyebrow, and the colonel added, "Hennessey and I may be familiar with some of the names, or their current circumstances."

"We've added what we've been able to piece together with the ones so far. There are one or two who will not be expecting a personal visit."

Tremayne added, "After we deliver Miss Montrose to Wyndmere Hall."

Garahan watched the men closely to see if anyone would try to dissuade him. No one did.

Bayfield was the first to offer his assistance. "I shall be on hand to speak on your behalf when the Watch is summoned."

Masterson nodded. "If need be, I can warn Coventry ahead of time."

Hennessey chuckled. "The captain is a stickler for not getting into brawls."

Relief filled Garahan. "Aye," he agreed. "Thank ye, men. Now then, we'll have a brief word with Wilcox before ye head to yer posts."

"While you speak to Miss Montrose?" Tremayne suggested.

Garahan shook his head. "I'm thinking she needs a bit more time to come to terms with the fact that until we deliver her to Wyndmere Hall, it is her duty to do as she is told."

Not one of the men argued with him, but he did note the speculative glances between them.

Bloody hell! Was he the only one who expected her to obey without question?

While Wilcox filled the men in on which of the footmen were capable of handling weapons, he wondered if he should speak to the lass sooner rather than later.

Resigned, he motioned to Tremayne, who stepped away from the men listening to Wilcox. "I'm going to ask Mrs. Minnover if she'll accompany me to speak with Miss Montrose. I'm thinking she's had enough time to consider her precarious situation and should be ready to listen to reason."

"You may want to omit the word *obey* when speaking to Miss Montrose."

Garahan was about to ask why, but thought better of it, remembering Da never used the word when speaking to his ma. "Ye may be right. I shall return and let ye know if the lass agrees to the idea of an outing with her maid—and a private guard."

Tremayne's lips twitched. Garahan decided to ignore the fact that the man was fighting the urge to smile.

"I'll be at my post."

Garahan strode to the door to the servants' side of the town house, intent on finding Mrs. Minnover. Hand to the doorknob, he hoped the lass would be more agreeable if the staunch housekeeper accompanied him. But he hesitated. What if she refused to listen to reason?

He knew what he would do. He'd hate to be the one to confine her to the town house...but if that was what it took to protect her, so be it!

CHAPTER THIRTEEN

BARON HARDWELL FROWNED at the man standing before him. "What do you have to report. Poston?"

The man removed his cap and twisted it in his hands. "The men who attempted to gain entrance to Montrose House last night were escorted to Bow Street."

"They were unable to get to Miss Montrose?"

"I… I don't know, your lordship."

Not one of the last four fortune hunters Hardwell had sent to Montrose House had managed entry. Infuriated that his plans were not being followed to the letter, the baron shouted, "Find out! I refuse to pay for insufficient information." Locking gazes with Poston, he promised, "Fail me, and it will be the last thing you do. Understand?"

"Aye, your lordship."

Instead of summoning the butler using the bellpull, Hardwell stalked to the door, yanked it open, and barked at the footman, "Have Poston leave via the rear entrance, and when Wilson arrives, show him in immediately!"

Alone, he walked over to the sideboard and poured brandy into one of the crystal glasses on the highly polished silver tray. Both the crystal and the silver had been in his family for generations. The knowledge that he stood on the precipice of disaster— empty coffers and ruination—had his blood boiling! No one must discover the part he'd played in encouraging Oliver Lippincott, the former Duke of Wyndmere, to begin an affair with Lady Hampton. He cursed himself for not believing Lord Hampton actually cared enough for his wife to insist she end the affair. Hampton discovered the lovers *in flagrante delicto*, shot Wyndmere in the back as he was leaving his wife's *boudoir*, reloaded...and put the pistol to his own head.

Hardwell refused to feel an ounce of guilt for his part in the debacle—which in his estimation, it was, while others were of the opinion that the murder/suicide was a tragedy. Bleeding hearts be damned! He'd had to leave London immediately, or else get caught up in the web of lies and deceit. If he could not be located, no one would be able to point the finger at him. Enough time had passed that most had forgotten about the whole affair. The former duke was dead and buried, and the current duke had a pristine reputation, putting family and duty to the Crown above all else.

Pity.

Hardwell had nearly succeeded in leading Oliver's youngest brother, Earl Lippincott, down the primrose path to where it turned a sharp left and headed straight into the bowels of London and into Hell. But the bloody current duke had somehow managed to pull the earl out of his downward spiral. If the duke had not interfered, Hardwell would be as rich as Croesus!

It was time to make the duke pay for his interference. Hardwell had learned from his earlier attempts to discredit the former duke and add to his coffers by starting with those closest to His Grace. He would not make the same mistake again. So he'd decided to begin his campaign with the duke's new ward, Miss Emily Montrose. His unsuccessful attempts were maddening. It was time to change tactics and employ those better suited to plying their violent trade where cries for help were ignored under the cover of darkness on the docks, or in the alleyways in the stews. If innocent bystanders tried to aid to any of his targets, they would disappear—permanently!

The knock on his study door interrupted his thoughts. "Enter."

"Wilson, your lordship."

When the butler retreated, the baron studied the burly man who stood before him, cap still on his head and a defiant look in his dark eyes. Rather than mention the lack of deference by keeping his cap on, Hardwell ignored it. He had performed the first job without a hitch—Montrose had ended up in the street and run down by a carriage. Though Wilson was rumored to be more than a bit unstable, he was the perfect man for this job, too. "No one is the wiser as to the last job you handled for me. I trust the down payment will suffice again."

Wilson gave a brief nod.

"Tomorrow afternoon at two o'clock, Miss Montrose and her maid will be going for a drive in the park. She will have three guards. Two on horseback and one riding beside the coachman. Will that be a problem?"

"What should I do with the maid?"

Hardwell glared at him. "There must be no witnesses."

Wilson nodded. "And if Miss Montrose resists?"

"Subdue her however you see fit. She must not return to Montrose House!"

"Do you have a destination in mind?"

"The Saracen's Head. I will arrange for a room at the coaching inn for my *niece*, Miss Montrose. They will be expecting her *cousin* to deliver her."

Wilson nodded. "The inn near Newgate." He held out his hand for the bag of coin. When Hardwell handed it over, Wilson tucked it into his frockcoat pocket, and left without another word.

Satisfied that the deed would be done. Hardwell poured another brandy, savoring it while plotting how he would deflower the duke's ward.

CHAPTER FOURTEEN

"MORNING, MISS!" HELEN called cheerily as she opened the curtains to let in the morning sun. "I trust you slept well."

Emily brushed the hair out of her eyes and stared at her maid. What had put her in such a chipper mood this morning? "I don't remember."

Helen nodded. "Mum always says that if you don't remember how you slept, you slept deeply." After disappearing into Emily's dressing room, Helen returned with another of the mourning gowns that had been hastily purchased—an unadorned black gown—and chemise and draped them over the back of the fainting couch next to the dressing table.

"Water's hot," she said. "Would you like me to help you put your hair up before you wash?"

Emily pushed back the covers and slipped out of bed, smiling at the way her maid bustled about her bedchamber while she began the arduous task of combing her fingers through the braid she fashioned every night, loosening it. It kept her waist-length hair from becoming tangled while she slept.

"Shall I brush your hair for you?"

"I think I can manage, thank you."

Emily smoothed her hair over her shoulders and fastened her favorite blue ribbon around it. For a moment, just a moment, she remembered the smile on her father's face when he handed her a brown paper package, urging her to open it. The rainbow of ribbons had them both laughing, until he hugged her close and rasped, "Always watch for the rainbow after the storm." Had it been a warning? Had he known last month that someone was plotting his demise?

Helen's voice snapped her out back to the present. "The water should have cooled enough for you, miss."

"Thank you, Helen." Setting aside her dark thoughts, Emily reached for her maid's hand and squeezed it. "I'm sorry I haven't been able to see beyond my own sorrow to note how badly Father's passing affected you, too."

Her maid's eyes glistened with unshed tears. "He was the best of men, miss." She wiped the backs of her hands over her eyes, drew in a breath, and slowly exhaled while she regained her composure. "Mrs. Christian said for me to hurry back—she'll have your breakfast ready for you." With a quick glance about the bedchamber, she asked, "Would you prefer to eat in your room again today?"

Noting the way her maid strove to set aside her emotions in order to do her job, Emily realized she too should be more diligent doing the same. Father had always managed to keep his emotions in check—and for the most part, so had Mum. As head of the household, it was her duty to follow the example they had set.

Shame filled her. Her unsettled emotions had her lashing out at Garahan when she should be more understanding, headstrong when she should have been more agreeable. The unwelcome thought that the duke and duchess may not want to have her thrust into their lives gave her pause.

"I haven't even thanked him," she whispered.

"What did you say, miss?"

"Er…nothing. Thinking aloud." It would be proper to send a note to His Grace, thanking him for sending Garahan and the others to safeguard her and accompany her on her journey north.

She would wait until she arrived and had observed their household before offering her help to the duchess.

"I understand," Helen replied. "About breakfast—"

"Please let Mrs. Christian know I shall be down in half an hour."

Her maid relaxed, why hadn't Emily realized Helen had become pensive as of late?

"She and Mrs. Minnover will be so pleased. They have been overset worrying about you, and believe our planned outing this afternoon will go a long way to bringing the roses back to your cheeks." Helen's hand covered her mouth and her eyes widened.

Emily knew then that her acting out of character had not just affected the men who'd sworn an oath to the duke to protect her, but the household staff as well. Normally Helen would share her thoughts when the two of them were alone.

Wanting to return to their former ease with one another, Emily said, "I won't tell anyone. In truth, I should have realized how difficult I must have been to be around." Drawing in one deep breath, and then another, she felt as if she'd regained a portion of her former self. "Mrs. Minnover and Mrs. Christian may be right about our drive in the park this afternoon. I am looking forward to it."

"I am too, miss." Helen had her hand on the door when she whirled around. "I shall be right back to help you dress."

"Take your time. It will give me a few moments to pen a thank-you note to His Grace."

The maid nodded. "We're so relieved that his lordship asked the duke to watch over you. Wilcox was especially concerned for your welfare, miss."

"Was?" Emily asked. "But isn't now?"

Her maid was quick to answer, "He trusts Garahan and the others to guard you until his lordship's affairs have been settled." She grabbed hold of her apron and began to wring it. "They'll miss you, but know that I'll keep them informed of how you are doing once we arrive at Wyndmere Hall."

Emily noticed a hint of worry in the depths of her maid's eyes. "I never even thought about the upheaval in your life, Helen. Will it be a hardship for you to accompany me?"

Helen shook her head. "I would have put up a fuss if you didn't take me with you. Who else knows in the chill of winter that you prefer a cup of chocolate and something sweet to eat to start your day, or that you cannot stomach mutton? You favor adding dried rose petals to your bathwater instead of lilac or lavender, and enjoy spending time in the gardens and out of doors—especially in the rain."

"How often has Mrs. Minnover chased me back indoors if she discovered me walking among the flowers and herbs while a soft rain fell?"

"Far too many to recall."

"Forgive me if I haven't said it recently, but I'd be lost without you, Helen."

"Thank you, miss." Her maid's smile warmed her heart as she opened the door, slipped through, and quietly closed it behind her.

Emily realized in that moment that although she had lost the most important person in her life, she had others who cared. It was time to assure them that they were appreciated, as they too had felt the loss of her father.

After washing quickly and donning her dressing gown, she settled at her grandmother's writing desk. Quill in hand, she felt a moment's hesitation—she'd never written to a duke before and had no idea what to say—until it dawned on her that she should simply thank the man. Dukes were human, too. Weren't they?

She was about to sign the note when she heard the knock. "Come in, Helen."

Her maid seemed lighter in spirit when she entered the room. "Have you finished your letter?"

"Just," Emily answered, signing the note. "After I fold it and seal it, I shall have to ask Wilcox to post it for me."

The maid waited for Emily to finish. "I overheard Garahan

mention they were in constant communication with the duke and his man-of-affairs."

Emily nodded and raised her arms over her head as Helen helped her dress. "I seem to recall hearing that, too. When I speak to Wilcox, I shall ask if he thinks it would be all right to send my note along with Garahan's correspondence."

"I'm not quite sure how you manage to coil your hair on top of your head without my help, but I must say, you look lovely— as always, miss."

Surprised by her maid's reaction, when she knew her mourning gown made her fair skin even paler, Emily brushed at a strand of hair that got stuck on her eyelashes and said, "I look a bit on the sickly side."

Her maid disagreed. "You look lovely no matter what you wear."

Emily linked her arm with Helen's and suddenly felt a bit lighter in heart and spirit, confiding, "I'm famished!"

They were laughing as they descended the main staircase together.

GARAHAN LOOKED UP at the lilting sound of feminine laughter. The pair drew his eye, though it was Emily's fiery auburn hair that caught his eye. She was lovely even wearing another of her black gowns. Both lasses were comely, but she was the one who'd captured his attention from the first. Eyes blazing, prepared to do battle with him for—as she put it—forcing his way into her home after she'd refused to see him. The lass had grit!

Lost in their conversation, they did not notice him standing at the bottom of the staircase until he bade them good morning. "It's wonderful to see ye meeting the day with a smile, lass. Ye as well, Miss Helen."

The hint of rose staining Emily's cheeks only added to her

appeal. The curve of her cheek had his fingers itching to test his theory that her skin would be soft as a rose petal. Her full lips drew his gaze whenever the lass was speaking. Would her supple mouth give beneath his questing lips—

Bloody hell! He could not allow his mind to wander where it had no business going. She was far above his station in life. What could he ever offer her but a life worrying that each time he was on special assignment, one of his brothers would deliver the news that he'd given his life protecting the duke and his family?

Shoving those thoughts aside, he asked, "Are ye looking forward to yer outing this afternoon?"

"Yes." She glanced at her maid. "Helen and I are looking forward to a drive through the park."

He frowned at the thought of what may happen after they entered the park. To ensure there would be no questions when the carriage pulled up in front of the town house, he reminded her, "Ye know that Tremayne, Bayfield, and I will be accompanying ye."

When she did not respond right away, he added, "'Tisn't negotiable."

She narrowed her eyes, and just when he thought she'd challenge him, she replied, "I understand. Helen and I will be grateful for your company. Won't we?"

Her maid nodded as she slipped her arm free. "I'll just let Mrs. Christian know that you will be in the dining room."

"I'd rather eat in the small parlor that looks over the gardens. If it's not too much trouble."

Garahan had not expected her maid to disagree, and was relieved when the young woman assured her mistress that it would not be. His gaze followed Helen until she opened the door to the servants' side of the town house, then he turned to Emily. "I'm happy to see ye're in a fine mood this morning." He paused and realized he may have been overzealous in his duty to the duke. "I...er...need to apologize if I appeared to not consider yer feelings, Miss Montrose. I was more concerned with your safety than yer need to venture out of the town house."

She surprised him by laying her hand on his forearm. "Thank you for apologizing, Garahan. I must apologize to you and the others. I have only just realized that I have been too quick to challenge everything that you've tried to do since you barged into my life."

"I did not barge," he reminded her.

"What do you call it when a gentleman enters someone's home without an invitation to do so?"

He raised his eyes to the ceiling then back. "Faith, lass, how many times need I remind ye I'm no gentleman?"

Her eyes sparkled with a mischievous light. "Faith," she replied. "I have noticed."

They were both laughing when Wilcox strode toward them, staring at Garahan's arm. The lass must have noticed too. She quickly dropped her hand. He immediately missed the warmth of her touch.

"Trouble, Wilcox?"

The butler was quick to respond, "Nay, miss. Helen mentioned you have a note you'd like me to post."

"Aye, Wilcox. I am overdue sending a thank you to His Grace. If you could see to it today, I'd be grateful."

Garahan was relieved that the lass would remember to do so. Ma would approve. "We've missives for His Grace as well. It'd be no trouble to include yers with the rest of them."

"I wouldn't want to be a bother."

When she lifted her chin at just that angle and tilted her head, silently questioning him, he knew he would never forget Miss Emily Montrose. His gut ached as he realized when he delivered her to the duke's front door, he would be leaving more than Emily behind... He'd be leaving his heart.

"'Tis no bother, Miss Montrose." He would have to brace himself for that day, in the not-too-distant future, when he would look into her soft gray eyes, knowing it would be for the last time. Until then, he would do his duty, until she was safe within the walls of Wyndmere Hall. Patrick O'Malley, the head of the Duke's Guard—and his cousin—would expect no less from him as he accepted his next assignment.

"Thank you, Garahan."

Her gaze dipped to his mouth, and he felt the punch in his gut, as if his brother James had delivered the blow. Where in the bloody hell had his ironclad control gone? "Ye're welcome, lass."

"After breakfast, I plan to spend a little time in the garden before meeting with Mrs. Minnover about the rest of the week's menu… If you need me."

It was on the tip of his tongue to tell her he'd always need her. He bit down hard on the inside of his cheek and swallowed the words. Never in his life had a lass affected him the way the fiery-hearted woman staring up at him did. Time to push his emotions where they belonged—deep inside of him, under lock and key.

"I appreciate knowing where to find ye, Miss Montrose. Enjoy yer breakfast. Mrs. Christian baked cream scones this morning. They were delicious."

The lass smiled fully, and his heart tumbled to his feet. Time to leave—now!

He bowed then stalked down the long hallway to the side entrance. If he stayed one more moment with her, looking at him as if he'd hung the moon and the stars, he'd be tossing her over his shoulder and looking for a quiet place where they could be alone, and he could finally discover if her lips tasted of sweet cream or his ma's currant cake—right before he took her to the heavens.

"Bloody *feckin' eedjit!*" He shoved the door open and nearly rammed into Tremayne.

"What's wrong?" the other man demanded. "Has King changed his mind and reassigned the men he promised will be in the park?"

Garahan shook his head. "Nay. He believes as we do that today's outing would be the perfect time for Hardwell—or whoever the bloody bugger has hired—to make a move. I've decided to ride beside the coachman. You and Bayfield can ride on either side of the carriage."

Tremayne waited a beat before agreeing. "You don't think there will be trouble… You are expecting it."

"Ye don't?"

"At some point, though not today. Mayhap if we venture out again in another day or two. Some may recognize his lordship's carriage, though not many will be expecting Miss Montrose to venture out of her home so soon after her father's death."

"True, but don't forget the wager."

Tremayne shook his head. "I cannot wait to get my hands on Hardwell."

"Ye'll have to get in line behind meself," Garahan grumbled. "I need to speak with the coachman before I take up me post." His gaze swept the area around them. "Are the others at their stations?"

"Aye. Ready and waiting."

"For?"

Tremayne met Garahan's gaze. "Anything."

CHAPTER FIFTEEN

EMILY FELT A hint of unease at the censorious look from Wilcox as he opened the front door. She should not have gone against Garahan's orders and insisted on using her father's landau for the drive.

Stepping into the warmth of the afternoon, she sighed, lifting her face to the slight breeze. Such a lovely day for a drive, but she would rather stay home than be stuck inside the close confines of her father's town coach beneath a roof and tiny windows.

"Where is his lordship's closed carriage?" Garahan boomed from behind her.

Heavens, the man moved silently—and quickly. Helen grabbed hold of her arm, and Emily laid her hand on top of her maid's to reassure her before responding, "In the carriage house, I would imagine."

"And why would that be, Miss Montrose?"

His brown eyes no longer held the warmth she was accustomed to. They were very nearly black with what she sensed was frustration. Mayhap anger. Striving for courage she was not quite sure she felt, she answered, "I asked the coachman for the landau. If I am going to be enjoying the ride, I prefer the open carriage to a closed one."

"Did ye not agree to do as I asked until ye arrive at Wyndmere Hall?"

The intensity of his glare put her back up. She simply lifted one shoulder and broke eye contact with him.

Garahan walked over to the carriage. "Return the landau and bring the town coach."

When the coachman agreed without question, Emily felt her ire bubbling too close to the surface. She was mistress of Montrose House—the question should have been put to her. How could he ignore her wishes on this first outing since the night…

She simply deflated at the memory of her father being carried inside.

Garahan noticed. "Ye must understand that I cannot keep ye safe unless ye're in the town coach."

"I'm afraid I do not see what difference it makes."

Garahan glanced at Tremayne and Bayfield, who walked over to stand on either side of him. The united front of her assigned guards had her biting her lower lip, but she refused to be intimidated by their size, their frowns, or their stance. "I am not trying to be difficult, but would appreciate one of you explaining why we cannot enjoy a ride in the park with the top folded down and—"

"Anyone walking, or riding—on horseback or in a carriage—will observe ye out and about. Word will spread, and there will be an influx of fortune hunters who will try their hand gaining admittance to yer home. 'Twould be sending the wrong message."

Striving to keep the irritation from her tone, she asked, "And what would that message be?"

"That ye are no longer in mourning, despite what we have been telling anyone who arrives to pay a visit…uninvited."

She swallowed the retort she had been ready to blast him with. The man was only doing his job. Hadn't she decided just this morning to stop countermanding his dictates and do as he requested? "I hadn't thought of that."

"The message would be loud and clear, Miss Montrose,"

Bayfield said.

Glancing from Bayfield to Tremayne, whose gaze silently questioned what she had been thinking, she sighed. "I do beg your pardon, gentlemen."

Garahan grumbled beneath his breath, while Tremayne and Bayfield shared a meaningful glance. Thankfully, not one of them reminded her—yet again—that they were not members of that particular class.

Helen leaned close and asked, "Do you have your hartshorn?"

Grateful that her maid knew her so well, and knew the rocking motion of the larger carriage made her stomach turn and her head light, Emily replied, "Tucked into my reticule."

The sound of carriage wheels and the jingling of the team's harness had Garahan striding forward to have a word with the coachman.

Rather than ask, as she would have the day before, she silently wondered, *What now?*

Garahan turned and walked over her. "Thank ye for yer patience, Miss Montrose. I'll be riding next to the coachman. Tremayne and Bayfield will be riding on either side of ye."

"Of course. Thank you."

He seemed pleased with her response, though for how long? Time, and their drive in the park, would tell.

Wilcox stepped forward to hand Emily and then her maid into the carriage. "Mrs. Christian promised to have your afternoon tea ready upon your return."

She thanked Wilcox as he closed the door. As she settled in the carriage across from her maid, she doubted anyone would recognize the town coach. Her family did not come from aristocracy and had no family crest painted on the side. She suspected Garahan—wearing his customary unrelieved black from head to toe—would be more likely to be noticed and worthy of mention by members of the *ton*.

She chided herself for worrying about what might happen, when she should be setting her worries aside and enjoying the day and the ride. Her mood lifted the moment the carriage left the cobbled roads behind and traversed the winding paths in the park. Enjoying the view—even though the window was small—she wondered how different her life would be while under the duke's guardianship in the Lake District. It was so far removed from her life in London. Though solitary by choice, she might find that she would enjoy meeting the people who worked for the duke. Mayhap she could be of some help to the duchess.

The distinct sound of shots being fired nearby jolted her out of her reverie. Before she could open the window to see what was happening, Garahan shouted, "Take cover!"

THE FEMININE GASPS from inside the carriage that followed the simultaneous crack of rifle shots through the stillness of the afternoon had Garahan's worst fears unfolding. *Ambush!*

Tremayne fired into the woods from his position, guarding the left side of the carriage. Bayfield aimed and fired in the opposite direction, as more gunfire sounded just out of sight.

Ignoring the searing pain in his upper arm, Garahan steadied the coachman, who was slumped on the seat beside him, with one hand. "Easy now—ye've been hit." He reached for the reins with the other. Had Emily or her maid been hit by a stray shot? The team was restive, and he had to set that worry aside while he wrestled for control of the frightened beasts.

Tremayne leapt from his saddle onto the seat beside the injured coachman.

Garahan nodded to him and secured the team. "Stay with him while I check on the women."

Tremayne grunted in reply as he whipped off his cravat and tied it around the coachman's bleeding thigh.

Worry pierced Garahan. It was too quiet inside the coach. Had either of the women been injured? Bloody hell, he should have realized the amount of coin involved in the wager involving Miss Montrose would only encourage something like this to happen. But how had the attackers known Miss Montrose would be riding in the park today? By God, he would not stop until he had the answer!

Garahan vaulted off the side of the carriage, pulled the door open, and slipped inside.

Emily's pain-filled eyes held the answer to his question, but he asked it anyway. "Where are ye hurt, lass?"

"It's nothing."

She answered quickly…too quickly. He swept his gaze from the top of her head to her toes but couldn't see anything immediately wrong. He turned to her maid. "Are ye all right, Miss Helen?" When the maid's eyes filled with tears, he sighed. He'd have to coax the truth from the frightened women. "Tremayne's binding the coachman's wound, and Bayfield will be back momentarily to stand guard, while the others contain the situation."

"Situation?" Emily asked.

Helen's face paled. "Others?"

"Aye. King's men were stationed along the pathway, hoping to prevent what just occurred." He clenched his jaw, angry with himself for not ignoring Masterson and Hennessey outright. He never should have given in and allowed Miss Montrose a bit more freedom. It was his job to protect her, not go along for the ride, straight into an ambush!

"King?"

He attributed her confusion to the shock of the attack. "Aye. Do ye not remember that I've mentioned him before? Gavin King heads up a division in the Bow Street Runners."

She frowned. "Does he always have men in the…" Her voice trailed off as her expression changed to one of horror. "You're bleeding!"

"'Tis nothing."

Her eyes widened, and he knew he could not continue to

ignore the wound. 'Twas a bit more than a scratch. It had soaked through the sleeve of his frockcoat and was dripping onto his hand. Much like Tremayne had earlier, he tore off his cravat and wound it around his upper arm. The back of his sleeve, as well as the front, were soaked with blood—an entrance and exit wound.

Small, soft hands brushed his aside. "Here. Let me." She bit her bottom lip in concentration as she tightened the makeshift tourniquet. Her eyes lifted to meet his. "Can you hold this end, while I pull the other? We need to make it as tight as possible."

The need to touch her face, press his lips to hers to thank her, nearly unmanned him. Clearing his throat to speak past the tightness in his throat, he answered, "Aye, lass."

They worked together until she was satisfied. When she reached for the end of the cravat he'd been holding, their fingers brushed against one another's. Heat shot straight through to his soul...and he knew. Sorrow followed elation. Miss Emily Montrose was the one woman he was fated to love till he breathed his last...but she was destined to marry her social equal.

Bayfield leaned into the carriage, studying Miss Montrose and her maid, looking for signs of injury before he narrowed his gaze on Garahan's arm. "Anyone else injured?"

Emily rose to her feet, lost every ounce of color in her face, and dropped onto the seat. Garahan waved Bayfield out of his way. "I'll ask ye again, lass. Where. Are. Ye. Hurt?"

"I didn't think I was," Emily answered.

He'd have to accept her word, though he had a sneaking suspicion the lass was putting on a brave front. But was it for her maid's benefit, himself, or Bayfield? He swore ripely.

"There is no need for such language, Garahan!" she admonished him. "I did not know anything was wrong until I tried to stand."

"If I am to protect ye, lass, ye'll have to tell me the truth—at all times!"

Bayfield leaned into the carriage again. "King's men have captured two sharpshooters. They promised to send word when they have finished interviewing the men."

Garahan struggled to contain his frustration. He was torn in three directions: discovering the extent of Emily's injury, returning to Montrose House as quickly as possible with the injured coachman, and the need to be present when the prisoners were interrogated on Bow Street. Taking them in order of urgency, he said, "The coachman needs to be seen by a physician."

"So do you, Garahan," Miss Montrose said.

"'Tis insignificant," he protested.

Tears welled in her soft gray eyes, magnifying her worry. Worry for him? "The bleeding hasn't stopped," she whispered.

He shrugged. "I know."

Bayfield spoke up. "I'll ride ahead and send someone for the physician. Our duty is to see to your protection and your safety, Miss Montrose," he reminded her.

"Ye've either twisted yer ankle or yer knee, if ye cannot stand, lass," Garahan grumbled. "Ye'll have to agree to have the physician attend to it."

She opened her mouth to speak, but must have realized the futility of arguing. "Very well."

Garahan stepped down from the coach. "I'll be driving us back to Montrose House. We may draw a bit of attention if anyone notices that the coachman is riding—not driving. Tremayne tied a tourniquet around his leg. The wound could be worrisome, if we do not have it taken care of right away. Will ye be able to wait to argue with me until after he's seen to?"

Frustration replaced the sorrow in the depths of her eyes. "Yes, of course. Is there anything I can do for him?"

Garahan schooled his features as he answered, "Pray."

CHAPTER SIXTEEN

T WO HOURS LATER, the physician had removed the pistol ball from the coachman's leg and given strict instructions to the housekeeper and the cook for his care. Garahan already knew what the physician would caution against. Familiar with the damage a tiny lead ball could do, he could have recited the physician's warning himself. As the ball was not lodged in the coachman's thigh for any length of time, wound fever would be a greater worry than lead poisoning.

Garahan hadn't moved from his position outside Miss Montrose's bedchamber, where he continued to stand guard. He had Tremayne carry her into the town house to avoid bleeding on her.

Wilcox and Bayfield approached. "The physician is waiting to patch you up, Garahan," the butler said.

Garahan looked over his shoulder at the closed door. He had not heard a sound, though he knew both Emily and her maid were in the room. "He should see to Miss Montrose first."

Wilcox shook his head, and Tremayne snorted. "If you weren't so worried about Miss Montrose, you'd realize that the risk of your losing more blood would render you useless guarding the duke's ward."

That had Garahan's mouth opening, and then closing, without him uttering a word. He squared his shoulders and met

Tremayne's probing gaze. "Please let Miss Montrose know that I shall return as soon as I'm able. I don't want her to worry."

Wilcox glanced from Garahan to Tremayne and back before agreeing. He knocked on the door and was bade to enter. The sound of low voices drifted through the closed door. A few minutes later, Wilcox reappeared. "Miss Montrose wanted me to thank you for letting her know where you'd be. She is most anxious that the physician see you and take care of your wound."

Tremayne frowned. "Don't hurry back."

"Bugger it," Garahan mumbled, following the butler.

Wilcox paused. "I did not quite hear what you said. What was that?"

Garahan knew the butler would not take offense when he repeated—louder this time—"Bugger it!"

The combination of snort and cough did not quite hide the fact that Wilcox was holding back his laughter. "Had I been in your place and been shot, I'd probably say the same. Let's get you taken care of so the physician can tend to Miss Montrose."

"Why wouldn't the physician listen when I demanded he take care of her before me?"

Wilcox shook his head. "Dr. Barry has been taking care of this family since his lordship retired from the military. He is well accustomed to dealing with all types of injuries and would know that the coachman's was the most dire."

Garahan did not argue with the man on that point. "Aye, but—"

"The bleeding in your arm has slowed, but not stopped. You have lost more color. Even I know that it would dangerous for you to lose any more blood, Garahan. By the way, I asked Tremayne to drop off a spare shirt and frockcoat earlier."

He was saved from replying when Honeywell called out to them, "Dr. Barry is anxious to put you back together."

Garahan bit back what he wanted to say. The younger footman did not deserve the edge of his frustration. He'd been a huge help since the first day Garahan and the others arrived at

Montrose House. Hoping to make light of his injury, he said, "Ye make it sound as if I'm held together by a thread, when anyone who's familiar with the Irish know that we're held together by the strength of our forebears, the heart of our people, and the magic of the Fae."

The men were laughing when Dr. Barry appeared in the doorway. "Garahan! Good. Let's take a look at your arm. The fact that you are still steady on your feet has me thinking the lead ball went straight through your arm without doing too much damage—aside from blood loss."

Garahan hated needles. "Ye might not have to put a needle and thread to me arm. Ye can sear the wound closed with a hot knife."

The physician made a humming sound in his throat as he helped Garahan remove his frockcoat. It was saturated. "Had we been on the battlefield—and yes, before you ask, I was a surgeon in the military before retiring to London—I would have done just that, as it would be the fastest solution. However…"

Garahan had slipped his shirt off and was surprised at the damage the lead ball had done to his arm. He dug deep for his steely control. "'Tisn't a pretty sight, is it?"

The physician agreed. "Have a seat while I clean the wounds. At least I won't have to search for a lead ball."

Garahan's head went light at the suggestion, but he couldn't afford to let his aversion to being sewn back together get the better of him.

A few moments later, the physician had cleansed both wounds to his satisfaction. His experience on the battlefield enabled him to work quickly and efficiently. "I'll go over what you can and cannot do for the next fortnight."

Garahan only listened with half an ear as he carefully slipped his shirt and coat on. He did not give a bloody damn what the physician wanted him to do. He'd been shot before—well, grazed, but that was close enough to know what to do and when to do it. "Thank ye, Dr. Barry. I'm anxious that ye see to Miss

Montrose. She's in considerable pain."

He followed the physician out of the room and back upstairs. Tremayne lifted his eyes to the ceiling, but did not comment on the fact that Garahan was ready to resume his position outside of Miss Montrose's bedchamber until after opening the door for Dr. Barry. "How's the arm?"

Garahan didn't answer right away. The irritation of the pain from his injury—and the stitches he'd suffered through—combined with the anger that had been on a slow boil since he ordered the landau to be replaced by the town carriage. He grunted.

But Tremayne was like a flea on a dog. "How many stitches?"

Garahan glared at the former dragoon. "Enough."

He wondered if Tremayne would comment on what he sensed the other man had observed—that Garahan's feelings for Emily went deep. Tremayne's next words confirmed it. "If you don't want word to reach the duke that you're besotted by his ward, you'd best snap out of it!"

Garahan's temper erupted. "The ambush should never have happened! Miss Montrose never should have been injured."

Tremayne nodded. "She must have been injured sometime between when you warned the women to take cover and when you opened the door to the coach. Most likely when she landed on the floorboards. Mayhap Miss Helen landed on top of Miss Montrose."

Garahan scrubbed a hand over his face. "Which never would have happened if whoever attempted to take one of us out had not been in the park today."

"King's men will get the truth out of them."

"The attack had to have been connected with the wager concerning Miss Montrose."

"We agree on that, but we need proof. Which we will have later today," Tremayne assured him. "By the by, I've heard from Cameron. I alerted the men and Wilcox to expect him within the hour."

"What about the witness," Garahan asked, "Miss Michaela?"

"As far as I know, Cameron is coming alone."

"Mayhap we'll have all of the information we need to subdue the mastermind behind the rumors, the wager, the endless stream of fortune hunters…and today's attack."

"Do you plan to send word to the duke?"

"After I speak with the physician. I won't be sending the missive until we know the extent of Miss Montrose's injury and how long she'll need to fully recover."

Tremayne blew out a breath. "About Miss Montrose. Bayfield has noticed your reaction to the duke's ward, too. If you don't want Hennessey and Masterson to comment on it, best rein in what you're feeling."

Garahan knew Tremayne had the right of it. "I will. After we know how Miss Montrose is doing, and I write to the duke, meet me in the stables."

Tremayne stared at him, then finally asked, "Why?"

"I'm after soaking me head again."

Tremayne's lips twitched. "Need my help?"

Garahan snorted with laughter. "I might at that."

Garahan accompanied the physician downstairs a short while later. Wilcox stood waiting with the man's top hat and frockcoat. "Thank ye for seeing to Miss Montrose, the coachman, and meself, Dr. Barry."

The physician smiled. "All in a day's work, Garahan. I've left extensive instructions with Mrs. Minnover and Mrs. Christian to send for me if the coachman's condition—or yours—changes."

"What about Miss Montrose?"

"It isn't a serious sprain, and as long as she follows my instructions to the letter, she will make a full recovery."

Relief filled Garahan as he followed the physician outside. "I'll be sending a missive to His Grace, who will no doubt be anxious when he learns his ward has been injured, yet relieved to know ye've taken such good care of her."

"I have never met His Grace, but please send my best to him in your message, and do remind him that with proper rest, Miss Montrose will be back on her feet in a few weeks' time."

"I will."

He stood back while the footman open the carriage door for the physician. After he departed, Garahan made his way to his lordship's study. Seated at the massive desk, he quickly penned the note to the duke, explaining the current circumstances. Rather than seal the missive, he returned the quill to its holder and rose to his feet. It would be best to wait to speak with Cameron first, then he could add that bit of information to the missive. His Grace would want to know all aspects of the situation at Montrose House.

Staring out the window, he replayed the events in his mind. He was grateful King had been able to spare a few men and had them stationed where they would not be noticed. Then again, not one of them had noticed the sharpshooters in the park either. The list of what he needed to accomplish before they left for Wyndmere Hall was growing.

He was anxious to find out if there was a direct connection to the wager that had been placed by Hardwell and the attack this afternoon. He needed to know what Cameron and Miss Michaela knew about Lord Montrose's death—which was no longer considered an accident by those in the know, and frustratingly still shrouded in mystery.

The knock on the door had him turning away from the window. "Enter."

Wilcox opened the door, announcing, "Cameron to see you, Garahan."

He strode over to greet the man, and was struck by the thought that Cameron could fit the description of the man who brought Lord Montrose home after the accident. He decided to wait to put the question to him. "Tremayne and me brother have mentioned ye."

"Don't believe everything either man has to say about me," Cameron warned. "Tremayne said ye wished to speak to me."

"Aye, as Miss Michaela isn't in a position to meet with us. I understand from me brother—and Tremayne—that ye were instrumental in taking care of me sister-in-law after ye rescued her off the streets when she dove out of her would-be captor's carriage."

Cameron smiled. "Mrs. Garahan is a plucky lassie. Miss Michaela was the one who saw her leap from the moving carriage and was there to get her off the street before the carriage stopped—or someone else swooped in to nab the lassie."

"Ye have me thanks. Melinda has added to me brother's life. I've never seen him so happy—well, unless he's in the middle of a bare-knuckle bout, winning."

Cameron chuckled. "Thought I'd be going a round or two with James, but alas, there wasn't time."

"I have a feeling James would be more than willing to accept yer challenge if ye're interested."

Cameron grinned. "It would be a pleasure." He handed a sealed note to Garahan. "Here is Miss Michaela's signed statement of what she saw that night. 'Tis addressed to Gavin King of the Bow Street Runners."

Garahan accepted the note and slipped it in his waistcoat pocket. "I'll deliver it personally."

"I'll let her know that ye offered to before I asked it of ye, as she bade me to do."

"When did ye arrive on the scene? Did ye see who pushed Montrose? Bloody hell, Tremayne wanted me to wait until he arrived to find out what ye knew."

A cry of surprise and the sound of a scuffle out in the hallway had the men rushing to the door.

Garahan strode from the room and jolted to a stop. "Tremayne, what in the bloody hell do ye think ye're doing? Set that footman down."

Tremayne did not look away from the much shorter man dangling from his grasp, nor did he let go of the footman's cravat, even though the man's face was turning an alarming shade of red.

Garahan didn't have time to argue. The blow to Tremayne's extended forearm was swift and powerful. Tremayne released his hold, and the footman slid to the floor, gasping for breath. Though his fists ached to pummel Tremayne, Garahan knew the man would never have acted in such a way without cause. He glanced down at the footman and noticed him trying to slink away. "If ye don't want to be dangling from me fist next, ye'd best not be moving."

Cameron moved to stand beside the footman and met Tremayne's gaze. "He won't."

Garahan noted the shared look and surmised that Cameron and Tremayne were more than just comrades who'd served together. He'd extract those details later. "Do we need to take this outside, Tremayne, or can we speak of it now?"

Anger poured off Tremayne in waves. "The only way we could have been ambushed in the park was if someone knew we would be there ahead of time."

Garahan inclined his head. "Aye, that thought occurred to me as well. How did ye know 'twas him?"

"The coward boasted to Honeywell about the bag of coin he'd received for passing on the information to the man who hired him."

Garahan nodded. "Honeywell? Whose father served in the King's Dragoons?"

"Aye," Tremayne replied.

"Honeywell must take after his father," Cameron said. "Honor and duty before selfish gain." He glanced down at the other footman, frowned, and nudged him with his boot. "Who paid ye?"

When the young man hesitated, Cameron bent over, but before he could grab the footman, the young man stammered,

"B…B…Baron Hardwell."

Wilcox chose that moment to step forward. "I have sent for the Watch."

Garahan thanked him. "How long has this one been in service to Lord Montrose?"

Wilcox glared at the young man before answering, "His lordship hired him on last month. We didn't need another footman, but his lordship was always willing to help those in need of employment, especially if their family had ties to the military."

Garahan stared at the young man until he started to fidget. "What's yer name?"

"Billings," Wilcox answered for him.

"Stark," the footman said at the same time.

Wilcox's look of disbelief told the rest of the story. "Then your father did not give his life in battle?"

Stark shrugged. "I needed a way to get in."

"So ye lied," Garahan said. He should not have been surprised. Not everyone was brought up with the same principles as his family.

"I knew other chaps were being hired on, and I needed the blunt," the footman said.

"Does your da know—"

"Don't have one," Stark interrupted.

"What of yer ma?"

"Don't have one of those either."

That would explain why the lad was headed down the wrong path. Garahan was torn between seeing the footman was brought to justice for his part in the ambush, and wondering if the lad's life would have been different if he knew who his parents were.

Cameron was the first to break the silence. "We may ask the Watch to go easy on ye if ye agree to work with us."

Tremayne's frown was fierce. "He already works with us!"

Garahan shook his head. "He works for Hardwell—not us. Mayhap we should see if he's willing to change to the side of the righteous. Well, lad?"

The footman's face lost every ounce of color. "He'd kill me."

"Hardwell?"

"Why don't we continue this discussion in private?" Tremayne suggested.

"No!"

"Ye have a reason not to speak with us?" Cameron asked.

The fear in Stark's eyes was real. "If you break my hands, I won't be able to earn a living."

"Who said anything about breaking yer hands?" Garahan demanded.

The young man hung his head. "The baron."

"Wilcox, when the Watch arrives, have him come to the study."

"Aye, Garahan."

The group walked in silence to the study. When they were inside, Tremayne closed the door behind them, and Garahan said, "We're after protecting ye, lad, provided ye tell us the whole truth."

The ugly truth poured out. Hardwell had hired Stark off the street the night he'd tried to pick the baron's pocket. Under threat of having his hands broken, the footman agreed to seek employment at Montrose House, and relay any and all information regarding his lordship and his daughter back to the baron.

"I'm thinking we bring Coventry or King in on this discussion," Garahan said.

Tremayne seemed to be thinking it over, while Cameron agreed with Garahan. Finally Tremayne said, "If he hands over the coin Hardwell paid him to King and agrees to continue to pass along information to Hardwell."

Garahan knew what Tremayne intended. "So we can spring a trap on Hardwell and catch him in the act!"

"Doing what?" Cameron asked.

"If my guess is right," Garahan answered, "abducting Miss Montrose."

The grim faces staring back at Garahan should have been a

relief. Instead, it added to the depth of his worry for Emily. Hardwell would only succeed in taking the lass over his dead body!

By the time Wilcox knocked on the door to the study, the men had convinced Stark to trust them. Garahan finished his note to the duke, and two more—one to King and one to Coventry to apprise them of this latest development.

"Enter!"

Wilcox opened the door and announced, "The watchman is here to see you."

"Show him in," Garahan said.

The burly man striding into the room had Stark swaying on his feet. "Do you plan to come along quietly, lad, or do I have to bind your hands?"

"How do ye know he's the man ye're to apprehend?" Garahan asked.

"The guilt and apprehension in his eyes, and the way he's not steady on his feet. As if he knows what's to come and may pass out on me." Keeping his voice calm, the watchman asked, "What's your name?"

"Ssss...Stark."

"Well then, Stark, what'll it be? Easy or hard?"

"Easy, sir."

"Well now," the big man said. "No one's ever addressed me so formally before. Thank you for the consideration." He glanced about the room and stared hard at Tremayne, Cameron and Garahan. "The lot of you look as if you'd take great pleasure in beating someone to a pulp. Would you all care to accompany me?"

Garahan chuckled. "Faith, but ye're not that far off the mark. 'Tis a pleasure to meet ye. Me name's Garahan. I'm one of the Duke of Wyndmere's private guard."

The watchman's eyes widened at the duke's name.

"Lieutenants Tremayne and Cameron were formerly with the King's Dragoons."

"I should have recognized the badges of honor you both carry," the watchman said. "Beg pardon for mentioning your scars."

Tremayne and Cameron shared a glance before Tremayne answered, "No need. We were just discussing the possibility of a bare-knuckle bout before you arrived."

The watchman's eyes gleamed. "I've been known to enjoy the challenge of a no-holds-barred, anything-goes fight."

"Me brothers and cousins would be more than happy to take ye on. What's yer name?" Garahan asked.

"O'Hanlon."

Garahan slapped him on the back. "I should have guessed. What county are ye from back home?"

"Mayo."

"Me brothers and I hail from Tipperary. Our Flaherty cousins are from Dublin, and the O'Malleys from Cork and Wexford."

"I had heard that His Grace hired a stout group of Irishmen. It'd be a pleasure to meet them—and go a round or two."

"It's settled, then—I'll send word to James and we'll see when we can arrange it."

"I'll look forward to it. Now then, Stark, let's be off."

"I believe Wilcox was a bit too hasty sending for you," Garahan told him. "Stark has had a change of heart and plans to amend his ways, starting now. Haven't you, Stark?"

"Yes, yes I have."

"Well then, no harm done." With a hand clapped to O'Hanlon's shoulder, Garahan said, "Why don't I walk ye out and fill ye in on the particulars?"

The watchman eyed the group one more time before he agreed. Once they were in the hallway, O'Hanlon asked, "Does this involve the duke?"

"Aye. 'Tis why I didn't want to say anything in front of the others."

"I understand. If you have need of me, you've but to send for me." He paused by the front door Wilcox had opened. "I'm glad that young man decided to change his ways. Too many young men these days would rather line their pockets, stealing from others, than work their fingers to the bone to scrape enough coin by to live off."

Garahan sighed. "We Irish know what it's like to have to work till we drop."

"For less than a fair day's wage," O'Hanlon added.

"If ye ever decide ye're looking for a change in employment, let me know. The duke could always use another good man such as yerself."

The watchman grinned and held out his hand. "Count on it, Garahan! It's been a pleasure."

Making his way back to the study, Garahan hoped O'Hanlon would give serious consideration to coming on board. They could use a man like him to add to their ranks.

CHAPTER SEVENTEEN

R AGE COURSED THROUGH Hardwell's veins as his heart pounded in his chest. He grabbed the crystal decanter of brandy and tossed it against the fireplace. It shattered on contact. Brandy-coated shards glittered on the stone, the floor, and in fibers of the thick antique carpet that was one of the last items he had not been obliged to sell.

His contacts only dealt with foreign entities when arranging the very private sale of the contents of his ancestral home. No one would ever be the wiser as to what happened to the entailed items attached to the barony. He should not have to be bothered with such trivial thoughts as selling valuable family treasures, but he'd underestimated the Duke of Wyndmere's Defender, and the rest of the men guarding Montrose's daughter—the men who were part of the duke's one-eyed man-of-affairs's band of scarred misfits.

He needed answers. What in the bloody hell was keeping Wilson? He'd sent for him hours ago. Had he already left London intent on spending the coin Hardwell had paid for a failed job? The only part of the plan that had been executed as planned was that the coachman and Garahan had been shot. There was a rumor that the coachman may not survive the blood loss from the lead ball taken in his thigh, which pleased him. The *on dit* circulating that Garahan hadn't appeared to be affected by the pistol ball in the arm, and in fact had been seen outside Montrose House, locking for all intents and purposes as a man without a care in the world, did not.

Slamming his fist on his desk, Hardwell ignored the pain shooting through his hand. There had to be a way to salvage the coin he could not afford to spend, and the perfect plan that had fallen apart.

Grabbing a second crystal decanter from the sideboard, he lifted it high, but at the last moment decided to drink the contents rather than shatter it against the fireplace.

Three glasses of excellent port later, he smiled, remembering Poston. In his anger, he'd nearly forgotten his lackey was due to arrive anytime with news concerning the men he'd paid to slip inside Montrose House and ended up on Bow Street. Although Poston was not in the same class of criminal as Wilson, he could be coerced into doing Hardwell's bidding with threats.

While he waited for Poston, he received word from the young man who'd infiltrated Montrose House's staff. Miss Montrose and her guard would be traveling to Wyndmere Hall at week's end.

If he could not locate Wilson, he'd either have to use another of his connections to do the job—or bloody well abduct her himself!

The knock on the door to the study had him barking, "Enter!"

"Poston to see you, your lordship."

"Send him in." A few moments later, Poston was shown into Hardwell's study. "Do you have the information I require?"

"Aye, your lordship." Poston shuffled from foot to foot, and could not look Hardwell in the eye for more than a few seconds at a time.

"Well? Don't just stand there!"

Poston's gaze met his, but he quickly looked away. "The men were caught trying to break into the back entrance of Montrose House."

"Caught?"

"Aye, by Miss Montrose's guards—after midnight!"

"Blundering idiots," Hardwell murmured. He waved at Poston, who stood there blinking for a moment before realizing he'd been dismissed.

Without another word, his lackey beat a hasty retreat. Hardwell had used the man a number of times when he needed information at a bargain price. He was glad that he hadn't given in to the urge to have Poston disappear—permanently. He may have a use for him one more time.

Yanking on the bellpull, he waited for his butler to reappear. Pointing to what was left of his grandfather's decanter on the fireplace, he ordered the man, "Take care of that." He strode past the butler and said, "If anyone calls for me, I'll be in my upstairs study."

"Yes, your lordship."

Satisfied with his amended plans and the news from Stark, Hardwell retreated to his private sanctuary.

CHAPTER EIGHTEEN

G ARAHAN STOOD WITH his hands behind his back, ignoring the pull of the threads reminding him his arm could not heal fast enough to suit him. "Do ye think Hardwell will question the information ye fed him?"

Stark seemed to be standing straighter. "Nay, or he wouldn't have asked me to see if there might be any another footman, gardener, or stable lad who would be interested in earning a bit of coin on the side."

While the change in Stark's demeanor pleased Garahan, he was not ready to leave the younger man to his own devices—especially with regard to his ongoing relationship with Hardwell. They needed Stark's help to outwit Hardwell and see that the man's plans were fully derailed. "When did ye receive the missive from him?"

"A few minutes ago." Stark couldn't hold Garahan's steady gaze. He looked away.

"If ye're worried that none of the other lads will be willing to work with ye, ye'd be wrong. They'd do anything for Lord Montrose's daughter. Hardwell's schemes and slurs against Miss Montrose must be brought to light. He must be stopped."

"I've never had anyone believe in me before, Garahan. It's a heavy responsibility doing the right thing."

"Aye, lad." Garahan placed a hand on Stark's shoulder. "'Tis at that, but we trust ye."

"You haven't told Miss Montrose about me, have you?"

"Not as yet, though I will after we are assured that Hardwell has been caught in his own web of lies and deceit."

Stark's Adam's apple bobbed up and down, and he had to clear his throat to speak. "I won't let you down."

"Faith, I know ye won't. Now then, I'm thinking Honeywell and Brewster would be ones to ask. Honeywell's on the second floor standing guard outside Miss Montrose's bedchamber, and Brewster's in the north alleyway."

"What do you think Hardwell wants us to do?"

Garahan opened the door to the servants' side of the house and said, "Well now, if I were Hardwell, I'd want to ensure that I had a few men ready to convince Miss Montrose to go with them, once her guards have been taken care of." He waved to the cook as they walked along the hallway to the door to the servants' staircase, then opened it and motioned for Stark to precede him.

"You don't think he plans to hurt Miss Montrose, do you?"

The worry in the lad's expression and his question were a relief to Garahan as they ascended the stairs. "Between meself and Coventry's men, we aim to see that no one harms a hair on Miss Montrose's head."

At the top, Stark opened the door and hesitated. "What if Honeywell refuses to help me?"

"He won't. Ye'll see."

The footman in question turned toward them as they approached. His expression guarded, he nodded. "Is something wrong, Garahan?"

"Nay. We need yer help."

With a glance at Stark before answering, Honeywell nodded. "Whatever you need."

"We'll be speaking to Brewster next. We need the both of ye to make the journey north to Wyndmere Hall."

Pleasure shone in the young man's eyes. "I'd be honored, and can assure you Brewster will be, too."

"I thought ye might be," Garahan said. "Now then, there will be a bit of intrigue involved, as we'll be asking ye to do Hardwell's bidding."

Honeywell's expression hardened. "After what you told us in the meeting earlier? Are you out of your mind?"

Garahan sighed. "Haven't ye ever heard that ye keep yer friends close…and yer enemies closer?" The lad shook his head. "Well then, now ye have. Ye don't need to actually meet with the man. He's arrogant enough to believe that his promise of coin will convince anyone in need of it will do his bidding—no matter what he asks."

Honeywell's rigid stance relaxed. "What do I need to do?"

Garahan grinned. "There's a lad. Now then, I need to speak to Tremayne and the others, but the gist of it is, yerself, Stark, and Brewster will be accompanying Miss Montrose as part of her staff. Yer duties will be similar to what ye do now, with the exception that ye'll be required to carry a weapon, as we do not know what—or who—we may meet on the journey north."

"What about Hardwell? Do you believe he will mount another attack?"

Pleased that the lad had grasped the heart of the matter—and worry—he grinned. "We'll be ready and waiting. Come along, Stark. We need to speak with Brewster before ye send word to Hardwell that 'tis all arranged."

Stark waited a beat, and Garahan sensed he was screwing up his courage. "Thank you, Honeywell. I know you have no reason to trust me," Stark said, "but I aim to prove that you do."

Surprise flashed in the footman's eyes. "I'm willing to do all I can to help you earn that trust."

"Come along, Stark," Garahan urged. "We don't want to keep Hardwell waiting for a reply—he may think ye plan to double-cross him."

Stark descended the staircase behind Garahan, protesting, "But I haven't given him any reason to before now!"

"'Tis what any black-hearted man would think—and Hardwell's heart is black as coal!"

A QUARTER OF an hour later, Brewster agreed to join them, and Stark had sent the reply off to Hardwell. The only possible drawback would be if the lass got the idea in her head that she didn't have to continue to follow the rules: no rides in the park, excursions to Bond Street, or ices at Gunter's.

Garahan swore beneath his breath. He'd just have to keep after her to toe the line. The thought of spending more time with the lass had his heart pounding and anticipation coursing through his veins. He'd have to summon every ounce of control if he were to survive spending more than a few moments at a time alone with her.

Miss Emily Montrose was a temptation he could ill afford.

CHAPTER NINETEEN

EMILY BRACED A hand to the arm of the ladder-back chair and slowly stood. When she was steady on both feet, she drew in a calming breath, took a step forward, and felt her ankle give way.

The door burst open. "Lass, are ye all right?"

She did something she rarely did unless she was alone…she swore ripely!

Garahan's cough sounded suspiciously like a snort of laughter.

"Are you so cruel that you would laugh a someone else's misfortune?"

"God help me, lass. Never!" He bent down on one knee and asked, "Where does it hurt, besides yer ankle?"

She stared at the floor as mortification heated her cheeks. She could not tell him that her bottom ached from the impact with the arm of the chair before hitting the floor.

"Don't try to move. Let me lift ye up." Without waiting for permission, he scooped her into his arms, settled her against his chest, walked over to the fainting couch, and gently placed her on it. "Have you tried the crutches Dr. Barry dropped off for ye?"

"My arms ache from trying to use them."

"Poor lass. Shall I ring for one of the footmen and have tea sent up for ye, or would ye rather I carry ye downstairs to the sitting room? You'd be in the thick of things and able to order everyone about like a queen from yer favorite yellow and blue flowered settee."

How did he know the color of her favorite settee? *Because he is observant, and watches you like a hawk.* She felt the first smile in days lifting her lips. "It was Mother's favorite spot in the sitting room." Smiling up at the too-handsome-for-his-own-good Irishman, she said, "If it's not too much trouble, I would love to be anywhere but stuck in my bedchamber."

"Do ye need to grab a shawl or yer reticule, or a favorite book?"

"It would probably be a good idea to bring all three with me. If you wouldn't mind walking over by the dark blue velvet chair, I left my shawl and reticule there."

He did as she bade him and then asked, "And yer favorite book would be where?"

"Beneath the ladder-back chair. I was reading and dropped it. Then decided I did not want to disturb you and ask for help."

"Ah," he said, leaning down so she could retrieve the book. "So instead ye tried to stand on yer injured ankle and risk the possibility that ye'll have to spend an extra week with it wrapped and elevated."

She wanted to smack him on the back of the head with her book, and only her mother's lessons in deportment overcame the need.

"Miss Montrose, ye're an absolute delight when I can see the wheels turning in that head of yers. Although, I'm thinking Mrs. Minnover and Mrs. Christian would take exception to ye walloping me in the head with yer book."

"How did you know—" She bit her bottom lip and looked away. "Forgive me."

"Well 'tisn't as if ye followed through with what ye were thinking and smacked me, is it now?"

He chuckled, and she scoffed, "What is so amusing?"

"I'm thinking Michael O'Malley's wife would have whacked him without giving it a second thought."

"O'Malley?"

"Aye, me cousin and another member of the Duke's Guard. His wife Harry—er…Harriet, was a widow, raising her son on her own and used to handling whatever life tossed in their path. She's not one to bow to convention."

When he fell silent, she prompted, "Until?"

Garahan's jaw clenched. "Until the night a band of marauders were set loose on their farm and that of a few others—intent on destroying them and Viscount Chattsworth."

Her eyes widened. "Then it was not a rumor of those attacks right before the viscountess gave birth to their son?"

"Nay. Now then, a change of subject to a happier one seems in order. Would ye open the door for me, lass?"

"Miss," she reminded him as she threaded her fingers through the thick, dark hair that touched his cravat. His sharply indrawn breath had a surge of power flowing through her.

"Aye, Miss Montrose."

She twirled one of the strands around her pointer finger as she rested her cheek against his shoulder. Heat poured off the man in waves. He was not immune to her! Mayhap she could convince him to agree to an experiment. His lips had been distracting her, tempting her to ask for a taste, but she didn't know how without causing a scandal.

She'd only been kissed a few times, and not once had she felt a smidgeon of the attraction that pulled at her whenever Garahan was near her. Before he delivered her to the duke's front door, she craved one kiss—just a brief taste of those beautifully sculpted lips. They appeared firm…*and* soft… Which was it?

The need to discover their texture tempted her to test her theory. They were halfway down the staircase when she trailed the tip of her finger along his bottom lip.

He jerked and leaned backward. "Are ye after killing the both of us, lass?"

She hung on for dear life as he regained his balance. Her heart was racing—and not because of the passion she'd begun to suspect only Garahan would pull from the depths of her soul. She'd nearly caused the man to tumble down the steps. "We could have broken our necks," she rasped.

He didn't say another word until he'd deposited her on the settee in the sitting room. With a stiff bow, he mumbled something about tea and stalked from the room.

Tears pooled in her eyes as she berated herself. How could she do anything so foolish? Why hadn't she realized the danger? *Because I didn't think he was all that attracted to me.*

The knock on the open door had her sniffing back her tears.

"Oh, miss, does your ankle pain you?" Helen asked, rushing into the room.

"It's my own fault. I dropped my book upstairs and foolishly thought I could stand up and retrieve it."

"Shall I send for Mrs. Christian? She would know what kind of damage you could have done to your ankle."

Resigned to hearing an earful from the cook, who no doubt had already heard Garahan grumbling on his way to his post outside, Emily replied, "Yes, thank you, Helen. I think that might be wise."

"I shall return in a few minutes." Before Emily could ask her to, the maid plumped two pillows beneath Emily's ankle. "There now, try to relax. When you stiffen up, the muscles work harder."

"They do?"

Helen shrugged. "I'm not sure if they do or not, but it seems to me that they would."

"Thank you for your concern and care, Helen. It means so much more than you realize."

Her maid smiled and hurried out of the room.

Alone, Emily wondered if Garahan would ever hold her in his arms again. The next time she wouldn't be so foolish as to caress his lips when they were descending a staircase... She'd wait until they were on a flat surface. Her mind wandered back to a few days earlier, when she'd walked into the stables and seen his very broad chest, *sans* waistcoat and frockcoat, his cambric shirt plastered to each and every one of his powerful muscles.

She'd nearly swooned on the spot and had been scooped up and ended in his arms then, too. Now if she could only sample the flavor and texture of his lips...the line of his jaw...the hollow of his throat—

"Here now, miss, are you in much pain?" Mrs. Christian asked as she rushed into the room.

Emily's mind felt like mush, and for a moment she had a bit of trouble forming an answer. Finally she managed, "I was just telling Helen that I should not have tried to test the strength in my ankle when I dropped my book upstairs."

"Garahan mentioned that to me on his way out to his post." Eyes narrowed, the cook asked, "Do you have any pain anywhere else?"

Only my backside...and my heart. "No, I'm fine."

"You're certain?"

"Aye. Thank you for looking after me, Mrs. Christian. I am sorry to be such a bother."

"You are not, nor have you ever been a bother, Miss Montrose. I thought you realized that."

Tears filled her eyes once more. "You have always been so kind to me. After Mother passed, I felt so lost, but you took me by the hand and brought me into the kitchen, where you let me help you bake a batch of cream scones."

"You stopped crying when your hands were busy," the cook reminded her.

Emily nodded. "Then we baked currant cake and a butter cake."

"His lordship was most appreciative—he had such a sweet tooth."

The tear snuck past her guard. "And you taught me how to bake his favorite—cream tarts."

"He would eat an entire tray of them, if I did not remind him it would spoil his appetite."

"His appetite was wonderful—and he was so very clever the

way he would distract you in order to sneak one or two of your special tarts. We'd go up to his dressing room and sit by the back window by the copper tub—the view of Mother's gardens made it feel as if she were with us in spirit."

"I know about the bits and pieces of sweets the two of you would leave as a tribute to the Fae."

"How did you find them? We broke them into such tiny bits and left them on the stoop of the faery houses Father helped me build."

"For a man who spent the bulk of his life barking out orders to his men, he was so patient when you dragged him into the gardens to serve bits of baked goods on the point of a leaf, or pour a thimbleful of mead or currant cordial for the faeries to enjoy at dusk."

"He never tired of sitting on the curve of the path, watching and waiting for the faeries to dance among the flowers," Emily whispered.

"He was the best of fathers… The best of men." Mrs. Christian waited a moment before adding, "He'd be proud of the way you have handled yourself with the solicitors."

"It was expected, and I did not want to let Father down."

The cook agreed, then added, "He would also approve of the way Garahan and the others have been so diligent protecting you."

Emily sighed. "He'd be vexed with me for being so difficult."

"I think he would understand," the cook assured her. "Don't spend too much time worrying over what you cannot change. Look to the future and change what you can. Now then, let me take a look at that ankle."

Emily was quiet while her ankle was unwrapped, the color and slight swelling noted, and then rewrapped. "Did I do more damage to it?"

Placing Emily's foot back on the pillows Helen had arranged, Mrs. Christian shook her head. "I do not think so, but I wouldn't recommend walking on it again for a least the remainder of the week."

"I promise not to."

"You will ring the bell that I left on the table next to your bed if you need anything, won't you?"

"And the second one you left next to the fainting couch," Emily promised.

"Excellent. Now, I'll see about your tea. I have a fresh batch of triple-berry tarts that just came out of the oven."

Emily sighed. "With clotted cream?"

"Just the way you prefer it, miss."

"Thank you Mrs. Christian."

"I'll be right back."

Emily watched her leave and wondered what life would have been like if she hadn't lost her mother a decade ago. She might not be quite as outspoken. Mother was soft-spoken. Then she shook her head. In order to gain her father's notice whenever he was home in between campaigns, she was boisterous. He would scoop her off her feet and, holding her in one arm, wrap the other around her mother and hold them tight.

She bowed her head. "I miss you both—terribly."

"Here we are!" Mrs. Christian said, bustling back in the room, followed by one of the footmen, who carried a large tea tray.

Emily was surprised by the number of tarts. "Are we expecting guests?"

The cook smiled. "Titania and Oberon have expressed an interest in taking tea with you."

Emily felt her spirit lighten. "We should be honored that the queen and king of the Fae would deign to take tea with us. Won't you and Helen join me? Mrs. Minnover, too?"

"I think we can take a break for a cup of tea with our favorite mistress." The cook asked the footman to tell the others their tea was ready and waiting. He nodded and left the room.

A short while later, the women were laughing as they spoke of flowers, faeries, and the restorative power of tea and triple-berry tarts.

CHAPTER TWENTY

"**Y**OU SEEM DISTRACTED."

Garahan frowned at Tremayne. "I'm thinking about the number of people making the journey to Wyndmere Hall with us, and how often we'll need to change horses."

"You agree that we'll be riding through a proverbial gauntlet." It wasn't a question. When the Irishman nodded, Tremayne said, "We will have to be on guard from the moment we leave. There are any number of places that would be perfect for a sharpshooter to lie in wait."

"I hope he gets it over with our first day out," Garahan said. "If not, we'll be on tenterhooks until Hardwell makes his move."

Tremayne agreed. "The baron has invested too much time and coin on his band of blackguards to wait until the last day."

Going over their strategy in his head, Garahan scanned the perimeter as he patrolled the north alley. Tremayne fell silent, prompting Garahan to ask, "Do ye think we need Masterson and Hennessey as additional outriders?"

"It would definitely be to our advantage. We could have either man ride ahead with one of the footmen. At any sign of trouble, one of them could ride back to warn us."

Garahan's gut clenched. "While the other stays to fend off an attack." He met Tremayne's level gaze. "But you think he'll have three men ready to launch an attack."

"Aye."

"Then two isn't enough. We'll need to have three men riding at the front."

"Adding two more men ought to round out our numbers and give us the added protection and the ability to send three men forward—and to the guard the rear."

Garahan felt one the knots in his stomach ease. "I'm thinking we should ask King if Jackson and Thompson could accompany us. They've assisted us in the past and are familiar with the lie of the land both on the journey north and surrounding Wyndmere Hall."

"I'm surprised the captain hasn't thought of adding to our number."

"Given all that's occurred since we formed the guard, Coventry probably has, and is waiting for us to put the request to him. He's not one to overstep once we've been assigned to our quarterly posts. I'd best send word to Coventry and King right away."

"I'd suggest a meeting with Coventry and King before we leave," the dragoon said. "We should include the men who will accompany us."

Tremayne's probing look had Garahan bracing for another comment about the woman they were protecting.

"Have you spoken to Miss Montrose about the journey?"

Garahan shrugged. "Not as yet. I'm waiting until after we meet with the men."

"Miss Montrose and Miss Helen will need to understand what is expected of them when we stop to change horses," Tremayne reminded him.

"They will," Garahan said. "I intend to inform them that they must have one of us with them at all times. I've been working with the list Coventry sent of the inns where His Grace has horses stabled. The teams will be perfectly matched, and accustomed to pulling a town coach."

"His Grace takes care of his family and his guard," Tremayne said. "As of late, he has been including myself and the others who work directly with Coventry to the list of men who have use of his horses."

"One less thing to worry about," Garahan mused. "Would ye let Wilcox know that I'll need Brewster to deliver missives to Coventry and King in the next quarter hour?"

"I will."

"Oh, and let him know that they'll be arriving for a meeting. We'll need Brewster, Honeywell, and Stark to attend as well."

"Masterson and Hennessey should be arriving for the shift change any moment," Tremayne said. "Is there anything you'd like me to tell Miss Montrose before I assume my post on the second floor?"

"Not before our meeting."

Their relief arrived, and the men separated, each intent on accomplishing their assigned duties and tasks.

TWO HOURS LATER, having received replies from King and Coventry, Garahan had his protection plan in place. The information from Coventry made the task that much easier. Their journey to Wyndmere Hall was laid out in detail, down to at which inns they would change horses, where they would be stopping for their midday meal, and where they would bed down for the night. After the meeting, he planned to speak to Miss Montrose and advise her when they were leaving, and lay down the rules for their journey.

He was writing a missive he planned to send to the duke immediately following their meeting when he was interrupted by the knock. He set the quill aside. "Enter."

"Coventry and King to see you."

He rose from his seat behind the desk. "Thank ye, Wilcox. Are the others on their way?"

"Aye. Tremayne and Bayfield have arranged for a few of the stable hands and footmen to take up your posts until you relieve them once your meeting is over."

Once the butler left, Garahan greeted Coventry and King. "Has Hardwell resurfaced?"

"Not since it was reported that he was seen in the park the afternoon you were ambushed," King replied.

"Bloody coward's hiding from us." The intensity in Coventry's eye assured Garahan that he wasn't the only one anxious for Hardwell to show himself. He had a score to settle with the man…and he intended to be the one who brought him to justice. But first he planned to even the score for the injuries they had suffered. One way or another, Hardwell would pay!

The others arrived, and Garahan laid out his plans. Coventry approved, and King agreed to loan out Jackson and Thompson. It wasn't until Coventry asked if he'd spoken to Miss Montrose about the journey that Garahan wondered if he should have. "Not as yet, though I cannot imagine it would take long for her maid to pack Miss Montrose's trunk."

King snorted, and Coventry cleared his throat before replying, "I used to be of the same opinion—however, since marrying Miranda, I have learned that my previous assumptions about women were incorrect."

Garahan frowned. "How long will it take to pack her trunk?"

Coventry stared off into space for a moment before answering, "I'm afraid I could not say, as the workings of a woman's mind are still a mystery to me."

"But ye've been married for a time now. Haven't ye learned anything?"

The captain's contented look should not have surprised Garahan. James, and the others stationed in London, had mentioned the deep affection between Coventry and his wife. "Aye, that I'm still not certain I understand the winding paths my wife's mind takes on a daily basis."

"We're leaving in two days," Garahan reminded them.

Coventry and King shared a look before King said, "Have you spoken with the physician? Does he agree that Miss Montrose is fit to travel?"

Garahan rubbed at the knot forming at the base of his skull. "She's improving every day and will spend most of the journey riding in the coach."

"I would not leave without the physician's approval. Best summon him first," King said. "Then speak to Mrs. Minnover."

"Why the housekeeper?" Garahan asked.

Coventry was the one to answer. "She will be able to give you an idea of what will be involved in packing Miss Montrose's possessions."

"Possessions?" Garahan's mind reeled. "I thought she'd only need to take a few gowns in a small trunk."

"The duke will be responsible for arranging a suitable match for Miss Montrose," Coventry advised. "She may want to take some of her belongings with her, as I doubt she will return for some time."

"If I were you," King said, "I would alter my plans to include a smaller coach which could haul two, possibly three, of Miss Montrose's trunks, as well as additional traces, leads, mayhap a spare wheel—"

Garahan's gut clenched. "Ye think they'll try to disable the team as well as the coach?"

King nodded. "I would be prepared for any eventuality. My sources indicate Hardwell has been waiting for this opportunity for a few years. He will not give up easily."

The thought of their team of horses or coach overturned on the side of the road had not occurred to Garahan. He'd been brooding about what would happen after they delivered Emily to Wyndmere Hall. The hard fact that she'd be expected to marry a nameless, faceless lord had had acid burning the lining of his stomach. He wanted to shout that she had yet to properly grieve for her da and should not be thrust into marriage so quickly, but he had no say in the lass's life beyond keeping her safe until they arrived at the duke's country estate.

Clamping down on the feelings rioting inside of him, he turned to Stark. The footman looked worried. Garahan knew why and wanted to assure the lad that they would protect him, too. "We've already set the wheels in motion and let it be known that we will be leaving in two days' time. Hardwell must not suspect that he is being fed information that will have him playing into our hands." He nodded. "Stark has already passed along the word that we travel in the town coach with two outriders."

The Bow Street Runner and the duke's London man-of-affairs's expressions did not change, but Garahan noted a slight lessening of the tension in their stances. They were relieved but did not want it to show. That was fine with him. The less everyone knew about the subterfuge planned, regarding the baron and his hired thugs, the greater their chance for success.

"As to that," Coventry said, "I would have the smaller coach precede the coach carrying Miss Montrose and her maid."

Garahan thought about it and agreed. "It would appear that the outriders were protecting the smaller coach...and therefore the focus of Hardwell's attacks."

The change agreed to, King turned to the footmen. "We are in your debt, men. Thank you for volunteering."

"Ye're free to return to yer duties. Thank ye, men." As the younger men took their leave, Garahan raked a hand through his hair. "Tremayne, would ye have Wilcox send for the physician?" Addressing the others, he said, "The rest of ye men can return to yer duties as well."

Coventry's men filed out, leaving Garahan with King and Coventry.

"The information Miss Michaela provided is damning," King said. "There is no doubt in my mind that Lord Montrose was pushed. We have her description of the perpetrator. It isn't Hardwell. One of his hired lackeys, no doubt. It may take a bit of time to locate the man without additional information. I agree with Cameron's suggestion that we allow her to maintain her anonymity. She is providing a valuable service to young women who have been coerced, or forced to work on the streets. With no other option, they are unable to provide for or protect themselves."

"When will ye be bringing Hardwell in for questioning?" Garahan asked. King paused, and Garahan knew, somehow, the baron would not be brought in just yet. "What could possibly keep ye from bringing the man in?"

"He does not fit the description of the man Miss Michaela saw push Montrose in front of the carriage. Until we have proof he is connected, he will remain free—but under surveillance. My men will get as close to him as is possible without being accused of harassing the baron."

Garahan's throat felt tight as he controlled the need to shout. "Who in the bloody hell cares if ye're accused of harassing the man? If ye don't harass him, he'll go free!"

"And all of the time and manpower spent gathering information will be for naught if a certain member of the *ton* who has Prinny's ear catches wind of it," King reminded him.

Garahan fought the turmoil of temper and worry bubbling inside of him. "All of the evidence points to the man. He must have hired someone."

King's eyes flashed with anger. "Aye, but we need that key piece of information or a witness. Suspecting and knowing in your gut is not enough to convict the man."

Garahan could see how difficult it was for King to keep his Runners from bringing the baron in and tossing him behind bars.

"Once we have the man responsible for the dark deed," King said, "we will go after Hardwell."

"Until then," Coventry added, "you will need to be vigilant in protecting the duke's ward. The sooner she leaves London, the safer she will be."

Shaking his head, Garahan had to ask, "I thought you agreed that Hardwell will plan to ambush us?"

"I believe he will," Coventry said.

"Given the length of time he waited to return to London to exact his revenge on the present duke, I would plan on more than one attempt," King warned.

"I included possible ambush locations on North Road, with the information about the horses and inns," Coventry said. "Any questions, contact me."

King and Coventry rose. "We will see ourselves out while you speak to the housekeeper," King said.

Garahan did not waste any time. There was more to accomplish before they left than he'd anticipated.

He located Mrs. Minnover in the kitchen. "May I have a word with ye? I need yer advice."

The older woman smiled. "Of course, Garahan. I need to speak to one of the upstairs maids—why don't you accompany me?"

As soon as he closed the door to the servants' staircase behind him, he asked, "How long will it take Miss Helen and Miss Montrose to pack her trunk?"

Mrs. Minnover hesitated. "That all depends. If there is a need for haste, she will have to make do with the two mourning gowns she has."

"That's fine—"

"But," the older woman continued, "we had planned on sending for Madame Beaudoine to have a few additional gowns made for her journey to Wyndmere Hall. Miss Montrose will want to be dressed appropriately when meeting the duke and duchess."

"Me cousin Sean's wife used to sew for Madame Beaudoine, and I've heard her mention a time or two that they had ready-made gowns that they would embellish and fit to customers who did not have the time to wait for one to be designed for them."

Mrs. Minnover seemed pleased with the suggestion. "I shall encourage Miss Montrose to send a message to the modiste, with her measurements—after all, it is an emergency."

"Best send word at once."

"There may be two or three additional trunks necessary for the journey."

Garahan nearly stumbled. "Two? Does she have that many

gowns and fripperies to pack?"

The housekeeper paused at the top of the stairs and turned toward Garahan. "Miss Montrose will be leaving all that she has known behind her to meet her guardian—a duke, no less, and a man she has never met. Would you begrudge her the right to pack her mother's looking glass, or her father's sword, or her grandfather's brace of pistols?"

He reached around the woman to open the door for her. "She's planning on arming herself?"

Mrs. Minnover sighed. "Her father's sword is a memento of his time in the military and the honor that was bestowed upon him—the title of lord."

"What about the pistols?"

"His lordship's father won them…"

The housekeeper trailed off, and he decided not to press the issue. "Is there anything else that you think Miss Montrose will be taking with her?"

"A number of books and a trinket box," Mrs. Minnover replied. "Miss Montrose has confided to me that she fears she will not be returning to Montrose House for some time."

"I wouldn't be knowing, though I can assure ye that His Grace is a fair man and would be open to listening to any request Miss Montrose makes. In the meantime, see that Miss Helen and Miss Montrose begin packing at once."

"I will." Mrs. Minnover paused with her hand on the door to one of the bedchambers. "I already know that you and the men will be diligent in protecting Miss Montrose and Miss Helen, but promise you will be careful, too."

Surprised by her request, though not irritated by her lack of faith in him, he agreed. "Ye have me word."

"Thank you, Garahan."

He nodded, turned on his heel, and strode back to the servants' staircase. With each step down, his aching heart felt as if it were being torn apart. His time with the lass, who was rapidly tearing his control to shreds, was dwindling. Before he knew it, they would load up two carriages and begin their journey north. His first prayer was that he could keep Emily safe. The second was that Hardwell would be lying in wait for them, so they could catch him in the act.

When he reached the last step, his heart cried out for the impossible—that somehow, someway, something would happen…and the lass would choose him.

"Aye, that'll happen when pigs fly."

CHAPTER TWENTY-ONE

EMILY AGONIZED OVER her decision, but finally chose the only former suitor she felt would be apt to let her spend her days in the country, while he spent his in London. She penned what she hoped would be a friendly, compelling note. Succinct, lest there be any question on the gentleman's part that she was interested in more than a marriage of convenience.

There was simply no question—they would not be blissfully happy in one another's company. Tolerate one another? That was definitely a possibility…as long as Giles would forgive her for refusing his suit six months earlier. In the back of her mind, she replayed the way he'd masked his emotions from her. She had been unable to discern what he was thinking. It had been obvious what Father thought. His fierce frown gave her a moment's pause, and had her wondering at the time if he would force her to accept the offer. Thankfully, he had not.

In the end, he had agreed to speak to Giles and deliver the unhappy news—or happy news, as far as Emily was concerned. She had no wish to marry anyone and planned to do as she pleased for the rest of her life. Father needed someone to keep him company, and she was more than happy to do so. Her heart had not been tempted by any one of the gentlemen she had been introduced to at the endless round of balls, musicales, and dinner parties. There had been two soldiers from her father's regiment who had gone out of their way to be charming, though neither one had been in a position to offer marriage.

Her life had been going along just as she'd planned once gentlemen ceased to seek her out at the balls she attended with her father. She'd felt nothing but relief when he finally agreed that she need not attend quite so many functions. In her opinion, they had been a tedious waste of time. Time that she could have spent curled up in a chair in the library with any one of the books she'd recently purchased.

All that changed the night her father was carried into their home bleeding…dying.

Pushing those thoughts to the back of her mind, she sealed the note and laid it on the desk. Rising, she walked over to the corner and tugged on the bellpull. A few moments later, she answered the knock on the door. "Come in." She smiled at her maid, reached for the note, and handed it to her. "Please ask Wilcox to have this delivered at once."

Her maid took the note and frowned, recognizing the name. "We need to finish packing. Mrs. Minnover said that Garahan is adamant about leaving the day after tomorrow."

"I may not be ready to leave just yet. It all depends on the response I receive from Giles."

Her maid's eyes widened. "You cannot refuse to leave, miss. I overheard Garahan and the men a little while ago. Time is apparently critical."

Emily lifted one shoulder, then let it drop. "If I am not ready to leave, they will have to wait, won't they?"

"I have a feeling you're going to regret sending this message."

She stared at her maid. "What makes you say that?"

Helen started to inch toward the door, but Emily's hand on her arm stopped her.

"You know something," Emily accused. "Tell me!"

"I promised, miss. I cannot."

"Whom did you promise?" Emily demanded.

"Lord Montrose," her maid whispered.

"Tell me."

Her maid let go of a sigh. "I had just entered the main part of the house when Giles and your father were walking toward the entry. They did not seem to notice me, so I stood off to the side."

"You heard something."

Helen nodded. "Giles seemed distraught that you had refused his offer, and his lordship was assuring him that you refused all offers and had no intention of marrying—ever."

"Well," Emily said, "that is true."

"Giles's expression changed from woeful to angry in a heartbeat. He raised his voice to your father and told him he should have kept you home rather than allowing you to turn the heads and hearts of those looking for a wife."

"I didn't know Giles had more than one emotion in him—complacency."

"His lordship thanked Giles for his offer, then waited with him while Wilcox opened the front door. As soon as it closed, he mumbled that he was pleased his daughter had shown the good sense not to settle for an empty marriage to a spoiled young man with no ambition other than to waste his time attending the rounds of social engagements and boasting with his cronies at his club."

"And?" Emily prompted.

"Wilcox agreed."

Emily's thoughts tumbled over themselves. Had she truly thought Giles would be a reasonable man? How could she have been so off the mark? "I wonder if my father felt that way about every offer I refused. He never said or did anything to encourage me to change my mind."

"I do not know, but it would not surprise me if he had. His lordship was a good man of strong principles."

Tears filled Emily's eyes, but she brushed them away. "He was honest and had more integrity in his little finger than any one of the gentlemen I've met in the last three years. Not one of them measured up to my father."

Her maid held out the note. Emily took it and tore it in half, and then again. "Thank you for telling me. I would have made a grievous mistake."

"I do not think Garahan would have let you make that mistake. He'd probably boot Giles out."

Emily's lips twitched. "Garahan would not have let Giles in the front door to begin with, though he may have been allowed to step down from his carriage."

"Garahan is a good man," Helen said.

Emily knew that now, though she had not thought so at first. More than that…he did not claim to be a gentleman. The memory of how he'd found her the night fortune hunters tried to break into Montrose House filled her. His broad frame and impressive size had been as much of a comfort as the way he'd gentled his hold on her, carrying her as if she were as fragile as glass. The way he argued with her and demanded she obey the rules so he could protect her seemed to be in direct opposition to his softer side. That he had hidden depths, she had no doubt. One thought filled her mind whenever he was near—he had the qualities she admired most in her father: honesty, integrity, and compassion for others.

"Aye," Emily agreed. "And he's been shot protecting me."

"Did you know he tried to convince Dr. Barry to see to your injured ankle before he tended to him?"

Her indrawn breath snagged in her lungs before she was able to exhale. "But he was bleeding!"

"Precisely what Mrs. Minnover said to him at the time."

She could not keep from asking, "And what did he say in response, Helen?"

"It was his duty to protect you to his last breath."

He had done his utmost to protect her, even when she fought against his orders to the point of compromising her safety. With the remnants of the note she intended to send to Giles in her hands, a cold certainty shot through her belly—there would never be another man in her life like Aiden Garahan.

She would never love a man the way she loved Aiden.

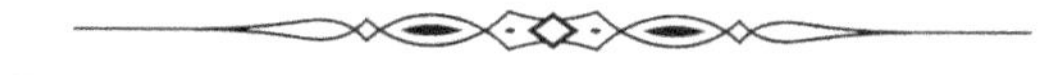

CHAPTER TWENTY-TWO

GARAHAN FROWNED AT the four trunks and the housekeeper. "We do not have room for two extra trunks."

The older woman stood her ground. "If you were not insisting that someone will be riding on the roof of the town coach, this would not be an issue."

Garahan ignored the jibe. "Can ye not send Miss Montrose's possessions another time?"

"Is that what you think the two trunks contain?"

"'Tis either her possessions or clothing."

For the first time since he'd entered Montrose House, the housekeeper seemed angry with him. "The smaller trunk contains linen strips for bandaging, healing salves, herbs for fever, and poultices—though you will need a ready supply of hot water for the poultices—calves' foot jelly, hartshorn, boiled threads, and needles."

"It sounds as if ye were thorough. Thank ye for ensuring that we'll have everything we need to patch one another up—if there is trouble. Though ye should not worry that there will be."

When Mrs. Minnover's eyes welled with tears, he held up his hands. "I did not mean to upset ye, when it's clear ye have the best of intentions. Me ma would agree with ye. 'Tis far better to be prepared." Eying the second small trunk, he asked, "May I ask what the other trunk contains?"

"Captain Coventry recommended you carry a ready supply of lead balls, wadding, and gunpowder."

"'Tis all the better that we have a number of former military men in our number to ensure we are prepared for any circumstance. I'll be thanking the captain the next time I see him." He knew what she needed to hear. "I won't break me promise. I will protect Miss Montrose and Miss Helen. Should anything happen to me, ye can rest assured that Tremayne, Bayfield, or one of the others will take my place." When she did not immediately reply, he grumbled, "Ye'll have to trust me."

"I do trust you." She managed a brief smile. "I'll go and see what is keeping the ladies."

He nodded and watched her head back into the house. They still had a bit of time before they had to leave in order to stay on schedule—though, God's truth, he wished they were already on their way.

"Garahan?"

He turned to see what Bayfield wanted. "Aye?"

"Are you certain it is a good idea to have a loaded pistol beneath the seat? Do you even know if Miss Montrose or Miss Helen has ever fired one?"

He grinned. "According to Wilcox, Miss Montrose is an excellent shot. Her father saw to that. I'd feel more confident if we had weapons at the ready. Both rifles and pistols have been known to jam on occasion. I'd rather not be left without a way to defend Miss Montrose and her maid—or the women to defend themselves if it comes to that."

"You have the right of it," Bayfield agreed, rolling his shoulders, impatience coming off him in waves. "How long before we can be on our way?"

"Mrs. Minnover went to fetch Miss Montrose and Miss Helen." He turned and saw Wilcox striding toward him with a hamper. "What in the bloody hell is in that?"

"Mrs. Christian has been baking up a storm since the wee hours of the morning. There's hearty meat pies and her cream scones still warm from the oven, a few bottles of ale and wine, and a small tea chest. Enough to feed everyone."

"We aren't planning a bloody holiday, Wilcox."

"But if one of your destinations cannot accommodate you, you will have rations. I've already thanked Mrs. Christian on your behalf."

Chastised, Garahan sighed. "Forgive me. I've more than food on me mind at the moment."

"His lordship would be grateful that the duke saw fit to send you and the others to protect his daughter. The ladies are nearly ready to go—they're just bidding farewell to the staff who will stay behind."

Garahan wondered if he'd have to deal with bouts of tears. He tried not to think about that possibility, or the fact that Coventry insisted that they not leave at first light, as Garahan had planned to. They were to leave by eight o'clock—an ungodly hour, according to those of the *ton* who'd only just arrived home a few hours earlier.

"I'll make one more round, checking that the men are ready and know their positions. Thank ye for everything ye've done for us, Wilcox." He held out his hand. When the butler shook it, he added, "Please thank Mrs. Christian and Mrs. Minnover for me."

"I will." The butler turned and disappeared into the town house.

By the time he'd spoken with Tremayne, Bayfield, and the others, the front door opened and Emily and her maid were walking toward him. Neither one was smiling—then again, neither woman was crying, though he could feel their emotions as if they were his own. Sorrow. Anxiety. Hesitation. Anticipation. Bloody hell, it was exhausting.

Compartmentalizing the emotions—as he'd learned to do at a young age—he opened the door to the larger coach for Miss Montrose, steadying her when she stumbled. "Have a care, lass."

"Thank you. My mind is elsewhere."

"Me pleasure." Once she was seated, he helped Helen inside

and closed the door. "We won't be stopping until it's time to change horses in two hours."

"How many miles do you expect to travel today?" Emily asked.

"Will we change horses at every stop?" Helen added.

He was pleased they were thinking of the journey and not the danger dogging their heels. But the fiery lock of hair brushing Emily's cheek had him fisting his hands. Would it feel like silk and carry the scent of roses? He buried the need to touch and answered, "We may be able to make eighty miles. I've sent along word to the inns we plan to stop at along the way, so they will be expecting us."

Turning to Helen, he answered her question. "Aye, we change horses at every stop. Our team is strong, but pulling a coach of this size is work. Never fear," he told the women, "we are well prepared for the journey and have more supplies than we could possibly need."

He had a word with the coachman, then strode over to the smaller coach to do the same with that driver. He mounted his horse, nodded to Tremayne—who would ride alongside the town coach for the first leg of their trip—and then Bayfield, who was seated beside the man driving the coach carrying their provisions and ammunition.

Garahan suffered one heart-clenching moment as the group departed the town house on Mayfair. He'd never felt this bone-deep connection to a woman before. Never felt this heart-crushing worry over protecting another... *God, please help me, and the others, deliver her safely!*

THE TENSION BETWEEN Garahan's shoulder blades increased exponentially with the number of miles they traveled. He did not expect Hardwell to spring a trap until they were well away from the crush of the city, but the lingering question remained: would the baron be bold enough to try to abduct Miss Montrose from the yard of a busy inn—or when they were on the well-traveled road heading north?

The stops to change horses, and use the necessary, went as planned. Not for the first time, Garahan began to have an inkling of just how wealthy the duke had to be to have teams of horses, as well as those strictly for riding. Their group required fourteen horses—two teams for the carriages, and horses for the outriders.

He'd never been responsible for that many lives on a journey before...out in the open! Garahan snorted at that notion. He wasn't responsible for Coventry's men—they were battle hardened and had survived horrific injuries. Gavin King's two Runners had years of working in the underbelly of London, the docks, and among the quality. The six of them were more than capable of taking care of themselves. It was Emily, her maid, and the three young footmen who depended on Garahan's fighting skills—both bare-knuckle and with all manner or weapons—to see to their safety. The Duke of Wyndmere had placed him in charge, it was his duty to protect the lot of them!

For the rest of the day, and the one following, the men changed positions seamlessly, and were becoming accustomed to guarding either coach. He would shift positions throughout the day, but spent most of the time riding alongside the carriage carrying the lass and her maid.

Garahan was relieved it had been uneventful so far, pleased that the women seemed to be traveling well and not suffering from the mode of travel. Not everyone's gut was equipped to handle the constant swaying motion of the carriage for long periods of time. The tales his cousin Finn O'Malley had shared of his journey to Cornwall with his pregnant wife Mollie had had Garahan insisting there would be two urns inside the town carriage...just in case they were needed.

He scanned their surroundings, alert to everything going on, from the way the breeze rustled the leaves of the trees along the side of the road, to the rumbling of the carriage wheels. Every so often, the memory of holding the lass to his heart popped into his head, but he ruthlessly shoved it aside.

The longer he was in her company, the more difficult it had been to remain detached. He had tried to distance himself from Emily while at Montrose House, but she'd managed to distract him on more than one occasion. It would not happen again. Her life depended on his ability to protect her, and the others, not to daydream about the curve of her cheek or the fullness of her lips.

He whistled sharply, and Masterson immediately turned his mount around, riding toward him. "Problem?"

Garahan would slit his own throat before he admitted he'd allowed his mind to wander to the duke's ward—even though it was for a heartbeat. "Just a feeling in me gut. Switch places with me."

Without hesitation, Masterson did as Garahan asked. They arrived at their next destination a short time later. The urge to switch places with Tremayne or Bayfield and have one of them escort the women into the inn was strong, but the need to keep his word to the duke—and Mrs. Minnover—was stronger.

The inn's hostler's eyes widened at the sight of two carriages and eight mounted riders pulling into the yard of the inn. Garahan dismounted and handed the reins to the hostler as the innkeeper rushed toward him.

"Welcome! You're the Duke of Wyndmere's party."

"Aye. Name's Garahan."

"We have been expecting you." The rotund innkeeper's smile was welcoming. "I have the meal for Miss Montrose and her maid in the private dining room, as requested. Will you be joining them?"

Garahan nodded. "There will be four of us joining them. We'll need food and ale sent out to the men who will be staying with the carriages."

The innkeeper glanced at the men dismounting. "I will have food brought out to your men. Are there any other servants in your party?"

"Just the fourteen of us."

The innkeeper rushed back inside to see to the preparations.

Garahan paused to speak to Thompson and Jackson. "I appreciate yer eyes and ears. The footmen are as green as they come in a situation like this, but have given their word they are ready to stand in between Miss Montrose, her maid, and danger."

"We've had a chance to talk with them. They show promise," Jackson said.

"I believe Stark has embraced the second chance you're giving him," Thompson said. "He can be trusted."

"'Twas me feeling as well, though it's good to hear ye agree with me." Garahan looked up at Tremayne's hail and nodded to him. Turning back to King's men, he said, "As we discussed, three men will accompany meself and the ladies in the private room. We'll rotate who accompanies me with each stop. Four of ye will eat in the main taproom—I'll leave that up to ye to choose. As we discussed earlier, the others will guard the coaches and the horses as they are being changed and after they have been hitched to the carriages." He paused, then pitched his voice low. "Pay special attention to the coach with our ammunition."

"My thoughts exactly," Jackson replied.

"I have a feeling we can expect trouble between this stop and the next inn," Thompson said.

Garahan's gut had been telling him that very thing. He nodded. "Feels like we've been sitting on a powder keg."

Tremayne approached the group. "Bayfield and Hennessey have inspected the horses and are well pleased with them. His Grace is an excellent judge of horseflesh."

"That he is. I'd like Stark, Hennessey, and yerself to join us inside."

Tremayne agreed. "Hennessey and Masterson are helping Miss Montrose and Miss Helen from their carriage."

Garahan turned and noted Emily had a slight limp. "It appears as if the Miss Montrose's ankle is a bit stiff from sitting. I hope she's not in any pain."

"I did not hear a word of complaint when I was riding with the coachman. Lively discussion inside the carriage," Tremayne said.

"How could you hear what they were saying above the rattling of the harnesses and the clattering of the coach wheels?"

Tremayne grinned. "It was the sound of their laughter."

One of the knots binding Garahan's gut eased. "If ye'd bring the others, I'll go inside first. Join me in a few moments."

"Aye."

The men separated to see to their duties while Garahan headed into the main taproom. He'd caught himself praying Hardwell would be waiting inside, and was disappointed that he wasn't. He walked the length of the dark hallway leading to the staircase, and the other one leading to the kitchen. Stepping into the private dining room Coventry had secured for them ahead of time, he was satisfied.

He did not plan to relax his guard until the moment he turned the lass over to the duke. Garahan would ensure the others were just as vigilant. No harm would come to the lass on his watch!

CHAPTER TWENTY-THREE

EMILY TRIED TO ignore the fact that she and Helen were still eating, while the four men who accompanied them into the private room had already finished and were standing guard, waiting for them.

She hadn't intended to linger over the meal of a thick stew, buttered bread, and a pot of tea, but she was tired of sitting, tired of the monotonous sway of the carriage and the clatter of carriage wheels. It would be selfish of her to complain when she knew the men in their large party were there for her protection. *Aiden* was there for her protection.

Her eyes instinctively sought his. Heat suffused her being when their eyes met, though his brief glance was more of a silent question. She shook her head to indicate nothing was wrong before turning back to Helen. "I'm not sure I should eat another bite."

Her maid's look of concern had Emily feeling guilty for not choosing her words more carefully.

Before she could explain, Garahan walked toward her and asked, "Are ye not feeling well?"

"Forgive me; I phrased that badly. I know how important it is for us to stay on your schedule and do not want to risk an unplanned stop if I overeat."

The look in his eyes warmed at her words. "A wise decision.

One I've made meself."

"Are you worried that with all that's happened since you arrived a few weeks ago, there is a chance that we have been followed?" she asked. "Will that man who sent those men to Montrose House because of that awful wager know we have left and are traveling to Wyndmere Hall?"

"Let me worry about that. Just know that I'll not let anything happen to ye, lass—nor to ye, Miss Helen."

Moved by the certainty, and sincerity, in his voice, she reached out to grab hold of his arm. Something dark and dangerous swirled in the depths of his gaze. The emotion pulled her inexorably closer.

He reached out to catch her before she fell off the chair. "Have a care, lass."

Rattled, she smoothed her skirts and settled firmly on the seat. "Er…yes… Thank you, Aiden."

His gaze held hers for one heartbeat, and then another, before he returned to the back corner of the room and his duty— guarding her life with his.

All too soon, the innkeeper returned to clear away the empty plates. "Would you care for more tea, Miss Montrose?"

She smiled at the man. He'd been solicitous, treating them as if they were royalty. It was a bit unnerving, but she did her best not to let it show. "No thank you. Our meal was delicious— please thank the cook for us."

Garahan held the back of her chair when she rose from her seat. "Tremayne and meself will see ye ladies to the necessary."

She felt her face flush with embarrassment. "Must you? Surely you do not think anything untoward will happen by the privies!"

"With the four of us guarding ye, we ensure nothing will happen."

"We are grateful," Helen said, nudging Emily. "Aren't we, miss?"

"Yes." It felt as if her face was on fire. "Forgive me for not realizing it is only due to your diligence that we were able to eat a peaceful meal. Thank you, Garahan."

Tremayne cleared his throat—loudly—Hennessey grinned, and Stark stared at his feet.

Emily was mortified that she'd ignored the other men. "Thank you, too, gentlemen."

Garahan rolled his eyes. "Lass, I keep telling ye—"

She swallowed the urge to laugh, lest one of the men think she were laughing at them. "I know, you've corrected me before, but I was taught that men were to be referred to as gentlemen."

"Not all men are gentlemen. Best remember that and be on yer guard until we reach the duke's estate."

"Even with the men guarding us?" Helen asked.

"Aye, and be aware of yer surroundings at all times."

Emily could not keep from asking, "Then why do we have so many men guarding us?"

"The men are a safeguard and here to ensure that if anything happens to me, or if I am unable to do me duty, another will step into me place and see ye safely delivered to the duke's front door."

She could not contain her sharp intake of breath. It was not the first time he'd said that to her, but it was the first time, she realized, that there was a very good chance Tremayne, Hennessey, or one of the others would be the one to deliver her into the care of the duke and duchess—while the smaller coach would carry the body of the man who held her heart to his final resting place.

Tears welled up and spilled over before she grasped the fact that she was crying. The handkerchief her maid held out to her brought her sharply back to the present. She whispered her thanks, blotted her eyes, and slipped her arm through her maid's. "Let us hope that will not be necessary, Aiden."

GARAHAN WATCHED THE emotions playing on Emily's face, and the moment his words hit home. It was a heady feeling that she was moved to tears when she realized the only reason another would take his place was if he was sacrificed his life for her, but he quickly dismissed it. He had to keep his mind on his duty and not the fact that the lass had feelings for him. No matter how either of them felt, nothing could ever come of the attraction between them. He was the duke's defender, and she was the duke's ward.

He motioned for Stark and Hennessey to follow them as they made their way outside to the privy. Garahan ignored Emily's sharp intake of breath as he knocked, then opened the privy door and scanned the small room. "'Tis safe—empty. Tremayne and I will be right outside if ye need us."

Her maid said, "If you don't mind, Garahan, I'll stand right outside the door should Miss Montrose need me."

He fought the urge to smile at her imperious tone. "Aye, Miss Helen."

The women didn't waste any time taking care of their needs.

"We'll see ye to the carriage. Have a word with the others and be on our way."

"Aiden?"

He ignored the tug on his heart at the sound of Emily's voice, at her using his given name. He turned to find her watching him with a devilish look in her eyes.

"Be sure to take care of your personal needs as well."

Garahan ignored Tremayne's snort of laughter and replied, "Rest assured, Miss Montrose, we will." Her mention of his using the privy was shocking enough to distract him from thoughts of sampling her sweet mouth, or the inside of her wrist where her pulse would beat faster when he pressed his lips there.

Once he closed the door to the town coach, he reminded Emily, "Stay put."

He heard her scoff and mumble something to her maid, but did not have the time for a battle of words with the lass. They needed to stay on schedule. The duke was expecting them.

Striding toward the back of the stables, he wondered what in the bloody hell possessed the woman to remark on whether or not he took a piss. His ma would have, but she had license to— she was his ma! He quickly took care of business, then stopped to speak to the coachmen and the youngest members of their group along the way.

When he finally made his way back to the town coach, Masterson was sitting beside the coachman. He signaled to Masterson, who hopped off the carriage. "I expected an attack at this inn."

Masterson's jaw clenched. "Hennessey and I did, too. If not here, the next obvious place would be along the road between this inn and the next." He waited a beat, then added, "We're ready."

His assurance did nothing to stem the acid slowly filling Garahan's gut. Masterson climbed back onto the seat and settled next to the coachman as Garahan walked over to his horse and mounted.

Determined not to let anyone see the unease roiling inside of him, he raised a hand in the air and lowered it. Harnesses jingled and horses' hooves added a rhythmic cadence, as carriage wheels clattered over ruts by the stables and in the front of the inn, dug by dozens of carriages that had visited before them.

Once out on the open road, Garahan was able to draw in a breath and exhale. It wasn't that he finally felt safe—it was the ability to see in all directions at once, without buildings or masses of people blocking the view of possible hiding places where Hardwell and his lackeys may be lying in wait.

The distance covered without mishap should have eased the knot between his shoulder blades the further they traveled—but instead, it increased the pressure. Hardwell's men had ambushed them in the park, for feck's sake! Anywhere along this stretch of road would be ripe for attack.

As if he'd conjured it, a rifle shot echoed from in front of them.

"Get down!" Garahan and the others closed ranks around the lass's carriage. They were ready to defend her.

Before he could ask if anyone had been hurt, or which direction the shot had come from, two more were fired. As planned, Jackson and Thompson sped off in opposite directions, intent on flushing out their attackers, while the coachmen coaxed more speed out of the two fresh teams of horses.

Another shot sounded, but this time Garahan noticed the smoke from the black powder hanging in front of the stand of trees on the right side of the road. "Tremayne, your right flank!"

The former dragoon reacted instinctively, taking aim and returning fire. The sound of branches breaking, a prelude to the sight of a body falling out of the tree, had Garahan issuing orders. "Hennessey, give Tremayne a hand with the body. Wait for Jackson and Thompson and meet us at the next inn."

Half a mile up the road, another hidden sharpshooter fired at the carriage, splintering the wooden seat just shy of Stark's leg. This time, Bayfield and Masterson set off after the gunman.

Instead of continuing on, Garahan ordered the coachmen to a stop a few hundred feet from where the last shot was fired. His pistol cocked, he turned so his horse was right up against the side of the carriage where Emily was seated. "Stay down—no matter what happens!" When he did not hear a reply, he repeated the command, and swore when she didn't answer him. "Bugger it, lass! Answer me!"

"I bloody well heard you the first time!"

Relief washed over him as he gave the order for those that were still with them to have their pistols cocked, aimed, and ready to fire. A few minutes later, Bayfield and Masterson rode up. Bayfield held the reins to a third horse with a man draped over it, facedown.

Before Garahan could ask, Bayfield shook his head. "Not dead—unconscious."

"Wasn't willing to come along until I slipped him a convincer," Masterson added.

Ten long minutes later, Tremayne and Hennessey rode up. This time it was Hennessey who led their prisoner on horseback with his hands bound behind him, blood dripping from a gash on his forehead. Tremayne answered before Garahan could ask, "He was moving when I fired. I missed him—hit the branch by his head."

Garahan studied the wound. "I don't see any sign of wood splinters."

"He was sitting on the branch and hit his face on the ground."

"Ah." He hid the worry from the others, though he was growing more concerned by the moment. How many other sharpshooters had rifles trained on the road between the last inn and the one they were overdue to arrive at? He checked his worry, remembering Coventry's inspired plan put into place ahead of time. If Garahan and his party did not arrive within an hour of their anticipated arrival time, the innkeeper was to notify the local constable.

He heard Emily arguing with her maid as Jackson and Thompson approached. Jackson had the reins to a horse that carried two men. Both were bleeding. One held a hand against his shoulder, blood oozing between his fingers. The other man had a hand clamped against his side to control the bleeding.

"We're too far away from the inn," Garahan grumbled. "We'll have to patch the prisoners up here."

Stark took that moment to speak up. "Why not let them bleed? It's what the baron would do."

Garahan didn't think the question was too bloodthirsty. After all, he understood the lad's need for revenge—even if it wasn't against the man who'd threatened Stark, but henchmen Baron Hardwell had hired. "Though it pains me to have to see to the care for those who would think nothing of putting a pistol ball between me eyes," he told Stark, "me brothers, cousins, and I swore an oath to the duke that we would shoot to injure—not kill—when protecting the duke, his family, and extended family."

"But Miss Montrose isn't family," Stark shot back.

"The moment Lord Montrose died, Miss Montrose became the duke's ward, and he considers her part of his family. 'Tis me job to keep her safe."

"Did you also have to swear that you'd see that they didn't bleed to death?" one of the footmen asked.

"Not at first," Garahan answered. "Wyndmere Hall was under attack, and we'd finally routed the attackers. The duke had us collecting the lot of them, and lending a hand binding their wounds while the lasses were occupied tending to our men."

"Lasses?" Stark's eyes widened. "Are there many at the duke's estate?"

"Not as many as before. Mollie, one of the maids, married me cousin Finn O'Malley, and last I heard, Francis had her eye on the local farrier. By now Her Grace would have had to replace at least two or three maids, so who's to say."

Garahan dismounted and opened the carriage door. "Anyone hurt?"

Instead of two women cowering in fear, he was greeted with eyes the color of summer storm clouds blazing with anger. "Do not ever swear at me again!"

He did not take offense, as his ma had often said as much to his da. "As long as ye answer me when I ask ye to."

Instead of a reply, she turned her head away from him. Not that it bothered him in the slightest—he had prisoners to see to, and there was the possibility that the local constable and one or two of his men would be headed this way, looking for Garahan and his party. "Miss Helen, see to it that Miss Montrose stays in the carriage."

"Aye, Garahan."

Masterson beat him to the small carriage and had the trunk containing healing supplies open. He looked over his shoulder at Garahan. "We don't have the instruments to dig out any lead balls, but we can stop the bleeding until we get to the inn."

Tremayne strode over to lend a hand. "There should be a surgeon or healer nearby who will be able to take care of the prisoners."

"Do we know for certain if any of the three that were shot is Hardwell?" Garahan asked.

"Only two were shot," Tremayne reminded him.

Garahan nodded. "The prisoners Jackson and Thompson delivered."

Tremayne's lips twitched. "Apparently, Gavin King doesn't follow the same strict rules regarding prisoners as His Grace or Coventry."

Jackson must have heard Tremayne's remark, as he called out, "Surprised a former dragoon missed his target." With a glance at Thompson, he grinned. "We hit what we aim at."

The last thing Garahan needed was a pissing contest between Coventry's men and King's. "Given that Tremayne was shooting blind, I'd say he accomplished what he aimed to do."

"Aye," Thompson agreed. "He shot the tree."

Tremayne glared at the man but, instead of taking it up a notch, turned his back on him.

"We're to work together," Garahan said. "If not, faith, it'll be the last time we ask King to spare the two of ye. Next time we'll request Franklin and Greeves. Understood?"

"Aye," Thompson answered, shoving his elbow into Jackson's ribs.

Jackson glared at Thompson, but muttered, "Understood."

Satisfied that there wouldn't be any more problems among the men, Garahan motioned for Honeywell and Brewster, who stood off to the side, ready to lend a hand. "I'll need ye to stand guard on either side of Miss Montrose and Miss Helen."

"Aye, Garahan!"

"Right away!"

The lads rushed over to the other carriage, drew their weapons, and stood with their backs to the doors and their eyes on their surroundings.

Once the prisoners were tended to, Garahan assigned a man to guard each one. Tremayne would ride on top of the small carriage with the man with the head injury. The man Masterson had knocked unconscious was riding one of the horses, while the remaining two prisoners rode double. When Garahan asked about the missing horse, he shook his head, not surprised that it had run off at the sound of gunfire. Apparently the baron must not be paying enough, or else the blackguards hired would have hit every target and ridden away to safety. Thank God that wasn't the case!

He gave the signal, and the party resumed their journey. Half an hour from the inn they were scheduled to have changed horses, they were flagged down by three men.

"Trouble, Garahan?" one of the men asked.

"A bit. Who sent ye?"

"The innkeeper. Captain Coventry's orders."

Relieved that it wasn't someone else working for Hardwell, Garahan nodded. "And ye'd be…?"

"Constable Cook, and my men, Dickson and Harald."

"I'd be happy to turn the prisoners over to ye," Garahan said.

The prisoners were transferred over to the constable, while Tremayne and Masterson explained the measures they'd gone to in order to ensure the prisoners would be alive.

Garahan added, "His Grace has always been adamant that any prisoners we capture will have the ability to be questioned."

"I thought that was a rumor," the constable said.

"'Tis the truth. The duke's a firm believer in justice being served. The prisoners—no matter if they attempted to kill His Grace, or kidnap his twin babes—were all able to answer any and all questions put to them before being hauled off to London, where they would be locked up to await their trial."

The constable frowned. "I am not certain I would be as magnanimous as His Grace were it my family."

"'Tisn't easy when ye're in the thick of things, protecting Their Graces and their family and extended family," Garahan mumbled.

The constable motioned to his men to join Garahan's men,

keeping the prisoners between them.

Garahan had returned to his position alongside the town coach when the constable rode over. "Thank ye for coming after us, constable."

"It's an honor to aid the Duke of Wyndmere and his ward," the lawman replied. "We'll accompany you to the inn. I asked the innkeeper to send for a physician, who will be ready and waiting to tend to anyone injured. While he tends to their wounds, you and your men can answer a few questions for me. Given who may be reading my report, I will need to ensure I do not leave any details out."

Garahan readily agreed and moved his mount closer to the constable, confiding, "I was not about to ask Miss Montrose or her maid to use their skill with a needle and thread on the prisoners."

The lawman immediately agreed. "The attackers were seen to, which is more than would have happened had it been any other party."

Garahan shrugged. What did the man expect him to say to that?

"Justice isn't always meted out by earthly means," Cook said.

"Me da would agree with ye."

They rode companionably for the last few miles. Garahan was more than ready for a tankard of ale, though he knew he'd have to settle for a watered-down brew. He needed to have a clear head for the last leg of their journey for the day. He planned to stand the first watch in front of the lass's bedchamber tonight.

From the pithy comments from inside the carriage as they rode to their next stop, he knew it was going to be a long night.

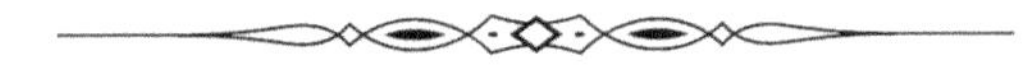

CHAPTER TWENTY-FOUR

EMILY'S IRRITATION SIMMERED until it was in danger of boiling over. Ever since the last stop, she'd been planning what she would say to the man responsible for making her so angry she couldn't see straight!

When he reached into the carriage to help her alight, he didn't even bother to look at her, merely extended his hand, expecting her to grasp it and follow along as if she were a child. Well, she thought, she was a woman, not a child!

She glared at his broad back, willing him to turn around so she could give him a piece of her mind. Not paying attention to where she stepped, she slipped and lost her balance. Before she landed on her face, she was cradled in Aiden's arms, held against his pounding heart.

"Are ye hurt, lass? Did ye turn yer injured ankle?"

The worry in his voice smoothed the edges of her anger until it was merely an irritating memory.

"Answer me, lass."

She traced the strong line of his jaw with the tips of her fingers and watched his eyes darken and swirl with emotions that had her breath hitching and her head going light for a moment. Would she finally feel his lips pressed to hers? Unable to resist, she rubbed the tip of her finger against the fullness of his bottom lip. The surprise in his eyes had her feeling a bit bolder as she slipped her hand up and around his neck, pulling him closer.

Time stood still as she held his gaze, wondering what he would taste of. Sandalwood and smoke? Leather and bright sunlight?

"Problem, Garahan?"

TREMAYNE'S VOICE BROKE the spell Emily had cast over him. He cleared his throat and eased back from the rosy temptation of her mouth. "Nay."

"What happened?"

"Miss Montrose slipped on her weak ankle."

Tremayne crossed his arms in front of him. "Mayhap you should remain in your room with your ankle elevated, Miss Montrose. We could have the innkeeper bring your meal to you."

"I'm weary of sitting and need to stretch my legs."

"You won't be walking anywhere tonight," Garahan said.

"If you've reinjured your ankle, you may have to stay off it for another sennight," Tremayne predicted. "One of the men in my regiment suffered a bad sprain, but we did not have time for him to rest or elevate it. A few weeks later, he stepped wrong. The man marching beside him swore he heard the bone break."

Garahan felt Emily shudder. "That does not mean the same will happen to ye," he told her, glaring at Tremayne.

"Just reinforcing your recommendation that she stay off her foot tonight," Tremayne replied. "With proper rest and care, you should be walking without a problem by the time we reach Wyndmere Hall."

"Thank you for your concern, Tremayne," Emily said. "I know you meant well and were not trying to scare me."

He grinned. "Do not get the wrong idea, Miss Montrose. I meant to caution you with a true tale of what happens when one ignores an injury. Don't let it happen to you."

"Oh, miss, are you all right?" Helen rushed over. "I found your reticule—it must have fallen off the seat when Garahan told us to take cover."

"I'll be fine, Helen. Thank you for finding it for me."

"What happened?" the maid asked.

Garahan quickly explained, "Miss Montrose slipped exiting the carriage and stumbled."

"I'm fine," Miss Montrose assured her maid. "Garahan is worried that I reinjured my ankle, so he's carrying me."

"If you are certain," Helen said.

"I am. Thank you for worrying about me." Emily pinched Garahan's shoulder to get his attention. When he glanced down at her, she asked, "Would you please do me a favor?"

"Of course, if it's in me power to grant it."

"Could you ask if there is an available bedchamber next to mine for Helen?"

"I'll speak to the innkeeper." He turned to Tremayne. "Tell the men I've put ye in charge and have them assume the same duties as when we stopped at midday. Send Bayfield and Masterson up as soon as the footmen are situated and know what is expected of them."

"You should be the one to give orders—that way there is no question who is in charge. I'd be more than happy to carry Miss Montrose to her room for you," Tremayne said with a wry smile.

Garahan fought the urge to plant his fist in Tremayne's face. "No need. Just follow me orders and send Bayfield and Masterson up."

Tremayne's eyes darkened to a wicked green, and it looked as if he would say something more. Instead, he spun on his heel and returned to supervise the men.

The innkeeper greeted them halfway to the door to the inn. "Hiram Blunt, at your service, and you must be Garahan. I've just spoken to the constable, but he did not mention Miss Montrose was injured. Would you like the physician to attend to her when he is through seeing to the blackguards who attacked your party?"

"If ye don't mind. I know His Grace would want to ensure she was fit to continue on to Wyndmere Hall."

"Was there another mishap on the road, and she was injured?"

Garahan did not need the innkeeper raising an alarm and calling even more attention to them. He changed the subject, and the innkeeper—smart man—understood. "Thank ye for sending the constable out when we did not arrive on time, Blunt."

"Given the strict instructions from Captain Coventry, I did not dare do otherwise."

Garahan knew exactly what the innkeeper meant. He'd felt the same whenever he received instructions from the captain. He was about to reply when the lass shifted in his arms, and her curvy bottom brushed on his abdomen. A bolt of heat shot straight to his loins. He mentally stomped out the fire raging inside of him so he did not embarrass Emily…or himself.

"Thank you for your concern," Miss Montrose replied. "I stepped wrong alighting from the carriage, but Garahan caught me before I fell on my face."

Full of sympathy, the innkeeper motioned for them to follow him. "Let me show you to your room right away, then."

"Do ye have Miss Montrose's maid staying in the room next to hers?"

"Servants are housed on the other side of the inn," Blunt answered.

"Oh, that will not do at all," Miss Montrose said.

The lass was back to sounding worried, and the slight catch in her voice hinted that her exhaustion and the attacks could be leading to a bout of tears. That was the last thing Garahan needed. "Do ye have another bed that could be brought to Miss Montrose's room for her maid?"

The innkeeper nodded. "We do. I shall see to it at once."

"We'll be needing hot water and linens for a compress for her ankle," Garahan added.

"My wife keeps herbs on hand for healing poultices. Just leave everything to me," Blunt said. "Follow me while I show you to your rooms. You and Miss Montrose's maid can see to her comfort while you wait."

"Thank ye." Thoughts of seeing to Emily's comfort was the last thing Garahan should be concerned with, but his mind went there anyway. It took a herculean effort to drag his thoughts back from sampling the skin at the base of her throat before trailing his lips along her collarbone.

The innkeeper produced a key, unlocked the door, and held it open for them, then handed the key to Garahan. "If you need anything, the bellpull's in the corner by the washstand. I shall return shortly." With that, he turned and headed back the way they'd come.

"After ye, Miss Helen," Garahan said. The maid looked startled, but preceded Garahan into the room. He watched her place Miss Montrose's reticule on the small table beneath the window that faced the stables and the woods just beyond. He'd make a point to speak to Bayfield about having two of the men scout the area behind the inn before dark.

"I'm sure I can walk—"

"Best not take the chance," he interrupted Emily. "Tremayne's right that an injury not properly cared for could end up being more serious." Though he knew it would not be wise, he turned and looked into her lovely gray eyes. The feelings he fought against rose to the surface. Miss Emily Montrose was a vision to behold. Whether she was frowning at him, lashing out at him in anger, or unsure of herself—as she was in this moment—while cradled in his arms, the want in her eyes was a temptation he fought daily.

Tremayne and Bayfield had noticed it from the first, and had subtly cautioned him to ignore his reaction to the lass. But he felt invigorated every time she argued with him. When he walked into her father's study and found her staring at Lord Montrose's favorite leather chair with tears damp upon her cheeks, he wanted to enfold her in his arms.

He eased her onto the bed and stepped back. No other woman affected him this way... No other woman ever would.

She's not for the likes of ye!

"Tremayne said you were ready to go over our detail for the evening."

He straightened at the sound of Bayfield's voice. He'd been staring at Emily while his mind took a side road he had no business going down. "Aye. The innkeeper is going to have the physician examine Miss Montrose's ankle before he leaves."

"Oh, but I don't—"

"Ye promised that ye'd do whatever His Grace asked," Garahan reminded her, yet again. "If he were here, he would insist that the physician look at ye."

Bayfield agreed. "His Grace brooks no arguments where his family's health and well-being is concerned."

"The constable's asking to speak to you," Masterson advised Garahan.

"If ye'll excuse us, Miss Montrose, Miss Helen." He bowed to the women, followed the men out of the room, and closed the door behind them.

Bayfield raised an eyebrow in silent question, but Garahan ignored the look. "Have either of you noticed how thick the woods are behind the stables?" Bayfield asked.

Bayfield and Masterson shared a glance, and Garahan nodded. "So ye'll be agreeing with me that tonight we'd best be keeping an eye out for trouble from that direction."

"And the south side of the inn's yard as well. It's larger than the other two inns we stopped at earlier," Bayfield added.

Garahan added Bayfield's observation to the ever-widening area of protection they'd need to cover. Turning to the most seasoned of Coventry's men, he asked Masterson, "What did ye note?"

The man's brown eyes held intelligence and a wisdom that Garahan had yet to achieve, if the tales he'd heard about the former colonel were to be believed. "Everything we've discussed since riding into the inn's yard have been excellent suggestions. We'll take the necessary precautions."

Garahan sensed the man had more to add. "But…?"

"But I have the bone-deep feeling that we need to be ready for attack from within."

Anger flared at the older man's suggestion. Garahan got in Masterson's face and growled, "Ye cannot mean that one of our men would betray us!"

Masterson waited patiently for Garahan to ease back before shaking his head. "I am not suggesting that at all. We know nothing about the innkeeper, the stable hands, the hostler, the serving wenches—"

"Nor the constable and his men, for that matter," Bayfield added.

Garahan raked a hand through his hair. "The thought crossed me mind when the three of them arrived on the scene, but I haven't had a chance to speak to anyone about it."

"No need," Bayfield told him.

"We took care of it," Masterson said. "Honeywell and Brewster seemed surprised. Stark did not."

Garahan felt the tension ramping up at the base of his skull. "He's an asset to our group, as he doesn't trust anyone."

"Even you?" Bayfield asked.

Garahan grunted. "He's trying not to, but he knows I'll keep me word and me promise to protect him from that bastard Hardwell. Bayfield, stand guard here. Masterson, take the position at end of the hallway by the servants' staircase."

Bayfield moved into position, but Masterson hesitated. "If I were going to make an attempt to abduct Miss Montrose," he said, "I'd wait until after midnight and use the servants' staircase."

Bayfield shook his head. "I'd climb the tree outside her window."

Garahan listened to their suggestions. "I'd prefer the tree, but climbing's a skill I learned to employ as a lad. If I was raised in the city, I'd use the servants' staircase. We'll have Tremayne stand guard in plain sight, beneath her window."

Masterson slowly smiled. "Forcing the blackguard to use the back staircase."

"Aye. Any questions?"

"Nay," Bayfield answered.

"Just one," Masterson replied. "Where will you be?"

"Me gut tells me to be as close to Miss Montrose as possible, but guarding them from inside the room would call her reputation into question. I won't do that. I'll stand guard out here. We'll have Hennessey at the end of the hallway by the servants' staircase, and Jackson at the bottom of the main stairs."

"We'll relieve them at eleven o'clock tonight," Bayfield promised.

"I'd like the two of ye to keep an eye on the younger men. I've already spoken to Jackson and Thompson about patrolling the inn's yard with an eye on the carriage with our ammunition."

Masterson and Bayfield approved, and knowing they did enabled Garahan to walk away from Emily now, when he desperately wanted to stay. He understood now what his cousin Patrick O'Malley meant when he'd confided that although the duke trusted every single man in his private guard, he always insisted Patrick be the one to stand guard where the duchess and the twins were concerned. Garahan felt that way about the lass.

He'd best find out what the constable wanted so he could relieve Bayfield and return to his post outside Emily's door.

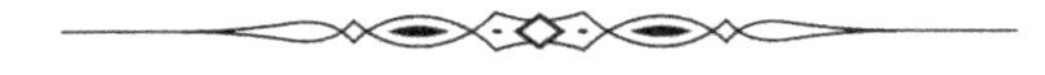

CHAPTER TWENTY-FIVE

E MILY JOSTLED HER maid awake. "Did you hear that?"

Helen wiped the sleep from her eyes. "Hear what?"

Deep voices rumbled right outside their bedchamber door! "That," Emily whispered.

A loud thud reverberated, and the maid reached for Emily's hand. "Was that a body?"

Another thud, across the hall from them this time. An odd sound that had Helen asking, "Did someone just get punched?"

Emily's heart stuttered in her breast. "Wait here." She crept over to the washstand and emptied the heavy ceramic pink and white pitcher into the matching bowl.

Helen grabbed her by the elbow. Another thud, this time followed by a loud crack. *God in Heaven! What was that?* "I have to help. It sounds like Aiden's in trouble." The sound of another scuffle taking place farther down the hallway cemented Emily's decision. "If anyone gets past me, toss the water from the bowl at them."

Her maid glanced at the bowl and back to Emily, and nodded.

Emily waited a moment, gathering her courage. With the pitcher raised high over her head, she flung open the door and conked the intruder on the back of the head with the pitcher.

"Bloody fecking hell!"

Oh, Lord, she'd hit the wrong man!

"Get back inside and lock the door!"

For a moment, shock had her rooted to the floor, unable to move. Helen grabbed her hand and pulled her into the room. Emily grabbed the empty chamber pot from beneath the bed while her maid struggled to close the door. A man tried to shove his way past Garahan into the room, and Emily swung, hard, pleased when she hit her target.

"Feck me!"

Oh no! "Aiden?"

"Miss Helen, shut the door and lock it!" he said.

Her maid managed to accomplish what Emily had not been able to. Arms wrapped around one another, with their backs against the locked door, they listened to the fighting on the other side of them.

Helen screamed when a face appeared in the window. Without hesitation, Emily hurled the chamber pot still clasped in her hand. The face disappeared right before the window shattered, and a familiar deep voice shouted a curse, followed by Garahan's name.

"Miss Helen!" Garahan called out. "Sit on Miss Montrose so she stops trying to help!"

Emily could not believe she'd hit Garahan twice. The first time she knew she drew blood, and the second time she may have damaged the stubborn Irishman's brainbox with the heavy pot.

Helen kept her arm around Emily, dragged her over to the corner of the room, and pulled her to the floor.

Tears stung the backs of her eyes, but she refused to give in to the weakness. "Helen, did you see who was at the window?"

"Aye, miss."

"It was Tremayne, wasn't it?"

"Aye, miss."

"Did I hurt him, too?"

"I'll live," Tremayne answered, stepping through the window into the room.

"You're bleeding!" Emily squeaked.

"I said I'll live. Wait here!" He unlocked the door, shoved his way outside into the fray, and slammed the door behind him.

"How many men are outside our door?" she asked.

"Beside the two you injured?" Helen replied.

Emily's mouth fell open, eliciting giggles from Helen. The maid's nervous laughter soon had Emily joining in. Neither one noticed when the voices and fighting stopped. She jolted when the door opened and Garahan called her name.

She drew in a breath and couldn't seem to let it go. Blood covered one side of Garahan's face. "Would ye hand me one of the drying cloths? I need to stop the bleeding."

She jumped to her feet and nearly tripped over them to get to the washstand. She had both cloths clutched in her hand as she dashed back to his side. "I am so sorry. I didn't mean—I was trying to… Oh, Lord, please forgive me?"

"Miss Helen, can ye see if ye can get Miss Montrose to hand ye one of the cloths?"

Emily stared down at her hands and realized the cloths were still clutched in her hands. Handing one to Garahan, she rasped, "Let me help."

"I think ye've helped enough."

Tears spilled over at his words. "I did not mean to hit you."

"I had things under control until ye opened the door the first time and broke that pitcher over me head."

"I didn't mean to hit you so hard."

"From the way me head's bleeding, I'm thinking ye did mean to."

"Well, I did, but I thought I was hitting the other man." Emily could not tell if the bleeding was slowing down, or if Garahan was simply spreading the blood in an attempt to stanch it. "Helen, please hand me my dressing gown."

Her maid handed it to her, but instead of putting it on, Emily surprised her by dipping the hem it into the bowl of water. She wrung it out and walked over to Garahan. "Sit down, so I can see how deep the cut is."

"I can take care of it meself."

"I said I was sorry," she grumbled, yanking on his arm to get him to sit on the side of the bed.

Tremayne was standing in the open doorway, holding on to their prisoner. "That's what she said to me, too."

Emily did not bother to look up when she said, "I thought you were trying to break into our room."

Tremayne snorted. "I was, but to make sure you and Miss Helen were all right before seeing if Garahan needed my help."

"I had things in hand before either of ye tried to help me."

She pressed the folded edge of her dressing gown against the gash. "Please be still."

Before she could ask, Helen carried the bowl over and set it on the table by the bed. "Thank you." Frustrated at working with the ungainly material, Emily ripped a wide strip off and dipped it into the water to rinse it out. She frowned at the bloody water, cleared her throat, and murmured, "I think we'll need fresh water."

"I got here as soon as I could."

Emily looked up and noticed Hennessey had a hold of another man—he had his hands bound behind his back, like the man slumped next to Tremayne. "Helen, would you please ring for someone? We'll need that water now. I cannot tell where the actual cut is underneath his hair."

"Yes, miss."

As her maid was tugging on the bellpull, Jackson appeared with the innkeeper in tow. "We've got the constable and one of his men tied up…" His voice trailed off as he took in the scene in front of him. "I see you have the constable's other man." When he noticed Garahan bleeding, he asked, "What in the bloody hell happened to you?"

Emily hadn't realized she'd started to cry until she couldn't see past the tears streaming from her eyes. "It is all my fault. I thought to help—"

Jackson interrupted, "By whacking Garahan in the head?"

Helen defended her. "Miss Montrose thought it was someone trying to break into our bedchamber."

King's man shook his head in disbelief.

The innkeeper's eyes were wide with horror. "My wife is adept with a needle. I'll wake her up and see about more water and fresh linens." Meeting Garahan's questioning gaze, the innkeeper shook his head. "I cannot believe the constable was a party to this. I've known the man for five years."

"It would seem that the constable was either in need of coin," Jackson said, "someone in his family is being threatened, or his past connections were on the wrong side of the law."

Blunt hurried out of the room to fetch his wife. While he was gone, Emily continued to keep pressure on the wound on Garahan's head. He kept trying to move away from her. "I know that it pains you, Aiden," she said softly. "But I must stop the bleeding. Please be still?"

Her plea must have gotten through to him. Once he stopped moving, she was able to hand off the saturated bit of her dressing gown and ask her maid to hand her another length. Helen folded it into a thick square before handing it to her.

IF SHE THOUGHT he would stop barking out orders, the lass was mistaken. "Hennessey, ye and Jackson take the prisoners and put them in one of the stalls in the stables along with the others. We'll need two or three men to stand guard."

"With the constable locked up, we'll need to send for someone to take them off the innkeeper's hands," Jackson said.

"Aye. We'll ask him to send for a messenger," Garahan said.

"Why not send Brewster?" Hennessey asked.

Garahan shook his head. "We cannot send the lad alone."

"Then send Bayfield with him."

Garahan paused, considering the possibility, but changed his mind. "That would leave us down two guards. I cannot compromise the women's safety."

Hennessey shook his head. "You cannot think to leave without having that gash sewn closed." When Garahan opened his mouth to speak, Hennessey added, "It's too deep to sear the wound closed with a hot knife."

"Forgive us for taking so long," the innkeeper said, returning. "Mrs. Blunt insisted the water needed to boil before she uses it." If he noticed the bits of broken pitcher in the doorway, he ignored them as he carried a tray over to the washstand.

His wife began to thread a needle. Garahan *hated* needles. To distract himself, he asked, "Do ye have a messenger that ye use, Blunt?"

The innkeeper mentioned two, and Jackson nodded. "Both reputable services, based out of London. Our best bet is to send word to King. If need be, we can leave two men behind to stand guard until someone arrives to escort the prisoners to London."

"See to it Jackson, and take the others with ye," Garahan said.

He watched Hennessey and Jackson take the men away, all the while keeping his eye on the needle-bearing woman's approach. He dug deep to appear as if the procedure would not bother him. "Tremayne, divide the men up between guarding the prisoners, the carriages and horses, the innyard—" The needle piercing the back of his head stopped him cold. He broke out into a cold sweat as the innkeeper's wife calmly began to sew the wound closed.

"You were saying, Garahan?" Tremayne asked.

Garahan's vision started to gray around the edges. The small hand that gripped his surprised him. He did not need to turn his head to know it was Emily's. Her emotions slammed into him at the contact. She more than cared for him… She loved him!

When she placed her other hand on top of their joined hands, effectively holding him in place, he heard her prayer in his mind and was filled with a sense of peace. The gray receded until he could see clearly again and finally answered Tremayne, "Have the men spread out between the yard, the downstairs, and outside the door."

Blessedly, Mrs. Blunt tied off the thread, placed a thick bandage against the stitches, and then wound a length of linen around his head.

"Thank ye for fixing me up, Mrs. Blunt."

The older woman smiled. "I'm sorry you were injured. Was it one of the prisoners?"

The sharp intake of breath and tug on his hand had him smiling. "Nay. 'Twas an accident. I was in the wrong place at the wrong time. I'll be paying ye for the pitcher."

"It was all my fault," Miss Montrose said. "I heard the commotion outside our door and thought Aiden needed help. I'll reimburse you for breaking the pitcher, Mrs. Blunt."

The innkeeper's wife did not seem to find Emily's explanation extraordinary at all. "A smart young woman learns to take care of herself." When Garahan was about to insist that he pay, Mrs. Blunt smiled at him. "Your defense of Miss Montrose, and Miss Montrose's ability to think on her feet and defend herself, is payment enough. It does my heart good. Neither of you need to worry about the pitcher. We keep extra on hand."

Emily let go of his hand, got to her feet, and wrapped her arms around the woman. "Thank you, Mrs. Blunt. I do not think I would have been able to keep my hands from shaking to sew the gash closed."

"There now," Mrs. Blunt said, patting Emily's back. "Nothing to fret over. I've had years of practice. Mr. Blunt is always doing something that needs my salves, poultices, and the occasional needle and thread."

"Accident prone," Mr. Blunt announced from where he stood in the doorway.

"I think what's needed is a hot cup of tea for you ladies, and a tot of rum for Garahan." She started gathering the soiled cloth and stared at it for a moment. "You must have been very worried about Garahan if you used such exquisite fabric to stop the bleeding. Was it a gown?"

"Dressing gown," Emily replied, meeting Garahan's gaze. "And I do care for him. He has saved my life more times than I can count in the last few weeks."

Watching the innkeeper's wife wash her hands with the water they'd carried in, he was surprised when Mrs. Blunt dried off, removed the shawl from her shoulders, and draped it around Emily's. "Now that the danger is past, and we've taken care of your man, it would be best to cover up. No telling whose eyes and ears have been witness to what happened here tonight."

"Nothing untoward happened—" he began.

Tremayne chuckled. "Except Miss Montrose breaking the pitcher over your head."

Garahan frowned. "And then she whacked me with the chamber pot!"

"Aye," Tremayne agreed. "She tossed it the window when she saw me there."

Mrs. Blunt's eyes filled with merriment as she patted Emily on the shoulder. "Well done, Miss Montrose." The older woman glanced at Tremayne. "Your arm's bleeding. Best let me have a look at you, too."

Tremayne tried to leave, but Mr. Blunt was blocking his way. "Can't have you leaving a trail of blood through our inn, now can we?"

With a glare at Garahan, Tremayne sat down and let the innkeeper's wife tend to him. As she cleaned out and sewed another wound closed, she said, "It's nearly time for me to put the bread that's been rising overnight into the oven. I'll have a hearty breakfast ready in half an hour. Do you think the rest of your men will be hungry, too?"

Garahan smiled. "Ye're a godsend, Mrs. Blunt, as every one of them will likely want to follow their noses to yer kitchen. Would it be all right if we sent them in in shifts?"

"It may be easier if we send food out to them as we did last night," Mr. Blunt answered for his wife.

She smiled at him. "Wonderful idea." As she wound the linen strip around Tremayne's forearm, she seemed to notice the slashing scar on his face. "Thank you for protecting our king and country."

Tremayne jolted at her words. "How do you know it wasn't from some accident as a child?"

She patted him on the shoulder as she rose to her feet. "My older brother had a similar scar. He served valiantly in the King's Dragoons."

"As did I," Tremayne said.

Garahan knew her brother gave his life. Emily surprised him when she said, "We'll remember him in our prayers, Mrs. Blunt. We have so many brave soldiers and seamen who've given their lives to protect us. My father served in his regiment for years. I know what the worry must have been like for you and your family."

Mrs. Blunt's eyes filled with tears, but she did not shed them. "Thank you, Miss Montrose. I'll just go start on breakfast, shall I?"

CHAPTER TWENTY-SIX

GARAHAN HAD NOT wanted to wait, though the few hours' sleep he managed did help to clear his aching head. He and the men agreed they could not take the prisoners with them, and the group was adamant not one of them would leave the prisoners behind for the Blunts—and their inn filled with people—to deal with. The innkeeper and his wife had been kindness itself in handling what could not have been a normal situation for them.

"Bugger it," Garahan mumbled before draining the metal cup of whiskey-laced tea, wishing it had been a straight shot of the Irish—no fecking tea. "King should have sent his reply by now."

Tremayne agreed. "There could be any number of reasons for the delay. I'll take these down to the kitchen and thank Mrs. Blunt for fixing the perfect cup of tea."

Garahan chuckled. "Best I've had in a while. I need to check with the men, ensure that the they've double-checked the wheels and their hubs, the harnesses, and the reins. Anything that could possibly cause more of a delay than the baron's henchmen—and the crooked constable."

When Garahan looked over his shoulder at the closed door, Tremayne grumbled, "I'll stand guard. Miss Montrose should have worked it out in her head by now that you do not blame her for coshing you over the head with that damned pitcher."

"Don't be forgetting clocking me across the face with the chamber pot," Garahan added. "The pitcher I understand, as it would be handy, but the fecking chamber pot?"

Tremayne grinned. "After she hit you, she hurled it at me. I ducked, and it only broke the window…not my head."

Garahan tried, but just couldn't see the humor in the situation. "How could she doubt that I could handle a couple of blackguards? Hadn't we handled more than our share trying to break into Montrose House?"

"Aye," Tremayne agreed. "We did."

"Why couldn't she trust me to protect her?"

"Be damned if I know," Tremayne replied. "Send Masterson up if you don't think I can handle guarding the women."

"I might at that." Garahan hesitated, then added, "If we don't hear from King soon, we'll walk our horses to the next inn. We can loop a rope around the middle of the prisoners…"

"And tie them together."

"Aye. They won't have the luxury of riding—they'll be on foot."

Tremayne grinned. "Humiliating and exhausting at the same time. I like it."

"Thought ye might. Hand me those mugs. I'll return them and send Masterson up to keep ye company."

GARAHAN STEPPED OUT of the rear entrance to the inn and walked toward the stables, where Jackson and Bayfield stood guard. The sound of horses rapidly approaching had the three men spinning around. They were armed and ready to defend against whatever was heading their way. But the four men riding into the innyard did not have pistols cocked, aiming for their hearts. They were here for a different purpose. Their bright red coats and identical bland expressions were a fine sight to behold. King had not sent a missive—he'd sent men!

The hostler and stable hands took care of the horses as Jackson walked toward his fellow Bow Street Runners. The men hailed him. "We hear you have a crooked constable and his men tied up in a horse stall," one said.

Garahan strode forward, ignoring the dull throb in his head. "Ye're a sight for sore eyes. Greeves. Franklin. Glad ye could make it." He waited for the other two men to dismount before extending his hand. "Name's Garahan. I work for—"

"The Duke of Wyndmere," one of the men said.

"King speaks highly of you," the second man remarked.

Greeves stepped forward and shook Garahan's hand. "You must have been guarding the door to Miss Montrose's bedchamber and were struck from behind."

Jackson grinned. "Not much slips past you, Greeves. Franklin, good to see you. Feldman, Dellbrook, meet Garahan."

Garahan decided a nod would suffice as a greeting, and immediately regretted it. The ache in his head was nauseating, but he beat the feeling back with a will of iron.

Jackson slid his glance to the north side of the stable. "I think it's time you meet the prisoners—Constable Cook and his two lackeys, Dickson and Harald. Not one bloody thing about Cook had my hackles rising—he seemed upfront, a decent sort. Don't know how I misjudged him."

Franklin leveled a look at Jackson. "He might have been coerced into Hardwell's schemes, and carrying the weight of whatever enabled the baron to convince the constable to join in his plan."

"We'll pry the truth from him," Greeves assured the others. "To give the horses a break, we plan to let the prisoners walk...for a bit."

Garahan snickered. "Me brother James has used that tactic before. Works well. I was planning to do just that if we hadn't heard from King by this evening." As they reached the door to the stables, Bayfield hailed him. "I need to speak with Bayfield before I join in when ye question the men. How long before ye plan to leave, Greeves?"

"Depends on how long it takes to extract the information we

need," Greeves replied. "Could be an hour, could be longer."

"I'd like to ask a few questions meself. I was a bit preoccupied earlier."

Greeves shook his head. "Only you would consider having your head sewn back together being preoccupied."

"I didn't say me injury required threads."

"Head wounds bleed—profusely," Greeves said. "Minor head wounds don't require bandaging."

Garahan frowned. He hadn't thought of that. Well, he might have, if his head wasn't paining him. "Fair enough."

The men parted, and Garahan walked toward the rear door to the inn, where Bayfield waited. "Has something happened?"

"Aye," Bayfield replied as the two walked inside the building and headed toward the anteroom off the kitchen. "Hennessey and Thompson just got back."

"Productive?" Garahan asked.

Bayfield knocked and waited.

"Come in!"

He opened the door and held it for Garahan. "Apparently it was good hunting."

"Was it now?" Garahan said, nodding to the men who stood guard by their prisoners. "Are these two the only ones ye flushed out, or did the others get away from ye?"

"Two. As you can see," Hennessey said. "We managed to wing them as they tried to escape. Mrs. Blunt is patching them up."

"Ah, ye are a treasure, Mrs. Blunt. How can we be thanking ye?"

She shook her head at him. "Just doing our part, Garahan. Did you drink the herbal as well as the doctored tea I left for you?"

"I appreciated the tea and didn't have the time to drink the herbal."

"Make the time, or your head will continue to pain you. It might not be as noticeable right now, but once you climb on the back of your horse and start riding, the movement of your horse will increase the pain tenfold. If you know what is good for you, you'll go and drink it now!"

Garahan grinned. "Ye sound just like me ma."

"Bayfield, be a dear man and escort Garahan back to whatever room he left the herbal."

"Aye, Mrs. Blunt." Bayfield grabbed hold of Garahan's arm and dragged him from the room.

Outside, Garahan shook free of Bayfield's hold, grumbling, "What in the bloody hell did ye do that for?"

"Mrs. Blunt threatened to put something in my food—or drink—that would purge my insides if I didn't ensure that you drank every drop of that blasted herbal."

Garahan grinned. "Did she now? She's more like me ma than I thought!"

"Odd how that explains a lot about you, Garahan."

"Isn't it, though? Best follow me, then—I think I left the cup on the windowsill in Miss Montrose's bedchamber."

"You're going to have to work harder at hiding what you feel for Miss Montrose. It was plain for all to see last night."

Garahan did not know what to say to that. Bayfield saw too much. "I was not meself last night."

Bayfield disagreed. "When a man's been injured, you usually see what's in his heart and on his mind. We'll be arriving at Wyndmere Hall in two days—"

"Unless there are any other delays," Garahan finished. "Interesting reply from King."

"Not the typical missive with a wax seal, sending his men, but effective just the same."

"Aye," Garahan said. "Four Runners arriving at an inn is sure to cause speculation."

"As will what occurred last night in the hallway. Even more cause for speculation would be the constable and three of his men tied up in the inn's stables. Never a dull moment with you around, Garahan."

"Faith, 'tis good to know I haven't lost me touch. Greeves and the men won't want to wait to question the men." Garahan cracked his knuckles and smiled. "See to it they don't get started without me."

GREEVES HAD A man by the throat with his back against the wall when Garahan walked into the stables. The herbal that tasted of pond scum had eased the worst of the pounding in his head, but did little to alleviate the frustration inside of him.

He noted the men who'd tried to ambush them were lined up against the wall along with the constable and his men. Three of them were bruised and battered. He was hoping to pound a few of the men to relieve the tension inside of him. "Ye started without me."

"We're hungry," Franklin grumbled.

Greeves let go of the man he held and took a step back. "Now that you're here, I'll let you continue the interrogation."

Garahan walked into the stall as the constable pushed to his feet and faced him. "Ye'd be wise to start talking." He refused to let the fear in the other man's eyes—or the stubborn silence—sway him from his purpose. Thoughts of what could happen to the lass if she was unprotected had his hand curling into a fist. His eyes never left the constable's as he delivered a left cross, followed by a hard blow to his solar plexus.

"Well now. Mayhap yer man, Dickson, will be more apt to talk." Garahan stood in front of the next man, looked into eyes the color of coal, and didn't bother to ask. His fist shot out, and the man slumped to his knees, blood gushing from his broken nose. Garahan moved to stand in front of the third man in line.

"I can't," the man rasped before Garahan even asked a question. "He'll kill me."

Garahan took a step closer and pitched his voice low. "If ye give me his name, Harald—"

Before Garahan could decide between a jab or an uppercut, a fist shot past his face, and the man crumpled to the straw-covered floor.

"Bugger it, Greeves!"

"Franklin's hungry," Greeves reminded him.

Garahan snorted with laughter while the last man in line looked at him as if he'd lost his mind. "Now then—"

Hennessey chose that moment to deliver the two new prisoners. Like the others, their hands were bound behind their backs. He summed up the situation: "Looks like no one's talking."

Garahan glared at the new arrivals. "Me patience is wearing thin, and Franklin's hungry. Ye'll answer me questions or take a beating."

One of the men snorted in response; the other spat.

Hennessey clocked the man. Unfortunately for the prisoner, the back of his head connected with his partner's nose. As both men doubled over, Hennessey shrugged. "He nearly creased my scalp when he shot at me."

Garahan nodded. "Understandable." He turned back to the last man standing—one of the sharpshooters. "Ye have a choice. Answer one question—"

"He'll kill my family."

The depth of the man's fear was palpable. Garahan understood the need to protect family. Felt it to the bone.

He scrubbed a hand over his face. The need to extract a name was greater than the need to take out his frustration with his fists. "What if I mention a name, and ye nod once if I'm right?"

"He'll know it was me."

Garahan glanced at Greeves, then Hennessey. When both men nodded, he turned back to the prisoner. "I'll send two men to wherever yer family is and protect them until we've captured the man behind these attacks. Ye won't have to be a part of it any longer. Greeves and the others will be laying a trap to catch the blackguard. We both know who it is. Don't we?"

The man closed his eyes for a heartbeat, then opened them. "Aye."

"Hardwell."

The man nodded and braced for a blow, relaxing when it never came.

Garahan shook his head. "Hennessey, bring—What's yer name?"

"Adams."

"Bring Adams with ye. I've a few more questions for him."

The man squared his shoulders. "You won't go back on your word?"

Garahan glared at him. "Ye don't know me, and for that reason only, I'll not be taking a swing at ye. I'm not like the baron. If I give me word, I keep it. Me brothers, cousins, and I made a vow to the Duke of Wyndmere to protect his family at all costs. Not even Hardwell could make us break our word."

"Not even if he threatened to kill your family?" Adams asked.

"Not even then." Garahan paused next to Greeves. "I'll ask Mrs. Blunt—she's the innkeeper's wife, and a stout-hearted woman—to have a meal ready for yerself and yer men. Mine will stand guard over the prisoners while ye eat."

Franklin grumbled, "About time."

"Ye're a man after me own heart, Franklin," Garahan said. "We'll use the rear entrance—there's a room where ye can eat in peace and not worry that yer conversation will be overheard by whoever's in the main taproom having their meal."

"Thank you, Garahan."

"Me pleasure. I'll be joining ye shortly."

As they stepped outside, Garahan grabbed hold of Adams. "Hold still." The man's fear had Garahan sighing. "I'm after untying yer bonds."

Adams stilled and waited while Garahan untied the ropes and tucked them into his frockcoat pocket. "Thank you."

"Don't be thanking me yet. Ye'll have to let us pick yer brain to find out the rest of Hardwell's plans, or we'll be tying ye up again and making ye walk to the Lake District."

Adams swallowed audibly, but did not refuse.

"Ye understand?"

"Aye. Can you wait until we are away from anyone who might overhear us?"

"That's the plan." Garahan and Hennessey flanked Adams as they walked to the back of the inn and ushered him to the door to the servants' staircase. "We can speak privately upstairs."

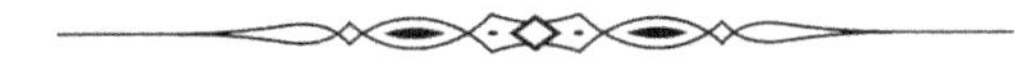

CHAPTER TWENTY-SEVEN

BARON HARDWELL STARED at Poston. "Well, what do you have to report?"

"There's a rumor Gavin King of Bow Street loaned two of his Runners to accompany Garahan and his men."

"What of the constable?" Hardwell demanded. "He should have Miss Montrose hidden away at my hunting lodge by now."

He stared long and hard at his lackey, until Poston was shifting from one foot to the other so fast, it looked like he was dancing.

"Bloody hell, I cannot wait! I'm going to have to go myself! I'll catch up to that dull-witted Irishman and Coventry's crippled crew."

"They aren't crippled," Poston said in a clear voice. "They fought bravely for our country."

"Why in the bloody hell would you think I care?"

Poston shrugged. "I was fifteen when I joined my regiment."

Hardwell frowned. "What of it?"

"I nearly lost my arm to infection, but one of the regiment's surgeons lanced the wound and saved it. I know what it's like to be sent home injured and not able to fend for myself." Poston squared his shoulders and said, "Not one of those brave men who were injured deserve your censure. You should be on your knees thanking them!"

Hardwell watched in amazement as Poston seemed to grow a

backbone right before his eyes. Considering how he would use that to his advantage, he said, "What are you going to do about it?"

Poston's eyes got a faraway look before he blinked, spun on his heel, and marched out of Hardwell's study.

"Bloody hell!" The baron did not have time to deal with that two-time failure. He stalked over to the bellpull and rang for his butler.

"Yes, your lordship?"

"Where is my valet?"

"Carrying freshly laundered shirts to your dressing room."

Hardwell did not like to have to do anything for himself—he preferred to be waited on hand and foot. But he was desperate to find out what happened to the men he'd hired. Could he have been wrong and chosen the wrong men? Had they missed their target on purpose? He hoped the constable was able to handle the abduction part of the planned ambush. Wilson had failed with the first attempt in the park.

Taking the steps two at a time, he reached the top and strode into his bedchamber, shouting, "Wellsmith!"

"In here, your lordship!"

He followed the sound of his valet's voice. "I need you to pack a small bag for me, enough for two days' travel."

"Am I accompanying you?"

"No."

"Where—"

"None of your bloody damn business! Now pack my bag!"

"At once, your lordship."

AN HOUR LATER, Baron Hardwell rode out of the city intent on catching up with the men he'd paid to create an ambush. Once he discovered what had happened, he would either congratulate the men...or have them killed.

Either way, the interfering Irishman had become too much of a problem to let live. Duke or no duke, Garahan would have to disappear—permanently!

CHAPTER TWENTY-EIGHT

EMILY'S HANDS TREMBLED. "What if he doesn't believe that it was an accident?"

Her maid shook her head as she continued to twist Emily's mass of hair into an artful topknot. After pinning it into place with dozens of hairpins, Helen took a step back and nodded. "There. You look more like yourself, miss. Would you like me to ring for more tea?"

Emily wanted to pull her hair out by the roots. "I need to speak to Aiden and apologize again. He has to understand that it truly was an accident."

"Miss, he knows," her maid assured her. "You apologized half a dozen times last night."

"He may not have heard me! His eyes seemed to be having trouble focusing on me when I apologized to him the fourth time. He may have been dizzy."

"I'm told it is normal when one suffers a severe head injury."

Emily covered her mouth with her both hands to keep from crying out. When she was certain she had herself back under control, she dropped her hands and whispered, "Severe?"

"It bled profusely and required threads," her maid reminded her.

"It was—"

"An accident," Helen finished for her. "Why don't I ask

Thompson if we can have tea in the taproom?"

"He'll refuse, just like he refused to allow us to venture downstairs to eat breakfast or our midday meal. All of the guards are treating us like prisoners."

Helen slipped her arm through Emily's and urged her to sit on one of the chairs by the window. "Isn't it wonderful how quickly Mr. Blunt was able to have someone in to replace the broken glass? I've never watched anyone repair a window before," she enthused. "It's almost an artform—a craft."

Though Emily should have been grateful her maid was trying to distract her, it only irritated her further. "Do be quiet, Helen, and pack our bags. You're driving me to distraction."

The hurt on her maid's face had remorse setting in, but Emily could fix it later. All she could think was that the man she'd lost her heart to had yet to accept her apology when he was clear-eyed. Ignoring the view out of the window, she watched Helen fold the clothing they had worn the day before and return it to their traveling bags. So much easier than having to haul a large trunk up and down an inn's staircase.

The knock on the door surprised her. Had Thompson changed his mind and decided to escort them downstairs for tea? She rushed to the door and swung it open to find Garahan frowning at her. The massive bruise across the side of his cheek and the bandage wrapped around his head reminded her of her folly in trying to aid the man.

"Going somewhere, lass?"

"Answering the door. Where's Thompson?"

"I relieved him and am taking the next watch."

The set of his jaw and lack of expression on his face had worry slithering into the pit of her belly. What little she'd eaten a few hours earlier curdled. She tamped down the nausea. "Shouldn't you be resting?"

"I could ask ye the same." Looking over Emily's shoulder into the chamber, he called out, "Are ye planning on leaving, Miss Helen?"

"Oh no, just doing what Miss Montrose asked me to—packing."

"We aren't going anywhere today. Save it for a bit later on, else ye may find yerself with time on yer hands and nothing to occupy it."

"If you would ease your restrictions and allow us to take tea in the main taproom, we would be able to pass the time until the evening meal," Emily said.

"No."

"But—"

"Do ye need anything else?"

"Tea!"

"I'll have it sent up." He gently took her arm and moved her a step back so he could close the door behind him.

"We want to enjoy our tea downstairs!"

"No need to shout, lass. There's nothing wrong with me hearing."

She banged the side of her hand on the door in frustration. The third time, tears of frustration blurred her vision, and her wrist connected with the hard edge of the doorframe. She bit her lip and cradled her hand to her breast, struggling to blink back her tears.

The door opened slowly. Garahan stood in the doorway like a dark, avenging angel. "Did ye bruise yer hand, then?"

She turned her back on him, walked over to the chair by the window, and sat down.

Helen looked from her mistress to Garahan and back again. "Neither one of us got much sleep last night. Please forgive Miss Montrose."

"Not one of the men guarding yer lives got any sleep at all, but they are not acting like a child misbehaving when they haven't gotten their way."

Emily shot out of her chair. "How dare you insinuate that I'm—"

"Acting like one of me nieces and nephews? Well, ye are.

Now show me yer hand."

WHEN EMILY TURNED her back on him for the second time, Garahan's frustration bubbled to the surface, dangerously close to spilling over. He drew in a breath, and then another, as he stalked over to where she stood.

"Miss Helen, would ye kindly ask Miss Montrose to turn around and show me her hand?"

The lass did not even give her maid a chance to speak, let alone do as he ask, before she whirled around, caught her toe on the heel of her half boot, and pitched forward.

He caught her against him and wished to God he had stayed on the other side of that door! Her curves fit against him like a dream. He struggled to control the need raging inside of him, replacing it with anger. *Bloody, buggering hell!* This was why he'd kept his distance from her last night. He'd wanted to hold her close and assure her he forgave her, but did not dare. It wasn't his place. She was the duke's ward.

At the soft gasp from behind him, he steadied Emily, dropped his hands, and took a step back. "Ye'll need to be controlling yer temper, Miss Montrose. It'll get ye into trouble one of these days."

"I do not…" Her words trailed off as her face flushed a delightful pink. Even angry, Emily was lovely.

Bloody fool—she's not for ye!

He gathered his control around him like a shield, reinforcing his guard against the temptation to yank her against him and plunder. He'd never truly been afraid before in his life, but he was mortally terrified he could drink from her lips and never quench the thirst inside of him. "If ye'd please satisfy me duty to protect ye by showing me the hand ye slammed against the door, I'll return to me post outside yer bedchamber."

He waited patiently for her to do as he asked. When she did, he told her, "Ye'll need a poultice to help with the bruising. Can ye move yer fingers?"

She wiggled them.

"Can ye make a fist and then open it?"

She did that more slowly.

"Now can ye move yer wrist?"

Her sharp intake of breath was what he'd feared. "Ye're lucky if ye either bruised or cracked the bone in yer wrist. The hand has more than two dozen bones in it." She stared at her feet, but he decided to wait her out. "Twenty-seven, to be exact. I found out that fact for meself the time I thought I'd broken a few of them."

"Twenty-seven?"

"Aye."

"How did break your hand?"

"Me brother James ducked, and I punched a rock wall. Though 'twasn't broken, just a wicked bruise on the bone."

She lifted her head. When her eyes met his, her unshed tears nearly broke his will to keep his hands to himself.

"Miss Helen, please ring for Mrs. Blunt. We'll be needing that poultice, and mayhap another visit from the physician." He withdrew his handkerchief from his waistcoat pocket and handed it to the lass. "Here now, dry yer eyes. Ye wouldn't want Mrs. Blunt to think ye weren't the same stout-hearted lass ye proved to be last night, would ye?"

"I'm not crying," she argued. Much to his relief, she ducked her head and blotted her tears.

When she tried to hand the handkerchief back to him, he told her, "I've a supply with me. Keep it for now. The dainty, lace-edged one I've seen ye carry cannot possibly mop up more than half a dozen teardrops."

The knock on the open door had him glancing over his shoulder. "Ah, 'tis herself. Mrs. Blunt, Miss Montrose has injured her hand." When the innkeeper's wife walked in, he said, "Do ye see how the bruise runs from the edge of her fist to her wrist and is purple and swelling already? She may have cracked a bone."

The older woman's gaze flitted from Garahan to Miss Montrose and back again. "Let me have a closer look."

Garahan watched and listened as Mrs. Blunt hummed low in her throat while she studied Emily's injury. She had her make a fist and then open her hand, then had her rotate her wrist—the same as he did. Mrs. Blunt noticed the lass's wince of pain. Then she asked her to wiggle her fingers. If Emily could do that, he reasoned, mayhap 'twas only a cracked bone, mayhap two.

"We always have plenty of hot water in the kitchen," Mrs. Blunt said. "It'll take no time at all to prepare a poultice for you, Miss Montrose. Do you mind telling me how you injured your hand? It may help me discern whether or not a bone is cracked, broken, or if it is badly bruised. All of which are quite painful."

Emily looked up at him before she answered. "It may have been when I tried to get Garahan's attention."

He snorted with laughter, but swallowed the rest of it when Mrs. Blunt gave him a telling look. Her next question to Emily surprised him: "Did you whack him in the side of the head again?"

Emily's eyes blazed with frustration. "It was the back of his head, and it was an accident."

Mrs. Blunt's lips twitched, further endearing the woman to him when she asked, "What about his face?"

"I meant to hit the intruder—not Aiden…er, Garahan."

"Why don't you tell me exactly what happened to your hand, Miss Montrose?"

Garahan didn't want there to be any blaming him when all he did was tell the lass no. "Miss Montrose asked if she and Miss Helen could leave the room to have tea in yer taproom. I refused."

"He slammed the door in my face," Emily accused.

He sighed and turned to face her. "'Tisn't true, and ye know it, lass. I closed it firmly." He turned back to Mrs. Blunt. "Her face was nowhere near the door. And that's when I heard her fist hit the door—twice. 'Tisn't that thick a door, so the sound reverberated a bit. The third strike was the one that did the damage. I'm thinking she hit the edge of the doorframe."

The older woman nodded slowly. "Miss Helen?"

"It happened just as Garahan said."

Emily fumed, but held her tongue.

He could not hold back his snort of laughter. "She was in a raging temper—and, from the fire in her eyes, still is."

She continued to hold her silence.

Mrs. Blunt's eyes twinkled with laughter. "I'll prepare that poultice and have it ready in a trice, and I'll fix a tea tray for you. Something sweet might just soothe the rough edges lack of sleep sometimes causes."

As the woman swept from the room, Emily glared at him, demanding, "How could you?"

"I always tell the truth, lass. Prevaricating only gets one in trouble. I'm going back to me post. As soon as Mrs. Blunt arrives, I'll let ye know."

Helen nudged Emily twice before the stubborn woman mumbled, "Thank you, Garahan."

He quietly closed the door behind him and grinned. Her eyes had gone dark as summer thunderclouds, stirring feelings he had no right to feel. Though, God help him, he loved her fiery spirit! He'd best reel his feelings back in before Mrs. Blunt arrived with the remedy and the tea tray. No need to cause more talk than there already was of midnight intruders, fighting in the hallway, and a guest breaking a pitcher over one her guard's heads.

They'd avoid further talk if she would only contain her temper and stay in her bedchamber with her maid. He had sent out two more men after Hennessey and Thompson returned. With a bit more luck, they'd flush out any other blackguards waiting to ambush them.

Going over the conversation he'd had with Adams in his head, and what the man had told them about Baron Hardwell, Garahan made the decision to turn the matter of whisking the Adams family to safety over to Coventry. He knew the captain would see to it. Garahan was also fairly certain that once he explained things to the duke, His Grace would be willing to add another man to those who had already been given a second chance working for the duke.

He looked up when he heard the door open at the other end of the hall. With a glance to ensure no one else lingered in the hallway, he strode toward Mrs. Blunt and took the heavy tea tray from her.

"Thank you, Garahan."

"Me pleasure." He shifted the tray to one hand and knocked on the door.

"Who is it?"

Mrs. Blunt smiled at the overly sweet tone. "I like Miss Montrose. She's strong willed."

"She is that," Garahan agreed. "Open the door, lass."

"My guard won't allow me to unless you state your name and purpose first."

"'Tis yer guardian angel, and Mrs. Blunt with yer poultice and tea tray," Garahan replied.

The door opened, and Emily stood there studying him. "I always pictured my guardian angel with light hair and blue eyes." Leaning to the side to look behind his back, she shook her head. "I don't see any wings."

The burst of laughter erupted before he could contain it. "Leave off, lass. I need to set yer tea tray down. Mrs. Blunt is a busy woman and has others to see to aside from yerself."

Her expression immediately changed from lighthearted to sorrowful. "Forgive me, Mrs. Blunt. I wasn't thinking and did not mean to take you away from your other duties."

"Not to worry, Miss Montrose." Mrs. Blunt glanced over her shoulder. "Thank you, Garahan. If we need you, we'll call for you."

It was his duty to protect the duke's ward, and his heart urged him to stay. "If it's all the same, Mrs. Blunt, the duke would want me to ensure that Miss Montrose is not unduly injured. 'Tis part of me duty to include that information, along with me observations regarding any treatment she receives, in me daily report to him."

"I see. In that case, please move just a bit to the left—you're blocking the light coming in the window." When he moved as directed, Mrs. Blunt thanked him and took Emily's hand in her own. "This may pain you, Miss Montrose, but the only way to discern if there are any broken bones is to manipulate your hand."

Emily nodded and relaxed when the innkeeper's wife asked her to. Mayhap the pain wasn't as bad as Garahan thought it would be. When Mrs. Blunt started to feel the bones in Emily's hand, he saw the lass flinch and bite her lip.

"A bit tender there?"

Emily nodded. Mrs. Blunt pressed on the bone near her little finger, and the lass paled. When Mrs. Blunt pressed her wrist, Emily lost every ounce of color. Sweat broke out on her forehead and trickled down her temples. Garahan anticipated what was about to happen and caught her as her eyes rolled back into her head. "Broken?" he asked, cradling the lass in his arms.

Mrs. Blunt nodded. "I'm afraid so."

"Can ye set the bone?"

"I have set larger bones before, but I do not want to risk misaligning it."

With a nod, he walked over to the bed and gently laid Emily on it. "Miss Helen, would ye sit beside her?"

"Of course," the maid answered. "Let me dampen this cloth for her forehead."

Mrs. Blunt thanked the maid, then turned to Garahan. "I have never seen anyone move as quickly as you did. Thank you for preventing further injury to Miss Montrose."

"'Tis me job."

She laid a hand on his forearm and lowered her voice. "It's more, and you and I both know it. I wish you luck."

God help him, he needed it.

She patted his arm and folded her hands at her waist. "I'll

have Mr. Blunt send—"

Mrs. Blunt was interrupted when the lass opened her eyes and called, "Aiden?"

He walked over to stand beside the bed. "I'm here, lass."

Her eyes cleared as she held his gaze. "It seems to be a habit."

"What does?"

"Your catching me."

"Aye, 'tis a bit more work protecting ye than I'd thought it would be."

"Oh?"

He didn't dare smile—didn't want her to think he was laughing at her. He was bloody relieved he'd caught her before she hit her head on the edge of the table—or the floor! "Now then, lass," he said. "Ye need to rest a bit before ye sit up. Miss Helen will make ye a cup of tea just the way ye like it. The two of ye can have a bite of those tarts Mrs. Blunt baked earlier while ye wait for the physician."

"Oh, but I don't need—"

"Ah, lass," he interrupted. "From yer reaction when Mrs. Blunt touched yer wrist, I'd say 'tis more than cracked."

She fell silent, and Mrs. Blunt added, "Rest for a bit while I go speak to Mr. Blunt. Helen and Garahan will help you to sit up when the dizziness passes, then you can have your tea in bed as if you were a queen."

Emily surprised him by agreeing with the kindly woman. "Thank you all for taking care of me. I think I would like having tea in bed—although I never have before. It will be a momentous occasion, won't it, Helen?"

"Aye, miss. Just close your eyes for a few minutes more and relax."

"Try not to get lathered up and in a temper," Garahan warned, "until after the physician sets the bone."

Mrs. Blunt grabbed hold of his arm on her way past him. He had no choice but to follow her. At the doorway, she frowned up at him. "Do not rile her. The poor young woman must be in terrible pain. If it's your duty to protect Miss Montrose, then it is also your duty to have a care with her feelings and emotions. Try to remember that."

Duly chastised, Garahan inclined his head. The woman had the right of it. "Aye, Mrs. Blunt. I will."

"Leave the door open for propriety's sake until you and Miss Helen have Miss Montrose sitting up in bed, then you can resume your post out here."

Garahan did not argue.

A few moments later, Emily was ready. Between himself and Helen, they easily scooted her up in bed, until she leaned against the headboard, with a pillow behind her back for comfort.

"I'll be outside if either of ye have need of me."

Not trusting himself to say more, he spun on his heel and walked through the doorway, grabbing the edge of the door on his way through and quietly closing it behind him.

CHAPTER TWENTY-NINE

FRUSTRATION ROARED THROUGH Hardwell as he journeyed north. Poston had more than grown a backbone; the man had found his *bollocks*, too—and spilled his guts to King on Bow Street. Stopping to change horses, Hardwell asked questions, but was met with a stony silence until he spun a story that he was Miss Montrose's cousin. Then the innkeepers at the first two inns were more agreeable, and confirmed his information that a Miss Montrose had been an overnight guest at the inn.

The innkeeper at the second inn had given him a suspicious look when he asked if her carriage had run into trouble along the way, but again, he pled concern as her cousin until the second innkeeper reluctantly gave him directions via a shorter route to get to the third inn.

His luck changed at the third inn. Between the shorter route—and traveling on horseback—he arrived ahead of Garahan's party.

Ordering a flagon of ale, he sat back and watched the innkeeper—observing that the keys to their rooms were kept elsewhere. It did not take him long to sweet-talk the information out of one of the inn's serving wenches that a bedchamber had been reserved ahead of time for Miss Montrose. Now all he needed was that key!

While enjoying a hearty meal of stew and a round of bread,

he indulged in a second flagon of ale and waited for any new arrivals, questioning them about trouble along their journey. The news that a number of brigands had been arrested for trying to rob a small party traveling together ate at Hardwell's gut. First, Poston had betrayed him to the authorities, who would no doubt be searching for him. Next, Wilson took the money—and, as far as Hardwell knew, had no intention of holding up the rest of their bargain. The possibilities that Bow Street Runners would find him before he was able to abduct Miss Montrose had him changing his plan—to save time, he'd compromise the chit and leave her to explain her way out of it.

He took a healthy swig, wiped his mouth with the back of his sleeve, and went over the final plan in his head. He would find that serving wench and either turn on the charm or coerce her into giving that key!

CHAPTER THIRTY

DESPITE THE PHYSICIAN'S wishes that he leave the bedchamber, Garahan stood guard by the door while the doctor prepared to set the bone in Emily's wrist. Though he tried to keep himself separate from the procedure to observe so he could report to the duke, when Emily's eyes beseeched him, he felt his control waver. God help him, the temptation to scoop her up and hold on to her until the physician was through had him shaking inside.

"Before you start," Emily said, "I'd like to ask Aiden a favor."

The lass had taken to using his given name more often, and it by turn warmed his heart or heated his blood to the boiling point. Right at this moment, it did not matter if she called him Garahan, Aiden, or *eedjit*—he'd do whatever she asked. "What will ye have me do?"

She motioned for him to come closer. He did so and bent his head to listen to her whispered request. "I don't want to cry, and I may pass out from the pain."

"Ye don't have to worry about showing emotion," he assured her. Was the worry in her eyes due to what the physician had to do to, or was it what waited for her at the end of their journey— her guardian and Wyndmere Hall? He wanted to ease her fears. "'Tis all right to cry, lass."

She looked up into his eyes, and for a heartbeat, he was lost in the warmth of her soft gray gaze. "I need someone strong to hang on to—someone whom I trust my life to… I need you, Aiden."

His guts shook as the elemental need he'd banked earlier roared to life at her confession. It was only his iron will that kept it from showing on the outside. He looked at Helen, Mrs. Blunt, and finally the physician. The unspoken question in the physician's gaze had him downplaying Emily's request and his own need. He spread his arms wide and looked down at himself, then backed up. "Apparently 'tis me size that has Miss Montrose thinking I'm built like a rock."

When the physician and Mrs. Blunt both smiled, he continued, "She asked to hold on to me while ye set the bone, if that is permissible."

"More than," the physician replied. "In fact, I was about to suggest she hold on to someone. It is imperative that she remain still until I'm finished setting the bone."

Garahan nodded as the maid moved over to make room for him. He reached out to grasp Emily's hand. The satin-smooth skin that pressed against his callused hand brought home just how delicate the lass was. At the physician's nod, he placed his free arm around Emily, anchoring her in place. "I won't be letting go, lass."

Mrs. Blunt placed her hand where the physician indicated, to hold Emily's other arm still, while he manipulated the bone.

Emily moaned in pain. Garahan heard it and felt his stomach flip. It brought rushing back the memory of the day his younger brother had fallen out of the tree they were climbing. The horrific sight of blood and the bone protruding through the skin of his brother's arm had had him jumping down, ripping off his shirt, and wrapping it around the injury. He had not felt lightheaded that day, but he sure as hell felt it now, watching the tedious process as the physician set her wrist bone.

He looked into her eyes and wished he could take away her pain. "The worst is almost over."

"Don't let go yet."

"I won't," he promised. Her pain still echoed through him, but instead of blocking it, he accepted it, hoping it would ease what the lass felt.

The physician realigned the bone and held it in place with two small slats of wood, then wound a strip of linen around it to secure it in place. He looked at Mrs. Blunt. "Do you have the sling I asked for?"

Mrs. Blunt let go of Emily to fetch it for him. Everyone was silent while the physician gently placed the folded cloth under Emily's arm and had her cradle it to her middle, before tying it behind her neck. "Now then. You'll need to follow my instructions to the letter, Miss Montrose."

She agreed and paid attention while he listed what she could and could not for the next few weeks.

Garahan thought the physician was finished handing out instructions, but the man surprised him when he turned to him and said, "I understand it is essential that you continue on to Wyndmere Hall."

"Aye. 'Tis."

"I would caution you not to travel for more than a few hours tomorrow. Miss Montrose may become nauseated riding in the carriage, due to the upset in her body humors."

"Is there another reason, other than her comfort, that ye recommend a shorter journey tomorrow?"

The physician was silent for a few moments. Mayhap the man was trying to come up with a stronger reason. "In order for Miss Montrose's wrist to heal properly, she must keep her hand immobile and get as much rest as possible."

"I will see to it that she rests as much as possible, and as long as she swears to keep her arm in the sling, it will be immobile for the rest of our journey. His Grace is expecting us, and we are already a day behind."

The man was clearly not happy. Garahan needed the physician to understand the gravity of their situation. "I am not normally at liberty to speak of me assignments, but I know the duke will understand why I am about to share pertinent information with ye. He'd want ye to release the patient into me care before we leave."

The physician nodded. "I would suggest a few days' rest before you leave, but am willing to listen."

"As the Duke of Wyndmere's ward, Miss Montrose has been victimized by a number of fortune hunters." He did not mention the wagers placed in White's betting book, or the men lined up outside Montrose House. "We were ambushed on the way here, but the guards and I routed them."

The physician blinked. "I see. So the danger is over?"

"Nay. 'Tis very likely we'll be facing another trap before we reach our destination. So ye understand that the sooner I can escort Miss Montrose to the safety of Wyndmere Hall, the better."

The physician cleared his throat. "Though I would not normally recommend it, I understand the urgency. There are times when I must bow to circumstances beyond my control." He reached into his bag and withdrew a small bottle. "Given your small stature, Miss Montrose, you will not need a large dose of laudanum to ease the discomfort you may feel. I shall pen the instructions I just mentioned and leave them with Mrs. Blunt."

"A wise idea," the older woman quickly agreed. "There is a writing desk with everything you require in the room off the kitchen. If you'll follow me?"

The physician paused in the doorway. "I wish you all a safe journey."

Once the pair left the room, Garahan slipped his arm from around Emily's shoulder and tapped a finger on the hand he held. "Ye can let go of me now, lass."

"Oh, yes, of course. Thank you, Aiden."

He stared down at her upturned face. "Ye're strong, lass. The pain will recede as ye heal. I know, as I've been stabbed and shot, more than once, and badly bruised a bone in me hand. 'Tis the truth that me hand pained me nearly as much as being shot."

He'd only share the story of his brother's broken bone later if he thought it would distract her from the pain she would no doubt be suffering on their journey north.

"Let Miss Helen know immediately if ye're suffering. Do not think it's brave to keep yer pain to yerself."

"Are you back to telling me what to do, Garahan?"

He snorted at her use of his surname. "So 'tis only Aiden when ye need a favor or are about to try to use yer feminine wiles to get yer way?"

She lifted her chin and glared at him. "Or when you annoy me."

He noted she did not deny using her wiles to distract him. "I know."

"You do? Then why did you ask?"

"I wanted to watch yer eyes darken to the color of storm clouds. Faith, I cannot help but wonder if lightning will shoot out and strike me from the tempest in yer eyes."

"Don't you have somewhere to be, Garahan?"

"I go where I'm needed, lass." He stared at her until she started to squirm on the bed. "Ye asked me to stay, so I stayed. Ye needed me."

"I did. Thank you for staying, Aiden."

"Ye'd be welcome, lass. I've missives to send before I speak to the men about preparations for our departure. Miss Helen, ye'll ring if ye need anything, or if either of ye need me?"

"I will. Thank you, Garahan."

He nodded and turned to go.

"Aiden?"

His heart tumbled in his chest. What he wouldn't give to hear her say his name just like that every morning—and every evening—for the rest of his life. "Aye, lass?"

"I would not have been able to take the pain without leaning on your strength. Thank you."

"Me pleasure, lass." Before she could call him back again, he yanked open the door and nodded to Tremayne, who stood guard, and strode down the hallway to the servants' staircase. For his own sanity, he had to leave. He had a duty to perform, and nothing would stand in his way!

Descending, he ordered his thoughts: first, he needed to speak to Masterson to find out if the men he'd ordered to ride ahead had returned, and if they'd uncovered another ambush. He needed their report. Next, he would have to pen two missives: one to Coventry advising him of the circumstances concerning Adams and his family, the other to the duke, explaining the same, and asking His Grace for a favor. If he could not gain the duke's agreement to protect Adams and his family, he'd handle that problem when he arrived at Wyndmere Hall by enlisting the aid of his cousin Patrick O'Malley.

Tomorrow they would leave the relative safety of the inn. The knowledge that Hardwell had a few more days to spring an attack was not a worry—it was a given. He and the men would be ready for it. There would be three rings of protection surrounding Emily. He hoped to God the baron made it through the first two, because he would be the last man standing, protecting the lass. And it would be his right to gut the bloody bastard!

He finally accepted what his heart kept trying to tell him from the start... He was *arse* over head in love with the lass.

CHAPTER THIRTY-ONE

"YOU DON'T LOOK well, miss."

Emily ignored her maid and concentrated on willing the bile back down her throat. She prayed her stomach would calm down, and wished she'd listened to the sound advice of Mrs. Blunt earlier that morning and eaten a slice or two of bread. An empty and uneasy stomach and her recent injury were a recipe for trouble when traveling.

Just another few miles, she told herself, and they would reach the inn where they would change horses.

The carriage hit another rut, forcing bile back up her throat, burning it. Sweat broke out behind her knees. She clapped a hand to her mouth and prayed she would not disgrace herself.

Helen shot to her feet and pounded on the roof of the carriage. "Stop the coach!"

The carriage rocked to a stop. The door swung open, and Garahan lunged toward her. "Hang on, lass."

Emily closed her eyes and willed the contents of her stomach to stay put for just a few moments more. But he brushed against her broken wrist, and the shaft of pain was her undoing. *Oh, Lord! Please do not let me cast up my accounts all over the man!*

He kept his arm around her and set her on her feet. "Go ahead, lass. There's no one to see. Ye don't have to hold it in any longer."

With his words echoing through her head, she dropped her hand and retched until her eyes watered, and her stomach and back ached from the effort. The sick feeling passed, and embarrassment took its place.

"Easy now," he soothed as he handed her a handkerchief. "Ye can wipe yer eyes—and blow yer nose."

"I cannot blow my nose with just one hand." Her irritation was short-lived, as her legs turned to water at the knees. When his arm curled around her waist, she leaned against him. "Thank you. I would have felt just awful if I'd retched on Helen."

"I'm thinking Miss Helen would have felt worse than ye." He paused as if he was not ready to let her go. "Do ye know," he said, "this is the second time since I joined the duke's private guard that a woman nearly retched all over me boots."

"Really?" Instead of feeling irritated that he continued to mention her embarrassment, she was intrigued. "Who would that have been?"

"Lady Calliope, Viscountess Chattsworth. 'Twas right after she and the viscount were married at Wyndmere Hall. She bolted out of the dining room door with a hand over her mouth. She was the same shade of green ye were when I opened the carriage door just now."

"What happened?"

"I grabbed the decorative urn next to me—and just in time, or me boots would have been a mess."

Emily was embarrassed for the viscountess. "Lady Calliope must have been mortified."

"Aye, but not for long, as I didn't show any reaction other than doing me duty—helping her."

"I think I know how she felt." Emily had experienced the same and had been swept off her feet by the man more than once.

"She was even more grateful when I caught her before she fainted at me feet."

"Thank for acting so quickly, Aiden."

His eyes searched hers, but she had no idea what the man was thinking.

"Did the urge come on ye sudden?"

Botheration—he *would* ask that. She could lie and tell him that it had, but she was not a very good liar. Besides, hadn't he warned her against—as he put it—prevaricating?

"Er… Not really."

"I see. How long did ye feel nauseated?"

"A bit."

"Do ye think so little of yer traveling companion—or yer da's carriage—that ye'd risk painting the inside of it with the contents of yer belly?"

His harsh words, and the mention of her father, had her wavering on her feet.

Garahan swept her into his arms and held her against his pounding heart. "Have a care, lass. I've half a mind to make ye ride double with me to keep an eye on ye, but the extra weight would tax me horse."

"Why would you even think I'd agree to ride with you?"

"Ye wouldn't have a choice. Each one of us is here for ye, lass. The men and I are doing our part, working together to keep ye safe."

She swallowed against the tightness in her throat, but the lump of emotion refused to budge. "Forgive me, Aiden," she rasped. "I'm not myself… To be honest, I haven't been since my father passed."

He shifted her until her head was beneath his chin. Resting it on the top of her head, he rumbled, "Poor lass. Ye haven't grieved properly for yer da. Miss Helen won't mind if ye do. She may even join ye, as she's missing him something fierce, too."

She realized he was right. Helen did miss him. "Do you ever get tired of being right?"

"Truth be told, no. I—"

"*Ambush!*"

Garahan sprinted toward the carriage. Emily heard a crack sound behind them, and felt his body jerk, but Garahan kept running. Bayfield was waiting by the carriage door, his rifle trained on a stand of trees on the other side of the road. Helen opened the door from the inside, and Garahan tossed Emily on the seat, mindful of her injured hand.

"Get down and stay down! We've got to keep moving!"

"Aiden, you're bleeding!"

"'Tis nothing, lass. Now get down!"

Worry lanced through her already aching stomach as she and her maid hunkered down on the floor of the carriage, which jerked to life a moment later as the coachman urged the team forward.

Emily couldn't seem to stop shaking. "Was anyone else hurt? What did you see?"

"Bayfield had dismounted and was standing guard waiting for the two of you to walk back over when he shouted," Helen replied. "I think he was the first to notice the glint of sunlight off the barrel of a rifle."

Emily wished her maid knew more, but at least it was something. She noticed Helen was shaking and wished she could wrap both arms around her, but at least she still had use of one arm to offer comfort.

After her maid stopped trembling, Emily asked, "Do you know if anyone else saw anything?"

Helen shook her head. "Why is all of this happening? Why won't they just leave you alone? Isn't it enough that your father is gone?"

Emily knew then that her maid needed her to be the strong one for a change. "Go ahead, Helen, cry. It only hurts more if you hold on to your tears. I know."

While Helen leaned against her and started to cry, Emily did her best to ignore the throbbing in her wrist, and the urge to sneak a look out of the carriage window. She knew her father had been like a parent to her maid—and the footmen, too! She dearly hoped that Wilcox, who had been instrumental in bringing the young men to Father's attention, would be able to ease their suffering as well.

A rifle shot at close range startled her. She reached out to steady herself without thinking. The impact where her wrist connected with the edge of the seat sent waves of pain from her hand to her shoulder. Agony stole her breath.

Helen kept repeating the same words, over and over, until it began to sink into Emily's brain. "Try to relax. Don't tense up. Just let the pain roll off you."

The carriage did not stop until they rolled into the yard of the inn where they would change horses. Although it did not take the hostler and the stable hands long to unhitch the teams of horses from the carriages, there were still the men on horseback. They would need to change horses, too.

A glance at her maid, and she knew Helen was as desperate as she was for a hot cup of tea. The carriage came to a full stop and the door swung open. Tremayne filled the doorway. "Allow me to help you down, Miss Montrose."

He held out his hand and she placed hers in his. "Thank you, Tremayne. Do you know where Aiden is?"

"Having his arm tended to."

"How is he?"

"He brushed it off, insisting the lead ball only grazed his shoulder."

"I felt his body jerk when he was shot."

"Garahan's strong. A mere lead ball didn't stop his older brother, and it won't stop him."

Taking him at his word, Emily smoothed her skirts and waited for Tremayne to help her maid down from the coach. He escorted the women over to the innkeeper, who showed them into the taproom.

"Do we have time for more than a cup of tea?" She tried to hide the hopeful expression on her face, but she was starving!

"Garahan said if you asked, we'd make the time. How is your wrist?"

Emily shrugged. "I'll be fine. Were any of the other men

injured?"

"Stark nearly was, but he ducked at the last second, or else a lead ball would have parted more than his hair."

Relief filled her. "I'm glad he was not hurt."

"If anything, it seemed to galvanize Stark. He's a bit fierce in his bid to protect you and Miss Helen."

Emily realized she had so many people to be grateful to. "Would you let Aiden and Stark know that I'm sorry to hear they were injured—or nearly, in Stark's case."

"Aye, Miss Montrose." He found a table near the back corner and hailed one of the serving girls.

Once their tea was ordered, Emily turned to Tremayne and laid her hand on his arm. He hesitated before he turned toward her, and she wondered if he did so because of his scar. She smiled up at him. "Thank you, Tremayne, for protecting Helen and me. Please pass my thanks along to the other men until I have a chance to personally thank them all."

"It would be a pleasure, Miss Montrose."

They finished their tea and, with Tremayne standing guard, made use of the necessary out back.

SEATED ONCE MORE inside the confines of the closed carriage, Emily wished she could feel the wind in her face, but knew they would have suffered far more injuries in an open carriage. Her need for fresh air was not as important as their safety. She would have to give Aiden his due. It was safer and more efficient to travel in the town coach.

Thinking of the handsome-as-sin Irishman, she wondered if he'd had to suffer through more threads having his shoulder sewn back together. As he filled her thoughts—and her heart—she realized that he'd been there from the moment he barged into Montrose House.

Though he had irritated her at first, she had become used to seeing him, hearing his voice. He had never been far from her thoughts. She'd spent too many hours wondering what the man was thinking—and the rest of the time she spent counting the moments until Aiden glanced her way or spoke to her. The music of his brogue had twined around her foolish heart until she gave in to his demands to obey his heavy-handed dictates. How in the world would she get along without having him near?

The monotonous sound of the carriage wheels rolling beneath them lulled her into a trancelike state. Not all that different from what the sound of Aiden's deep voice had done to her the first time he lifted her in his arms and held her against the impressive breadth of his muscled chest. She sighed.

"Are you in pain, miss?"

Emily glanced at her maid, who had been solicitous of her without being overbearing since they'd left that morning. "Not overly. Though I believe I am suffering more from hunger and the desperate need for another cup of tea. Mrs. Minnover and Mrs. Christian certainly spoiled us, didn't they?"

"They did."

Emily smiled at her maid's ready agreement. "I wonder what the duke's housekeeper and cook will be like?"

"Efficient, I would imagine," Helen answered. "You promise to let me know if you need to stop again?"

Emily's face flamed at the reminder. She should have realized her maid would not let the topic go. "I promise. I should never have waited so long before asking to stop. My belly had been churning longer than I realized."

"Garahan didn't even ask what was wrong." Helen's eyes lit with humor. "He ducked inside, swept you off the seat—"

"And steadied me while my stomach rebelled." Emily shuddered. "It was mortifying." She hesitated, then admitted, "I shouldn't have been irritable with him. But my wrist was pounding in time with the ache in my head." She did not mention the story he'd shared with her about the viscountess, because Emily doubted the woman would want her embarrassment repeated.

"I'm certain he understands."

"I do hope he is all right," Emily said. "He lost a lot of blood the other night. I'm not certain he can afford to lose any more."

"We would have heard if he was weak from blood loss, miss."

"You always manage to bring me back around when my thoughts are leading me astray. Thank you for being so sensible, Helen. I promise not to worry until we reach our next stop, where I can see for myself how Aiden is doing."

"Excellent idea."

Emily closed her eyes and dreamed she was in Aiden's arms once more.

CHAPTER THIRTY-TWO

GARAHAN DEALT WITH the inconvenience of the headache plaguing him, as he felt responsible for the fact that he'd pushed Emily when he knew she was in pain and needed to rest. If there were no threats dogging their heels, he would have gladly extended their trip, allowing Emily a day or two to rest and recuperate before continuing on to Wyndmere Hall.

But time was of the essence. And they were a day away from their destination. The fact that there had only been one man lying in wait for them, with his rifle trained on the well-traveled coach road north, worried him. He expected more than one ambush.

He made the rounds checking with the guards who would take their first shift guarding the carriages and the horses. "Why only one?"

"One what?" Masterson asked.

"Sharpshooter," Garahan replied. "There were plenty of places along the way that would have been the perfect spot for an ambush."

"You expected it," the former colonel said. "Our regiment was always more weary after a day's march when we expected cannon fire than when we knew we would simply be covering ground until the next time we would engage the enemy."

Garahan thought about it and had to agree. "Makes sense."

Masterson chuckled. "Trust an old soldier to tell you the

truth. I would still be serving in my regiment if I hadn't been injured at Salamanca. The fever would never have taken hold of me if I had been in fighting form… Instead, it ended my career."

"Coventry is lucky to have ye as one of his trusted men. We're lucky to have ye as part of our guard. Yer experience and advice have been invaluable." Garahan waited a beat, then asked, "What do you think the baron will do next?"

Masterson stared across the innyard at the newly arrived guests. "An unexpected attack—from within."

The hair on the back of Garahan's neck stood up. "Within?"

"Aye. It would be what I would do."

The bottom dropped out of Garahan's stomach. "If you're right, Hardwell could have gained access to Miss Montrose's bedchamber and be lying in wait for her to arrive."

"Brewster and Honeywell are escorting the women."

"I should have sent you or one of the other seasoned men." He spun around and tore across the yard, with Masterson hot on his heels.

The pair bounded up the stairs as a bloodcurdling scream rent the air. Garahan tried the door, but it was locked. He looked over his shoulder at Masterson, who nodded.

They kicked the door in in time to see Hardwell, straddling Emily on the bed, backhand her maid, who was trying to pull the man off Emily. Masterson went to check on Helen, while Garahan delivered a left cross that lifted the baron up in the air and off the bed, freeing the lass.

His hands were shaking when he gathered her into his arms and lifted her off the bed. Her quiet tears gutted him. "Where are ye hurt, lass?"

Her maid answered for her, "The baron sprang out from behind the door and coshed Brewster on the head when he opened it. Before we could see how badly he was hurt, the baron grabbed Miss Montrose and tossed her on the bed." Her tears fell. "He threatened to do unspeakable things to her, and said no one would care—or have her when he got through with her."

"The money," Emily rasped. "He planned to ruin me and force me to marry him for my inheritance."

Helen wiped her face with the backs of her hands. "And your dowry, miss!"

When Hardwell stirred, Garahan gently set Emily on the chair on the other side of the room. "Wait here." In two strides, he stood looming over the baron. "Ye're going to live to regret this day."

"You cannot threaten me! Do you know who I am?"

"Aye, the man I'm going to enjoy beating to death."

"You wouldn't dare."

Garahan grabbed hold of the man's cravat one-handed and hauled him to his feet. "I dare!" The satisfying crunch that followed the quick jab to Hardwell's nose was music to his ears. "That is for touching Miss Montrose!" The gut punch doubled the man over. "That is for hitting Miss Helen. Stand up, ye bloody bugger! I'm not through with ye!"

"What's going on in here?" a deep voice demanded.

Garahan glanced at the newcomer, taking his measure. "Who wants to know?"

"Morrison, and this is my inn! And you are?"

"Name's Garahan. I'm one of the Duke of Wyndmere's private guard, head of the protection detail for the duke's ward, Miss Montrose. Masterson and I heard Miss Montrose screaming and kicked in the door in time to see Hardwell strike Miss Helen, while he straddled Miss Montrose on the bed. He planned to violate her. I stopped him."

"It's true, Mr. Morrison," Helen said from where she stood by Emily. "He threatened horrible things to Miss Montrose." Tears streamed from her eyes as she added, "I tried to stop him, but he struck me."

Garahan nudged the baron with his foot before. "Baron Hardwell hit Brewster." He pointed to the man struggling to his feet and rubbing the back of his head. "He and Honeywell were to escort Miss Montrose and her maid to this chamber."

Morrison walked over and stared down at the still-unconscious man. "Baron Hardwell could only have entered this room if he had a key." The innkeeper stood back as two more men stepped into the room.

"What happened, Miss Montrose?" Tremayne demanded.

"Are you all right, Miss Helen?" Bayfield asked.

"Who are you?" Morrison asked.

"Tremayne and Bayfield," Garahan answered. "Part of Miss Montrose's guard."

"How many fingers am I holding up, Brewster?" Masterson asked, satisfied when Brewster swatted his hand out of the way.

Garahan ignored the men and walked back over to the lass. "Forgive me for not escorting ye meself."

"How could you know the baron would have been waiting for us?" Emily asked.

"I should have, when we didn't encounter trouble when I expected it," Garahan insisted.

"They would have been safe with Honeywell and me," Brewster replied, "if that bloody bastard hadn't somehow got his hands on the key to this chamber."

Garahan turned to the innkeeper and asked, "Care to explain how that happened?"

"We keep spare keys in the pantry. No one but myself and my wife are allowed access to the locked cabinet where we store the keys."

Garahan curled his hands into fists as the need to pummel the innkeeper washed over him.

Masterson caught his eye. "Later."

"Tie him up and send for Stark," Garahan said. "He'll confirm Hardwell's identity."

"What are you going to do with the baron?" Morrison asked.

"I should drag his *arse* with us to Wyndmere Hall. The duke will want to question him personally, but neither the duke nor meself would want to risk having him near the duchess or their twins—especially after the kidnapping attempts. We'll have to arrange to have him held by the local constable until he can be transported to London."

"I have a friend who works on Bow Street," Morrison said. "He owes me a favor and would no doubt send men to collect the baron and bring him back to London."

Garahan glanced at his men and then back at Morrison. "Well now, that's convenient, as I was going to send a missive to Gavin King for that very reason."

Morrison's lips twitched. "Haven't seen King in a number of years. It's about time I call in the favor."

Relief filled Garahan—Morrison knew King. "I'd be grateful if ye'd take Hardwell off our hands. I can leave one of King's men, Jackson, behind as part of the escort."

Morrison's eyes widened. "I thought I recognized him as I was running up the steps to see who was brawling in my inn. He's a good man to have guarding your back."

"That he is," Garahan agreed as Jackson and Stark entered the room.

Stark's expression shifted quickly from remorse at seeing the bruises on the women to one of hatred as he noticed the baron. "That's him—Baron Hardwell. He paid me to infiltrate Montrose House." He turned his back on Hardwell and walked over to the women. "I do not deserve your forgiveness, Miss Montrose, Miss Helen, but I do need to tell you how sorry I am."

"There are times in life when we think we only have one option," Miss Montrose said. "Even if we know it is not the right thing to do. But when you were offered the chance, Stark, you did the right thing. I forgive you."

"I forgive you, too," her maid echoed.

Garahan laid a hand on Stark's shoulder. "Ye did the right thing, lad." He turned to the innkeeper. "Morrison, can ye send someone up with a tea tray and hot water for Miss Montrose and Miss Helen? We have the herbs we need with us to fashion a poultice."

"Aye, right away. I can arrange to have my daughter sit with you ladies for as long as you need. My sister runs the kitchen, so she can't stay as long, but she keeps healing herbs on hand. I'll have her bring up two poultices and will send for a physician."

Garahan nodded. "Thank ye." He turned to his men. "Masterson, ye and Bayfield take that bloody bugger with ye and turn him over to the constable when he arrives. Jackson will accompany Hardwell. I'll send word to King and leave it up to him how many men he sends. The rest of ye return to yer posts. Tremayne and I will be standing guard for the rest of the night."

When they cleared the room, Garahan walked over to stand before Emily. "Forgive me for not anticipating that he would be waiting for ye in yer chamber. We expected the sharpshooters, and were prepared for them. But this…" He raked a hand through his hair. An apology would never be enough—he'd failed to protect the lass. "I cannot erase what happened, but I can promise ye, he'll pay for touching ye, lass." He stared at the bruise on her cheek and then glanced at her maid, who carried the same dark reminder of what happened before he'd been able to stop it. "Forgive me, Miss Helen. Ye're a brave lass for trying to prevent him for harming Miss Montrose. Thank ye."

He took two steps back to lock down the urge to reach out and enfold the pair of them in his arms. It wasn't his place. So he offered what comfort he could. "When we arrive at Wyndmere Hall, Constance and Merry, the duke's cook and housekeeper, will look after ye. They took care of the injured when Wyndmere Hall was attacked. Me cousin Eamon O'Malley has a bit of skill healing—not quite as much as our cousin Emmett, but between the three of them, they'll see that the physician's orders are followed to the letter."

He had his hand on the doorknob when he paused. "If ye have need of either Tremayne or meself, we'll be right outside."

Chapter Thirty-Three

TWO DAYS LATER, they arrived at Wyndmere Hall surrounded by her guard. The duke and duchess, and two of Garahan's cousins, members of the duke's personal guard, Patrick and Eamon O'Malley, were on hand to greet them.

Garahan dismounted and motioned for the men to do so. "Yer Graces," he greeted them.

The duke stared at the bandage around his head then glanced at the men sent to guard his ward. "Trouble, Garahan?"

"A mishap or two. Ye received the missive I sent about Miss Montrose's injury?"

"I appreciated your reports regarding the distressing situation in London, and other news that you kept me abreast of. I'm pleased that Miss Montrose rallied to make the journey instead of staying on at the inn where the injury occurred. It would appear something else occurred more recently."

"Aye, Yer Grace. I'll explain shortly." Garahan opened the carriage door, held out his hand to Emily, and whispered, "Don't be fretting. The duke and duchess will love ye and only want the best for ye."

She paused to look into his eyes and held on to him with a fierce grip. Because of her sling, her balance was off, and she started to pitch forward. Without missing a beat, Garahan swept her into his arms and carried her to the steps where Their Graces waited.

He set her on her feet and steadied her. "Are ye all right, lass?"

The blush on her cheeks said as much, but she managed to murmur, "Aye, thank you, Aiden."

The sound of his cousin clearing his throat had him glancing up to see a hint of censure on Patrick's face. He'd have to have that conversation with O'Malley sooner rather than later.

"Yer Graces, may I introduce Miss Emily Montrose. Miss Montrose, the Duke and Duchess of Wyndmere."

The duke frowned at her sling, and the bruise on her cheek, but bowed. "Welcome to our home, Miss Montrose."

"Welcome, Miss Montrose," the duchess said. "You must be desperate for a pot of tea. Constance has been baking up a storm in anticipation of your arrival."

"I beg your pardon, Your Grace, did you mean to say cup of tea?" Emily asked.

The duchess's engaging laugh was filled with warmth. "Not at all. After a journey of any length, I am always desperate for an entire pot of tea—one cup is never enough."

The duke chuckled. "My darling duchess cannot begin her day until she empties *her* pot of tea."

EMILY'S HEART FELT lighter as she listened to the duke and duchess speak fondly to one another, and all because of a pot of tea. Mayhap her time spent here would not be as disastrous as she feared.

"Thank you both for your generosity in opening your home to me, and for honoring my father's last wish that you step in as my guardian."

"The pleasure is ours," the duke replied.

"Did you bring a lady's maid with you?" the duchess asked.

"Oh dear!" Emily rushed back over to the carriage, and smiled when she saw Garahan helping her maid from the coach. The purple bruise marring Helen's cheek was stark against her pale complexion, and matched the one on Emily's own cheek. "There you are, Helen. Forgive me for not waiting for you."

Her maid thanked Garahan before moving to stand beside Emily. "I had to gather my composure a moment. When you stumbled, miss, I thought you would fall and do more damage to your wrist."

Emily linked her arm with Helen's and walked back to the duke and duchess. "I'd like to introduce my lady's maid, Miss Helen Langley. I could not have managed without her—even before I was injured. Helen, the Duke and Duchess of Wyndmere."

"We're grateful that you could accompany Miss Montrose," the duke said.

"I know from experience it is difficult to leave your home behind without the stout support of a longtime companion," the duchess added.

Helen and Emily smiled at the couple, and Helen rasped, "It is a pleasure to meet you, Your Graces. Thank you for extending your invitation to include me. I have been with Miss Emily for a decade."

"We're delighted that you could accompany Miss Montrose." The duke turned to his wife and said, "If you will excuse me, my darling, I need to speak with Garahan."

The sound of raised voices behind them had Emily looking over her shoulder. "Who is that man dressed like Aiden yelling at him, and who is the man walking toward us? Are they part of His Grace's guard, too?" As soon as she said Aiden's name, she worried that the duchess had noticed she'd used his first name twice now.

"The head of my husband's personal guard, Patrick O'Malley, is arguing with Garahan," the duchess said. "He is one of Aiden's cousins. Their other cousin, Eamon O'Malley—another of my husband's guard—is walking toward us."

"Oh dear. It was my fault we were delayed, but it was only one day—all because Aiden was adamant that His Grace would insist on having a physician's release to continue our journey here. Once when I broke my wrist, and then the other day when…" Emily's voice trailed off and she fell silent when the blond giant with piercing green eyes approached them.

"Yer Grace. Miss Montrose, Miss Helen. Garahan asked me to introduce meself."

"Eamon has a talent for healing," the duchess began.

"Not like Patrick's brother, Emmett—he has the gift," Eamon told them. The voices were louder this time, and he looked over his shoulder. "If ye'll excuse me." He strode over to join the others.

"Come along, now," the duchess said. "I am certain we will hear the particulars by the time we have emptied two pots of tea."

"Two, Your Grace?" Emily asked, tugging on her maid's arm when she noticed her standing stock-still and staring after Eamon O'Malley.

"Absolutely. One for you, and the other I will share with Helen after the two of you freshen up. If you like, we can have our tea in my upstairs sitting room—"

"And I'm sayin' ye know better than to compromise yer duty all because of a pretty face!" Patrick thundered.

Emily jolted to a stop. "Oh no!" Before the duchess could stop her, she rushed over to where Aiden and his cousin stood arguing while the duke stood listening with a dark look on his face.

"It's my fault," she called, stumbling for the second time.

Garahan steadied her. "Are ye all right, lass?"

"Yes, thank you, but—"

"Don't ye think that's a bit personal, addressin' her as lass instead of Miss Montrose?" Patrick asked.

"I do not see any harm in it," Emily replied. "We have been

living in one another's pockets for the last few weeks. Without Aiden and his men, I have no idea if I would have made it here in one piece! I am indebted to your foresight, Your Grace, in supplying me with a personal guard. Thank you."

The duke's stony expression softened. "Of course I sent a guard to you. I could not get away myself, and know that London is not always the safest of environs."

"Gettin' back to the point," Patrick boomed. "Ye're to show respect at all times."

"I did, and I have," Garahan said.

"Ye're a bit too quick to step in and scoop the lass off her feet."

"Why is it all right for you to call me lass, and not for Aiden?" Emily asked.

"I'll answer yer question later," Patrick replied. "Right now, I need to get to the bottom of why ye don't seem to mind me boneheaded cousin cartin' ye around."

"Bloody hell, O'Malley," Garahan barked. "She would have landed on her face if I didn't catch her."

"Ye could have put yer arm around her to steady her."

"I have done that on more than one occasion," Garahan explained.

"You are making it sound as if I'm unsteady on my feet—either that or I am not graceful," Emily interjected.

"Ah, lass," Garahan said, meeting her gaze. "Ye are as graceful as a rosebud in the spring, but ye tend to hurry about and get yer feet twisted up."

"A word, Garahan." The duke's expression was forbidding.

"Aye, Yer Grace."

"Aiden, wait!" Emily reached out to get his attention.

When her hand touched his arm, the duke frowned again. "I believe you are keeping my wife waiting. She has only just recovered her health. Please do not keep her waiting for you."

Horrified that she would cause the duchess to possibly fall ill, Emily begged the duke's pardon and hurried over to where the duchess waited patiently. "Forgive me, Your Grace. I am so sorry."

"You are forgiven. Ah, here are Humphries and Merry, our intrepid butler and marvelous housekeeper. Miss Montrose and her maid Helen will be staying with us," the duchess told the pair. "As you can see, she has suffered a mishap, which I assure you I will be getting to the bottom of by the time we've emptied two pots—maybe three—of tea with some of Constance's delicious lavender scones. Merry, would you show Miss Montrose and her maid to their chambers, while I check with Gwendolyn in the nursery?"

"Of course, Your Grace. It would be my pleasure. Welcome to Wyndmere Hall, ladies. Follow me."

Emily could not help but be swept away in the housekeeper's wake. To do otherwise would give a very poor impression. She dared a glance over her shoulder and was dismayed to note Garahan, Patrick, and the duke were gone. She could not let Aiden leave without saying goodbye to him. And from the sounds of their loud discussion, he may be leaving sooner than later.

"Your Grace, if you don't mind, I left something in the carriage and need to fetch it."

"Is it your reticule, miss? I have it right here."

Helen handed it to her, nearly foiling her plan. Then Emily remembered something.

She opened her reticule and let out a sound of distress. "They're not here."

"What? the duchess asked.

"A small bottle of laudanum the physician prescribed, and my hartshorn. I left them at the inn. On the washstand!"

"You did, but I packed them in the small valise that Garahan had me leave in the carriage," Helen said. "Why don't I fetch it for you?"

Emily put her hand on her maid's arm. "You know once I start to worry, the only thing that will help is when I feel that vial of hartshorn in my hand. I need to retrieve it. But thank you for offering."

"I'll go with you. We shall be right back, Your Grace."

Without waiting for permission, the two dashed down the steps.

Neither one of them noticed the speculative look in the duchess's eyes.

While Helen asked Tremayne where Garahan had disappeared to, Emily grabbed their valises from the carriage. She nearly dropped them when she saw the anxious look on her maid's face. "What is it? What's happened?"

"Garahan's leaving."

"But we just arrived! Did Tremayne say where?"

"He's borrowing a fresh horse from the duke's stables and heading back to London."

Emily's hands flew to her mouth. Tears welled up and spilled over. "No! I refuse to let him leave before I tell him I love him!"

Tremayne strode over. "Can I be of assistance, Miss Montrose?"

"Aye. Which way to the stables?"

"They're behind the house."

Emily's feet could not move fast enough. As she rounded the corner of the huge building, she saw the stables—and a horse and rider coming toward her at a fast clip. "Aiden! Aiden, wait!"

He slowed his pace but did not stop. "I cannot, lass. I've orders to return to London at once."

"But—"

He shook his head and rode away from her.

"Wait!" She ran after him, screaming his name. "Aiden, you can't leave! I haven't told you I love you yet!" Her balance was still off because of the sling, and she started to stumble.

The sound of hoofbeats pounding toward her had her looking up—in time to watch Aiden leap off his horse and reach her side as she was falling. He caught her to him and held her to his pounding heart. "Lass. Ye cannot love me! I have no rank. Me family are farmers. What could I possibly offer ye?"

She cupped his face in her hand. "Your love."

"What is the meaning of this, Garahan?" the duke demanded, striding toward them.

"Botheration, Jared!" said the duchess, joining him. "Could you not see the sparks? The signs that these two have fallen in love with one another?"

"Why aren't you enjoying a pot of tea with your feet up, Persephone?"

"I had a feeling something like this would happen if I left it to you and Patrick."

He narrowed his eyes. "Are you insinuating that I know nothing about love?"

She beamed at him. "Nothing of the sort, my darling duke. You know quite a bit. It is this situation we find ourselves in. You've never been guardian to anyone before, and I know how you strive to do the right thing—always."

"I'm pleased you have noticed."

"That being said, it's clear that one of your guard has fallen in love with your ward." She winked at Emily. "And it appears that your ward has fallen in love with him." She put her hands on her hips. "Just what do you intend to do about it?"

His frown melted away, and he tipped his head back and laughed. "I thought you'd never ask." He reached into his waistcoat pocket and withdrew a sealed missive. "I requested this as soon as I received Coventry's missive explaining things."

"What things?" Garahan said as he accepted the note from the duke.

"That apparently I will not be interviewing candidates for Miss Montrose's hand." He smiled. "Open it."

Garahan hesitated. "Ye did not have to go to the trouble of giving me a written reference, though I'm grateful, as I may need it looking for employment."

"As you are so fond of saying, *eedjit*! Open it!"

Garahan broke the seal and unfolded the parchment, and his mouth dropped open. "'Tis a special license—and me name's on it."

"I bloody well hope so. I'm not about to give Tremayne permission to wed Miss Montrose when she's in love with you."

"Thank ye, Yer Grace!"

The duke smiled. "My pleasure."

Garahan grinned. "Lass? Would ye have me?"

"I might consider it if you told me how you feel," Emily replied.

"I have nothing to offer ye."

"You have a strong back and capable hands that can fix anything. I happen to know for a fact that you have an extremely hard head."

He snorted with laughter and pulled her close. "I love ye, lass, and will to the last beat of me heart. Marry me?"

She wrapped her good arm around him and held on tight. "I thought you'd never ask."

"Now that that's settled," the duke said. "Why don't we adjourn to the library, I have something of import to discuss with you both." He held his arm out to his wife, who slipped her arm through his.

Garahan held her to his side as they followed the duke and duchess. Emily tugged on his arm before he could lead her into the house. "Do you suppose he has information about Hardwell's arrest? Do you think the baron will call in a favor from a member of the *ton*?"

"Trust the duke—if anyone can move mountains and see that justice is served, 'tis himself." He brushed a kiss across her upturned lips and sighed. "We'd best be going in before they send someone to fetch us."

The duke was standing in the doorway to the library waiting for them. "You have the rest of your life to kiss your bride-to-be. I have important news."

"About my father?" Emily asked, entering the room.

"Patience, lass," Garahan urged. "His Grace obviously wants to speak to us privately."

The duke closed the door behind them and nodded to his wife, who began to pour tea. He motioned for Garahan and Emily to take a seat before speaking, "It seems I am to continue paying for my brother's faults and failings… His mistakes. When I assumed the title after Oliver was murdered, I vowed to bring respect back to our family name. As it had been in Father's time."

He paused for a moment and glanced at his wife, who smiled, encouraging him to continue. "Refilling the coffers was far easier a task. It was almost as if Oliver tossed a pebble in a pond, and each ring that formed touched another person's life. His actions affected so many people, not only our tenants, and those living in the villages near our estates, but the shopkeepers and our staff."

He fell silent, and Persephone said, "What my darling duke is trying to say is that he has more than accepted it is his duty to repay those affected adversely, but to also repair any damage that has been done."

"By my brother, the fifth Duke of Wyndmere. It has become my life's work and will continue to be until the task has been completed and the wrongs have been righted—and, where necessary, seeing that justice has been served."

"You have kept your promise to my father, Your Grace," Emily said, "by sending Aiden and the others to protect me. Thank you, from the bottom of my heart."

"'Twas part of me duty as one of the duke's private guard, lass, to guard the duke, his family, and extended family with me life," Garahan said. "I've said it before, but by now, ye must know that I'm meaning what I said: that as his ward, ye're now under me protection as well."

"I owe both of you so much," Emily rasped, setting her teacup and saucer on the side table. "You've been shot, clubbed over the head, knifed—"

Garahan reached for Emily's hand and raised it to his lips. "All in a day's work, lass."

Her horrified expression had the duke and duchess sharing a look before they dissolved into laughter.

"There is one other thing, lass. Have ye considered the possibility that yer da could have come in contact with Hardwell at some point? Mayhap he was one of the witnesses to the former baron's death."

"I had not thought of that," she admitted.

"'Tis possible he was there when the former baron was thrown from his horse. More than one witness said they saw Hardwell approach the body—but not to render aid. Then they saw him leave." Putting his arm around her, Garahan added, "He didn't kill yer da, *mo chroi*, but he paid a hired killer—Wilson—to do the job and make it appear to be an accident. King's men are still searching for Wilson."

"Circumstances can harden a person's heart," the duke said.

"Aye," Garahan agreed, "and greed will blacken it until a person does the unthinkable—takes a life in exchange for coin."

The duchess refilled their teacups and offered more scones and tarts. When everyone had been served, she asked, "Have King or Coventry sent word that they have found the man who brought Lord Montrose home?"

The duke shook his head. "Between their contacts and those of the men in my guard, they have eyes and ears all over London and in the villages near our other estates. We'll hear something soon."

"I hope so," Emily said. "I need to thank him for his bravery and kindness to my father."

"Worry not—ye'll hear eventually. Never give up hope, lass."

Emily brushed the tips of her fingers along the line of his jaw. "Hope is that tiny flame inside of us that may dim in times of trouble or grief, but it never, ever goes out, as long as you have faith."

Garahan pulled her closer. "Ye had faith enough for both of us, lass, when ye chased after me, shouting that ye loved me." He leaned toward her. "I know I don't deserve ye, lass, but I'm keeping ye."

Emily pulled him closer. "If you ever change your mind, you

won't get far," she promised. "I'll chase after you until I catch you."

"Like ye did today?" The laughter in his eyes warmed her heart.

"Aye, my love." She pressed her lips to his, sealing her promise.

EPILOGUE

Two weeks later…

G ARAHAN SET HIS wife on his horse, mounted behind her, and pulled her onto his lap. "Are ye ready, wife of mine?"

"Where exactly are we going?"

"To our new home. I hope ye don't mind that it's a cottage."

She wrapped an arm around his neck and pressed a kiss to his cheek. "A cottage sounds perfect. Is it far?"

"Just over that rise. The duke had a few built after me cousin Patrick married their nanny, Gwendolyn. He gifted them with a cottage, too."

"But he doesn't even know me."

"He knew yer da, lass, and he is your guardian—for life. The duke is a generous man."

"Oh, Aiden," she sighed. "It's lovely." The cottage was whitewashed, with a bright yellow door and window boxes with flowers. "I love the thatched roof."

"I was hoping ye wouldn't mind living in such a small place after living at Montrose House."

"It's perfect." She tugged on his neck until he was close enough to press her lips to his…and for a brief moment, the world stood still.

He reined in his horse in front of the cottage, dismounted,

and held up his hands to help her down. He tied the horse off to the fence in front of the cottage and scooped her up. "Ye're a delightful armful, lass. Would ye open the door? I'm after carrying ye over the threshold."

Charmed and more in love than she'd thought possible, Emily did as he asked, and leaned against him as he kicked the door shut with his boot.

He walked past the table and chairs near the cookstove to the side of the bed. He set her on her feet, tilted her face up, and pressed a kiss to her lips. "I'll be right back. I have to see to the horse."

She shivered, but agreed.

He quickly returned. "Wasn't the horse hungry or thirsty?" she asked.

He chuckled. "Patrick rode over to take care of the horse for us."

"Oh, will he want a cup of tea?"

"Not unless he wants a black eye to go with it," Garahan grumbled.

"Why on earth would you suggest such a thing?"

"Unresolved disagreement. Now then, wife, 'tis me job to help ye undress." He slipped her sling off and said, "Turn around." She shivered and whirled around. He made short work of the buttons and eased her gown up over her head. "Need help with yer chemise?"

Emily felt a wave of shyness and didn't know how to answer him. She stared at her feet.

Strong arms wrapped around her, pulling her back against his chest. "We can go as slowly as ye need, lass. But I'm not certain how long I can hold out without touching ye. Ye've been plaguing me for weeks—I've been wondering if yer skin feels as soft all over as it looks, and if the hollow of your throat will taste of sun-warmed rose petals."

She sighed and confessed, "Ever since that day in the stables when I opened the door and saw you standing there dripping wet…" She closed her eyes and slowly opened them. "The damp fabric molded to the muscles of your massive chest had me drawing in a breath…and unable to let it go."

"I wondered what caused ye to faint, lass. Now that I know, I cannot say as I would be blaming ye."

She beamed at him. "You do not have a problem with confidence, do you?"

He laughed. "Nay, lass. Now, are ye wanting yer chemise on…or off?"

"I'm not afraid of the marriage bed."

"Off it is." He pulled it up and over her head and beheld the beauty of the woman who had challenged him on all levels, turned his head, and captured his heart. "I think me heart just stopped, lass."

Love for this woman tangled with need, and he wondered if he'd lost his mind altogether, until she whispered, "Your turn."

He tore his shirt off and reached for her hand. She smiled as she placed her hand in his, and he slowly reeled her in and wrapped her in his arms.

"You are so beautiful, Aiden. It's a good thing you're holding me. I cannot feel my legs."

"Poor lass. I've got ye. Now kiss me back."

Emily slipped her arm around Aiden's neck and tangled her fingers in his thick, dark hair…then poured her heart and soul into the kiss.

He swept her off her feet and onto the bed. He eased back long enough to step out of his trousers, then joined her on the bed, gathering her into his arms. "I'll be careful with ye, lass, but won't lie to ye. There's—"

"Pain our first time together," she interrupted. "I know—Mrs. Christian and Mrs. Minnover told me what to expect."

Unable to resist, he pressed his lips to hers. He traced the shape of her mouth with the tip of his tongue, until she sighed, and he slipped his tongue inside for a fuller taste. When she tugged on his hair and nestled closer, he felt the edges of his control fraying.

Needing to get it back so he didn't push her too far, too fast, he kissed the curve of her cheek and nibbled on her earlobe, inhaling the faint scent of roses. "Will ye let me kiss you?"

"Isn't that what we are doing?"

"Aye, but those were yer lips and yer face. I'm after a more sumptuous feast."

She frowned at him. "Feast?"

"Aye, lass." He traced the tip of his finger along her collarbone to the base of her throat and let it glide down between her breasts.

Her soft moan had him smiling. "Ye're a banquet for a starving man, lass. Let me taste ye." She hesitated, and he rasped, "If ye want me to stop, tell me and I will. All right?"

"All right." His tongue circled the nipple of her left breast, and she gasped. He stopped, and she brushed the tips of her fingers across his powerful shoulders. "Don't stop."

He obliged by worshiping one breast and then the other with his lips, his teeth, and tongue until she was writhing beneath him, moaning his name as waves of pleasure shot from her breast to her belly.

Just as she was catching her breath, his hands molded her breasts and slid down her curves, brushing over the very heart of her, teasing, tantalizing, until she begged, "Aiden, please!"

His control was at the breaking point, but he held on to it and stilled for a heartbeat to ask, "Please what, lass?"

"Don't stop."

He settled between her legs and let her feel how ready he was to make love to her.

Eyes wide, she let her hands glide up and down his back, lower and lower until she brushed the tense muscles of his backside and lifted her hips.

He entered her soft warmth and rasped, "I love ye, lass."

She bucked beneath him, and his control snapped. He drove into her, filling her to the hilt, then stopped, clamping down on his own need to wait for her. "The pain will lessen, I promise." He kissed her softly, tenderly, praying the pain would ebb soon.

"Aiden?"

Dear God, don't tell me to stop…

She moved beneath him, and he felt her passage soften to accommodate him. She pressed her lips to the base of his throat. "I love you."

Her words brushed his heart and snapped the chains around his control. He drove into her again and again until they were both mindless to everything but the pleasure they gave…and the pleasure they received.

"I can't—" she rasped.

"Ye can," he promised, taking her mouth as he drove into her one last time and felt her shatter, clutching him as they rode the crest of the wave of ecstasy until it tossed them over the edge of reason into the abyss of madness.

His heart was still racing when he slid his hand to her curvy bottom and then rolled over until she was lying on top of him. Linked body to body, heart to heart. She shivered, and he pulled the blanket over them, wrapped his arms around her, and felt himself drifting off on a cloud of euphoria.

She shifted her hips and leaned back, bringing him sharply back to the present. "Can we do that again?"

His delighted laughter echoed in their cottage and mingled with hers. "Ah, lass, I need a minute here."

She pinched his backside. "I was hoping we could practice until I get it right."

He snorted. "Any righter, and ye'll be burying me tomorrow."

Their lips met as he rolled again and slid deep…and then deeper still. "Is this what ye had in mind, lass?"

Her shocked gasp of pleasure rocked him to the core as they rekindled the passion between them until it threatened to consume them. This time he was the one who shattered first, emptying his seed inside of her.

He pressed his lips to her temple and brushed a strand of auburn off her forehead. "I love ye, lass."

"Mmm." This time, he pinched her bottom. She giggled, wrapped her arm around his neck, and kissed him deeply. "I love you, Aiden."

"Well now, that's more like it." When her eyes drifted closed, he whispered in her ear, "Can we do that again?"

About the Author

Historical & Contemporary Romance "Warm…Charming…Fun…"

C.H. was born in Aiken, South Carolina, but her parents moved back to northern New Jersey where she grew up.

She believes in fate, destiny, and love at first sight. C.H. fell in love at first sight when she was seventeen. She was married for 41 wonderful years until her husband lost his battle with cancer. Soul mates, their hearts will be joined forever.

They have three grown children—one son-in-law, two grandsons, two rescue dogs, and two rescue grand-cats.

Her characters rarely follow the synopsis she outlines for them…but C.H. has learned to listen to her characters! Her heroes always have a few of her husband's best qualities: his honesty, his integrity, his compassion for those in need, and his killer broad shoulders. C.H. writes about the things she loves most: Family, her Irish and English Ancestry, Baking and Gardening.

C.H.'s Social Media Links:
Website: www.chadmirand.com
Amazon: amazon.com/stores/C.-H.-
Admirand/author/B001JPBUMC
BookBub: bookbub.com/authors/c-h-admirand
Facebook Author Page: facebook.com/CHAdmirandAuthor
Facebook Private Reader's Page ~ C.H. Reader's Nook:
facebook.com/groups/714796299746980
GoodReads:
goodreads.com/author/show/212657.C_H_Admirand
Instagram: c.h.admirand
Twitter: @AdmirandH
Youtube:
youtube.com/channel/UCRSXBeqEY52VV3mHdtg5fXw